LEANN AND
THE CLEAN MAN

OTHER BOOKS BY
JEFF SHAW

Who I Am: The Man Behind the Badge, 2020

The Bloodline Series
Lieutenant Trufant, 2022
LeAnn and the Clean Man, 2023

THE BLOODLINE SERIES

LEANN AND THE CLEAN MAN

Jeff Shaw

AUTHOR OF
WHO I AM: THE MAN BEHIND THE BADGE

LANIER PRESS

LANIER PRESS *an Imprint of BookLogix*

Alpharetta, GA

ISBN: 978-1-6653-0596-9 – Paperback
eISBN: 978-1-6653-0597-6 – ePub

Library of Congress Control Number: 2023900853

10 9 8 7 6 5 4 3 2   0 3 0 1 2 3

♾ This paper meets the requirements of ANSI/NISO Z39.48-1992 (Permanence of Paper)

NOTE FROM THE AUTHOR

Although I have never been to Singapore, it is one of the those places I dream of visiting. I feel something magical, or exotic when I think of Singapore. There are other countries that have that same aura; Morocco, Hong Kong, and Macau to name a few. I think this is something imprinted on my consciousness, probably from watching old Hollywood movies when I was younger.

LeAnn and the Clean Man takes place almost entirely in Singapore, so I spent hours—days even researching every detail. I even reached out to people in Singapore for advice and I thank them for their input. That being said, I'm sure not everything is perfect.

Singapore has a multicultural population with strong roots in both Southeast Asia and the West. It was a former British colony up until 1957 and much of their influence is still evident.

One thing I found confusing, and you might as well—character names. In much of Asia, the use of the family name, or sur name comes first and the given name, often two names, comes second. Kwan Kim Lee, a character in this story is an example. Superintendent Kwan's given name is Kim Lee, or Kim as his friends and family call him. And then there is Tommy Fong, a character with a western name.

I hope you enjoy following LeAnn on her adventures in Singapore, if you do, please think of leaving me a review.

CHAPTER 1

SINGAPORE

Dawn broke in the eastern sky and the long shadows of tall buildings began to shrink as they swept across the Changi Airport. Although it was early morning, the traffic around Singapore's international airport was already heavy.

Hui Jie, a skinny man with a ruddy complexion and a sun tattoo rising from the collar of his uniform, stood inside the international gate, scanning the arriving passengers from Manila. The only woman coming out of the gate alone was too old—near thirty.

The next flight was from Brunei and experience told him this flight would have better odds. He needed a girl between the ages of twelve and eighteen, one traveling alone, and the more attractive, the better. His boss had beaten him the last time he brought him an ugly girl, and the scars were still fresh where the hammer had severed the tip of his index finger. The Laoban was a cruel boss sometimes, but he knew that he had deserved the punishment. He had been lazy that day, and he feared that showing up today without an attractive girl would cost him another fingertip.

A yellow-and-white Royal Brunei Airlines Boeing 737 turned on the ramp and taxied toward the gate until the cockpit filled the window. With his maintenance badge and ID card hanging on a lanyard, Jie emptied one trash barrel into another as the passengers streamed down the concourse on their way to customs. One after another they turned in front of him, close enough that he could smell them. He could reach out and touch them if he wanted. Finally, he saw a target, a young brunette woman, a college student wearing a Nanyang Tech sweatshirt. She was a pretty one, but not as thin as Jie liked them, and too Asian for his liking.

Asian women were everywhere, and Jie had developed a taste for the foreign ones, the ones from America and Europe, even the dark ones from the islands excited him. But this girl would please his laoban.

Jie followed her down the long corridor toward customs and watched her being processed through a glass partition. She showed the agent a Chinese passport then headed out toward the main terminal where a man and a woman greeted her. He silently cursed his bad luck. He needed a lone woman, one waiting for transportation. Snatching one away from friends and family would put everyone at risk. Jie glanced at his mangled finger as if he needed a reminder.

Turning back toward the gates, he would wait for the next flight. He knew most of the international arrivals by heart now, and the next flight was from San Francisco. This plane was one of the big ones and it would be a full flight. Half of the passengers would be Asians returning from vacation, and the other half would be a mix of North Americans arriving for the holidays.

Jie would wait.

CHAPTER 2

LEANN

LeAnn Haddad took one last glance at the crowd of travelers in San Francisco's international terminal expecting to see Lieutenant Trufant right behind her. The black detective was a head taller than everyone else—he would be easy to spot, but there was no sign of him, or anyone else looking for her. They would be easy to spot too. Passengers look at gate agents, departure monitors, or their luggage, but law enforcement officers scan the crowd, seeking an individual, someone they've seen before. No one was looking for Leila Moran, the alias she'd assumed for this flight.

Still, she was terrified that a hand would grab her by the neck and all her careful planning would have been for naught. As she stepped across the Boeing's threshold, the anxiety she'd battled all her life began raging.

In her distorted imagination, the cabin stretched for miles as hundreds of passengers stared at her. They knew that she was the one on the news, that she was a wanted murderer. She took a deep breath, knowing what she was seeing was impossible.

"Excuse me, if you're not going to your seat, can I get around you, please?"

The middle-aged man behind her was wearing a Rolex and two-hundred-dollar Nike running shoes. Despite the shoes, he was overweight and out of shape. Probably a tech executive with an attitude. He emphasized the word "please," but meant he wanted to push her out of his way.

Ignoring him, LeAnn took another deep breath and surveyed the passengers in the rear of the cabin, looking for any telltale sign of recognition. Only half the seats were filled and most of the passengers ignored her. Having heard the man, a few eyes did glance at her, but even they turned away as she studied each of them.

She had seen herself on the local news several times in the last few days. Her brother Ramzi had been murdered while in police custody, his throat cut as he was being treated at a local hospital.

LeAnn Haddad was the prime suspect.

They'd also linked her to three other homicides in New York. She knew if they found her, she'd be in handcuffs and behind bars before midnight.

Seat 26K, which she'd selected three days ago, was directly over the right wing. Looking at the ground from thirty thousand feet was not an option, but sitting in an enclosed aluminum tube with two hundred strangers was just as terrifying. Along with anxiety, she also suffered from claustrophobia and a fear of heights. Seat 26K allowed her to see the surface of the wing just a few feet away—a perfect balance, along with six Xanax at the ready in her pocket.

With her backpack stowed, she moved toward the window seat and sat, tucking her small frame into the seat, making herself less noticeable to any law enforcement officer looking for her.

Her ears popped as the pressure inside the plane changed, and the last of the passengers made their way toward their seats. She was safe now, and she tried to relax and dismiss the feeling of suffocation. It was hard to breathe without gasping in the tight, cramped cabin, and her seat seemed to be designed for a child. At 5'4" and one hundred and twenty pounds, she wasn't much bigger than some of the children still walking down the aisle. Deep breathing cleared the tightness in her chest, an exercise that dampened most of her anxieties. She was okay . . . until an elderly woman sat next to her and began talking the instant she was in her seat.

"Well, hello, my dear. I guess we'll be traveling together for a while. I'm Helen."

"Leila," she said, pulling her earbuds out of her pocket.

"A while" was an understatement. It was a seventeen-hour flight to Singapore. The woman prattled on as LeAnn listened to Tchaikovsky's *The Nutcracker*. Tchaikovsky provided her with two things: it muted any attempt the woman made to disturb her, which probably saved the woman's life. Second, with her eyes closed, she could visualize the dancers as they performed the ballet she attended every Christmas while living in New York City.

It was a soothing memory, one her psychiatrist had recommended. Use whatever comforts you, LeAnn, the woman had said. Killing anyone who annoyed her comforted her just as well, but it was often too messy.

In the middle of the "March of the Toy Soldiers," the engines of the big jet started, and she sensed the heat radiating off the woman's arm next to her.

Please don't touch me.

LeAnn could picture the woman's moist flesh inches away from her own. The sensation of a stranger and sometimes even a friend touching her was repulsive, and she pressed herself closer to the window.

Squeezing her eyes shut helped eliminate the image of the woman's arm. So often something like this would escalate into full-blown rage, and the way she satisfied that rage usually meant killing the source. She hated those emotions, but the act of killing was often euphoric—like a drug addict's high, she imagined. She never craved that euphoria, or that act of killing someone, but once someone triggered her, the violent cycle was almost inevitable. Nicole, Christa, and Olivia, three of her college classmates, had learned that lesson the hard way.

As she thought of those girls, the plane accelerated, pushing her back into her seat, and then it was airborne. Her anger toward her seatmate vanished as the sensations of freedom and confinement battled each other. She dug one of the Xanax out of her pocket and chewed the pill into a bitter paste, then swallowed it.

The *Nutcracker* again. With her eyes closed, she focused on the dancers performing in front of her and imagined she was the only one in the audience. A sea of empty seats spread out in all directions as the costumed dancers twirled and leaped across the stage.

At last, she felt at ease. The warmth from the anti-anxiety drug flowed through her, and she was at peace—until the woman woke her.

When LeAnn opened her eyes, the flight attendant leaned over the old woman, a bag of pretzels in her hand. "A snack, honey?"

"No, thank you," LeAnn said, smiling. "Just some water please."

Once the flight attendant moved to the next row, LeAnn whispered to the old woman, "Don't touch me again, and don't let them wake me."

The woman recoiled and edged farther away from her—perfect!

Nine hours later, a soft, cool breeze brushed several strands of loose hair across LeAnn's forehead, waking her from a deep sleep. The breeze lasted only seconds and came from the closed window shade. It was impossible, she knew, and the sensation passed as quickly as it had begun.

The breeze was a sign, and she knew her mother, the family matriarch, was finally dead. Diwata Haddad suffered from throat and lung cancer and had been in a Toronto hospital ICU bed for the last several days.

Raising the window shade, the top of the wing was right there; the ocean miles below was hidden in the darkness. Looking forward, there was nothing else to see, the plane was midway across the Pacific. She closed the shade, thinking of her mother. Deep down, she wanted to grieve, to experience the death of a loved one and the feeling of sadness she had read about. What she felt was a void, not unlike losing a favorite pair of jeans, even though they no longer fit.

I'm describing my mother like and old pair of pants!

Sometimes she envied those around her, those able to feel grief, but at the moment, she felt freer.

As the plane flew westward over the Mariana Islands, she

fished two more Xanax out of her pocket and washed them down with water this time.

"Having trouble sleeping?" the old woman asked.

Anger flashed and she wanted to slap the woman, but it would cause a scene she couldn't control, at least not yet. Instead, she began planning how she would kill her once they landed. Just toying with the idea eased her irritation. LeAnn had been in the Singapore airport several times and was familiar with the layout.

I'll follow her to a bathroom and kill her there.

She knew it was too risky. She was flying halfway around the world to her brother's safe house to avoid the police. Killing this woman could reignite what she was trying to escape. The Xanax and Tchaikovsky began working their magic, and the anger and the woman became insignificant.

Hours later she woke as she felt the plane decelerating, and a brilliant shaft of sunlight beamed through a window on the other side of the cabin.

Everyone around her was awake now. She stretched her legs as far as she could, feeling the stiffness in her knees from sleeping in an awkward position. The old woman next to her stared, started to say something, and changed her mind.

LeAnn opened her shade and saw the city below her. It was early and many of the streetlights were still on. A motor whined beneath her feet, and the plane slowed again as the pilot announced their arrival.

"I need to get my carry-on out from above you, do you mind?" she asked the woman.

"Can't you wait like everyone else?"

"No, I can't. That's why I'm asking you to move."

The old woman made a show of how difficult it was to get out of her seat, and LeAnn reached above her and grabbed her backpack. She was determined to be one of the first off the plane.

LeAnn hoisted the backpack onto her shoulder and glared at the woman. "That wasn't so hard, was it?"

CHAPTER 3

HUI JIE

A young woman wearing a red rain jacket was the first passenger through the gate. Without making eye contact, Jie tried to guess her nationality. She wasn't Chinese, of that, he was sure. Hispanic or Middle Eastern, maybe. She was short and thin, and Jie liked them thin. He looked behind her and saw two other girls that were also promising. These two were better-looking, thick with bigger breasts, but Jie was not a breast man. Jie loved a woman's ass, her *pigu*, and the girl in the red rain jacket had a perfect one. This girl, with her long dark hair, hair that brushed that perfect ass, excited him. She was the one.

Jie fell in behind the crowd of departing travelers and followed her. Once he was sure she was on her way to customs he went to the men's bathroom and took off his khaki uniform shirt and put it into the cleaning closet. The gray skull and red sun of his tattoo rising up from the collar of his T-shirt were reflected in the mirror. Most of the tat had been concealed by the maintenance uniform, but now it was visible. It would be easy to recognize and witnesses would remember it, but he was committed now. If things failed with this girl, he would come back and retrieve the uniform and start over.

Edging through the crowd outside customs, he spotted the girl, now third in line on the near side of the room, a stroke of good fortune and another sign that success was near. As she stepped up to the counter, he could hear her speaking English. He couldn't see her passport, but the customs officer was being thorough,

8

another good sign. Most of the customs officers scrutinized the North Americans and Jie hoped she was an American. A girl from the United States was worth much more than someone from Central or South America. The laoban would be pleased and might even offer Jie a bonus.

A second officer approached the girl and went through her carry-on, asking her more questions in his broken English. Jie couldn't speak English, but he knew it was a heated exchange and feared she would be taken away for interrogation. The officer called her an insolent foreigner in Mandarin and walked away. The first officer slammed the stamp down on her passport, startling the passengers behind the girl.

Jie pushed his way through the crowd in the main terminal to keep up with her while trying to blend in with the departing passengers. Holding a map of Singapore in one hand and his cell phone in the other, he looked like any other tourist heading towards the exit. It was a struggle to keep the girl's red jacket in front of him, to lose her now would be a disgrace. With his cell phone, he made the call. "We're coming out, a girl in a red jacket, thirty seconds."

Jie passed through the automatic doors and stood behind her in the taxi line, pulling a clear sandwich bag from his pocket. As the unmarked white van approached, he took a wet rag out of the bag. The van stopped right in front of her, the side door slid open, and in one movement, Jie reached around her, holding the wet cloth across her nose and pushed her toward the van's door. The girl elbowed him in the stomach, knocking the wind out of him, but he held onto the rag as he and the girl were pulled inside. The door slammed shut. Tan Khoo stared at Jie gasping for air and laughed.

Rolling off the girl, Jie looked out the back window and saw two elderly men watching them pull away, and another, younger woman pointing her cell phone in their direction. The rest of the crowd were looking at the line of yellow-and-blue taxis, oblivious to what had just happened.

The van's driver turned and looked at LeAnn lying in a heap on the floor.

"Good one this time, Jie."

CHAPTER 4

LeAnn

I'm dead . . . or I'm dying.

Blackness was all she could sense and even that felt like it was slipping away. If she let go of that black void, she knew she would die.

A screech of metal-on-metal brought her back to some sense of life. It was a real sound, and she waited an eternity for another sound, another sensation, but there was nothing, just an overpowering void.

If I can just call out, if I can say something, anything, someone will know I'm alive.

But speaking was impossible.

What is happening to me? I was flying . . .

An image of an airplane flashed.

I died in a plane crash somewhere.

She clutched at that image, one of sitting in a cabin surrounded by passengers. There was more . . . but remembering was too hard and the darkness claimed her again.

***

A man's voice echoed inside the void, but it was so far away.

If I can just say something, a single word, he will know I'm alive.

Forming a word proved to be impossible. She couldn't sense her lips moving, even her tongue was numb and useless.

I'm paralyzed, that's what has happened to me. I'm in a hospital.

Now another voice, this one much deeper, or was she dreaming? *I've got to open my eyes. If I can just do that, I'll be okay.*

Two men having a conversation. She heard the words, but nothing made any sense, just random words floating through her dream.

Goddammit, open your eyes!

A dim yellow light above her replaced the emptiness . . . finally. Then a gray blur formed in its center.

I want to see—but I'm so tired.

Closing her eyes was much easier, so much safer, until another voice, murmured behind her. It was a man's voice, and it was closer still. She tried to understand what he was saying—something about a smell, or "she smells."

Opening her eyes, the yellow blur above her looked different now. The yellow was brighter, and as she stared, the shape transformed itself into a light fixture. A cheap, corroded fixture, its bulb surrounded by a wire cage. Attached to the cage, a ragged cobweb full of dead insects fluttered in slow motion, like a flag waving in a light breeze, the husks looking like stars.

What kind of hospital is this?

Flat on her back and still unable to move anything but her eyes, she stared at the light, relieved that she could see and hear again. Someone was nearby, behind her. She could hear heavy breathing and scratching sounds like drawers opening and closing. She wanted to turn her head, to see who was behind her, but trying was futile. Again, she tried to ask for help, to form a simple word, but knew she couldn't, and the sensation of being paralyzed triggered a panic reflex—claustrophobia made her want to scream and that terror intensified until she blacked out.

I'm awake again, that's what's happening to me. I've been falling asleep and waking up over and over for how long now, how many hours or days?

Then she remembered being in a wheelchair. Someone pushing her across the floor and hands touching her all over. Something horrible had happened in that wheelchair.

Someone was breathing behind her again; the sound was shifting, and he or she was moving away. Again, she tried to speak. With her tongue, she could feel her lips now, it was progress. They tingled in some spots and were numb in others. Her mouth was dry, and her throat felt like she had swallowed sand, but she heard herself make a noise.

She tried to say hello, but it sounded more like a gurgle. She tried again and waited. Then she was in the wheelchair again and she couldn't remember how she got there. There were long gaps in her memory, but this was more than a memory, this was happening right now. Her head rolled uncontrollably on her chest, giving her a view of nothing but a dirty concrete floor passing underneath her. The person pushing her was wearing heavy boots. Leather soles slapping the floor sounded like it was a big man or woman. The chair stopped and a round stainless-steel drain was below her bare feet, her legs were bare too, and then a shower of freezing cold water soaked her. Someone poured water from a plastic bottle down her throat. She gagged uncontrollably until she blacked out.

**

She was comfortably warm now, and this time the lightbulb above her was on, casting an eerie yellow light on the ceiling around it. It's nighttime, she thought. There was a new memory now to go with the others, a trip to a shower, eating something soft from a jar and sitting on a toilet. She tried to lift her head again but was still too weak.

Staring at the lightbulb, she felt like she was in someone else's body, unable to control anything but their eyes. Above her, a small brown spider, just a speck in the amber light, was weaving a new web, its concentric circles spread evenly across gossamer spokes, like a tiny bicycle wheel.

Her eyelids felt heavy, she lacked the strength to keep them open … and the light vanished and the breathing behind her drifted into the darkness.

I don't want to sleep, I want to watch the spider work. The spider needs a name . . .

***

Minutes, or maybe hours later a door slammed, startling her, and she was able to move her head an inch to the right, only to see more of the same ceiling and another light fixture. The bulb in this one was missing.

"Hello," she said again, and this time she was able to make a rasping sound. It was weak, but someone should have heard her. She could move her head a little more now and looked to her left. There was an old, empty stained cot with heavy canvas bindings hanging loose and touching the floor. An IV pole stood at the head of the cot and a deflated clear bag hung from it.

She could see her own arm now; a clear tube snaked its way down to a port taped to the back of her hand. The tube was filled with a brown fluid the color of iced tea. Now the cycles of numbness and sensations of being paralyzed made sense. She had been drugged and if this was a hospital, it was not in the United States.

She lifted her head as far as she could and saw those same canvas bindings holding her arms to the cot. The mattress was old, stained, and damp. It smelled like urine, probably hers if she had been strapped to it for a week. The mattress was disgusting but what really horrified her, was the fact that she was naked.

Panicking, she began thrashing, trying to pull her arms free of the straps and cover herself, but it was useless, her arms were barely moving. She wanted to laugh or scream, but the best she could do was make that same pathetic raspy sound.

Someone moaned to her right. Turning her head, she saw a dark-skinned girl strapped to another cot, identical to the one on her left, but this girl was conscious and looking at her, then the girl moaned again as her eyes tracked something behind LeAnn.

A face loomed over her. A man's face, close enough she could smell his breath. He was Asian, in his mid-twenties, maybe as old as thirty with lighter skin than the girl on her right. A small cross tattooed above his left eye moved as he smiled. His lips and teeth were stained red, like blood. Spitting a wad of red mucus onto the floor, his smile faded as he gripped her forearm and squeezed it so tight, she could feel the pain penetrate the last of the drug still running through her IV.

His smile changed as his eyes swept downward.

LeAnn studied his face, not wanting to miss the slightest detail. She would need this image to focus her rage. His nose was too big for his face and had been broken at least once; his eyebrows were lined with scars, and another scar ran under his left eye below the cross and halfway to his ear. It was a jagged scar and an amateur must have done the stitching. He reminded her of a boxer who had lost too many fights.

Furious, she thought of all the ways she wanted to kill him, but right now, she couldn't lift a finger if she tried. With a syringe, the man injected a clear fluid into the IV's port and a warm sensation began creeping up her arm. Her terror was replaced by the familiar blackness. This time, she welcomed it.

***

She woke listening to something tapping behind her. The drug was wearing off. She could lift her head a little more now, and she was still naked. She had shaved her pubic hair the day she flew out of San Francisco, and there was at least a week's, maybe even two weeks' growth of black stubble between her legs.

Have I been here that long?

It didn't seem possible. It seemed like she was walking through San Francisco's airport just yesterday.

Above her, the spider was still at work, the web now twice as big as it had been yesterday, or was it the day before? The familiar metal scraped again behind her, and now a different man stood over her, another Asian, but with darker skin and a patchy beard.

He was younger and shorter than the first man, and unlike the other one, he was bone-thin. The same red saliva collected in the dark hairs around the corners of his pinched mouth.

Staring at his face, she remembered dreams or vague memories of both men touching her, running their hands over her . . . and there were other, more terrifying images. LeAnn screamed as long and as loud as she could, until black spots raced across her vision. Taking a deep breath, she cursed him: "You fucking bastard!" It was weak and garbled, but also satisfying.

The man was grinning now, his thin lips stretched tight, and then laughed out loud while his small, dark brown eyes darted between her breasts and legs. He needed to touch her. LeAnn saw the lust in his eyes; the look was unmistakable. Furious, she pulled uselessly on the straps and screamed again. Only killing them would ease this rage.

This sick bastard was enjoying himself. He grabbed his crotch and stroked the inside of her thigh. Drug-free now, the sensation of his fingers moving up from her knee were unbearable, but fortunately he stopped. She pulled again on the straps as the rage consumed her.

It was no use struggling, she didn't have the strength. She held his gaze and said, "I will kill you." It was an oath, a simple promise to herself that one day, she would watch this ragged man die.

He laughed again, and as he did, tiny drops of red spittle flew through a shaft of sunlight and landed on her chest. It was betel nut harvested from Areca palms. Feeling those wet drops on her chest was maddening, worse than the itching between her legs.

He turned to speak to someone, and as he did, a tattoo a of a large red sun rose above his collar. The center of the sun was dark gray and looked like the top half of a human skull. The sun had probably been bright red at one time, but was now dull and faded. He said something in Mandarin, and laughed. Living in Singapore off and on for ten years, she had learned enough of the language to understand he was saying he was going to fuck her again.

LeAnn liked to think she had a photographic memory, that she could close her eyes and see all the imperfections in her victim's faces. The lines, the scars, the pits, and most important, their eyes. This man's dead eyes lacked any sign of intelligence. He was stupid and easily manipulated, and that was something she could use, and his crooked, stained teeth and that pinched mouth would be easy to remember.

He injected something into her IV. The drug moved quickly through her vein, and she had a vague, ghostly image of him on top of her again.

***

One nightmare ended as another began.

There was the smell of brackish water and dead fish. The scent of machine oil reminded her of the days she and her family had fled Manila on an old freighter. She had been ten years old then, but she remembered all of it, and as if to confirm it, a ship's horn groaned somewhere close by, no less than half a mile away. She was in a run-down warehouse near a shipyard or a seaport.

A girl's voice startled her. The girl cried out in English. "Please, I need another shot! Please, it's been two days! I need another shot."

Behind LeAnn, two men were whispering. With her eyes closed, she listened to the one with the deeper voice say, "This one's ready to meet the Laoban. I'll call him."

The bigger man was on the phone now, speaking in Mandarin, his words unintelligible with the loud metal scraping sounds behind her. The girl cried out again, and the cry turned into a steady moan until one of the men moved behind her. It was the big man, the one with the cross tattoo, his heavy boots thudding against the concrete floor as he walked. The thin man made no sound at all.

LeAnn opened her eyes just wide enough to peek at the ceiling again and turned to her right to observe the girl. She was ten feet away, a light-skinned black girl no older than seventeen. She too was nude and identical straps bound her to the flimsy cot.

The girl looked toward her and they made eye contact. The big man spotted their exchange. It was too late to close her eyes; he knew she was awake. This was the first man she had seen, stronger and the smarter of the two, the one with the simple cross on his temple. He was filling a syringe from a small brown bottle and jabbed it in the girl's elbow. Her IV pole was now empty and stood behind her cot. The girl looked at her again and smiled, her glassy eyes now drooping and unfocused.

"Jie," the big man said, "we need to change these two mattresses if the Laoban is coming. Don't try to clean them, just throw them out and replace them."

The skinny man's name is Jie, the one with the sun tattoo, and I will kill him first.

Jie leered at her as he refilled the same syringe and stuck the needle into the IVs port. She waited, the cold sensation of the drug creeping up her arm, as it reached her shoulder, her eyelids grew heavy, she couldn't concentrate, each thought slipped away. She tried using these precious seconds to remember everything. She repeated the name: Jie, his name is Jie . . . Jie. Then the drug washed over her, taking every thought. This part of her nightmare was over, but another was about to begin.

In this nightmare, the man with the skull tattoo had raped her, again and again, then she realized it hadn't been a dream at all. There was a dull ache between her legs, and she inhaled the bitter stench of red betel juice. A slamming door erased any doubt of her reality.

Then a new smell overpowered the betel nut, a man's cologne, a cloying scent like new leather. Keeping her eyes closed, she listened. A man was breathing . . . slow and steady breaths. He was close, right next to her, she felt the heat radiating off his body.

Ready to spit on the man she knew was peering down at her, she opened her eyes to aim. It was a new face, a well-dressed Asian man in his early thirties with big, straight white teeth, and a clean-shaven face. This man's dark brown eyes were alive, intelligent, and then he winked at her.

"So, you're a Canadian, Ms. Leila Moran?" he said in perfect English. There was a British accent in his voice, giving his words a musical quality. He could have been a handsome man, but his big square jaw looked cartoonish, and his teeth were huge and too white, like the keys on a piano. Bedecked in an expensive white suit of fine silk, he appeared muscular, but she suspected it was expert tailoring. Underneath the jacket was a contrasting black satin shirt, a matching tie held in place by a thick gold tie chain and a black pocket square tucked in his breast pocket. He looked like a wealthy politician on his way to an executive business affair or a luncheon on a polo field, a startling contrast to the filth all around him.

He waited for her reply, the smile on his face slowly receding. He yanked at one of the straps holding her wrist. His hands looked soft, his fingernails manicured and coated in clear polish with big garish gold rings glittering on each finger.

"Who are you?" she said finally, refusing to answer his question.

His right hand struck her left ear and as his open palm raked her cheek, it felt soft and delicate. He was a weak man, and she knew for certain the tailored suit was a cover, its shoulders giving him the impressive look of a tough man. Still the sting of the slap cut through whatever drugs were still cruising through her veins.

"Answer me, girl! I don't like to repeat myself."

"Yes, I am. What's your name?"

"You don't need to know my name, Ms. Moran, and never ask it again. All you need to know is that I own you. You work for me, no different from Jie, and you will do as I ask. Soon you will want to please me."

"I won't."

"Oh yes, you will. I noticed you looking at my rings, Ms. Moran," he said, flashing them in front of her and making sure Jie could see them as well. "Do you like them? I'm sure you do. You see this one? Isn't this ruby extraordinary? Of course it is, and look at the diamonds surrounding it," he said, holding it beneath a sliver of sunlight. "This ring once belonged to a man that thought he was my equal. Now it is mine. Do you want to know why? Yes, you do," he said, answering his own question. "Jie," he said, switching to Mandarin, "show our guest your finger."

Jie's fingers shook as he stretched his arm out in front of her face. The little finger on his right hand was missing above the last knuckle, the jagged scar still pink.

"That's enough, Jie."

Jie sucked in a big breath and backed away, his face was the color of pale wax—and LeAnn knew he was terrified of this man.

"You see, Ms. Moran, Jie understands me, and so when he let me down, he knew he would have to pay a heavy price. I simply asked him to put that finger on the desk behind you. I didn't have to ask him twice. And when the hammer came down, Jie never said a word. As for the other man, my competitor, he did not understand me, and he will never wear this ring again.

"Each of these rings has a similar story," he said, waving his hands through the air again. "It's not the gold or the stones, as nice as they are; it's the stories, Ms. Moran. And Ms. Moran, I want you to know, you would be just as valuable to me if you also were missing a bit of a finger."

"So let me repeat myself this one last time," he said. All traces of humor and the counterfeit smile vanished and there was a deep coldness in the air around him now. "You will beg to please me, just like your friend Brianne does," he said, pointing to her right. LeAnn looked over and saw tears on the girl's face.

The man paced at the foot of her cot, the grin appearing and then fading again as if some inner battle was raging in his head. Then he turned and his eyes locked onto hers.

"Leila Moran, from Ottawa, Canada," he said, waving her passport in his right hand, and then slapping it into his left. "I haven't been able to find you on any social media platforms. No Facebook, no Instagram, and no humorous TikTok videos; you're a bit of an anomaly and I find that troubling."

"I'm going to kill you, old man!"

The resulting blow stung more than the last. LeAnn tasted blood, her jaw ached, and two of her teeth felt loose. Any harder and he could have knocked her out. Perhaps there was more strength in his body than she realized.

She glanced to her right at Jie and the other man, both men stood stiff like soldiers at an inspection. Jie glanced at her nervously, his cheek twitching and then he looked back at his boss. She understood Jie's fear, he was a coward. But the second man was no lightweight and the scars around his eyes showed he was no stranger to violence, and he too feared this man.

LeAnn stared at the man, etching the bastard's face in her memory. That perfectly combed jet-black hair, the whisps of white at his temples and groomed eyebrows. She would coat that leering face in his own blood one day, and she would kill him each night in her sleep for as long as it took until he was truly dead.

"Look at her eyes, Jie! Oh, you are a feisty one. You and I are going to get along just fine I think. Two weeks, maybe three, Ms. Moran, and you will be just like Brianne over there. You will beg to serve me."

Switching to Mandarin, the new man said, "Jie, how long has this one been our guest?"

"Fifteen days."

You've done well this time, Jie, but I want to fill the empty cot soon, and once Brianne is ready, we will need to replace her as well, work on that for me. Until then, take good care of Ms. Moran. Also, I want you to take Brianne to the house tonight. Clean her up and find her a pretty dress and have her there by seven o'clock sharp. We're entertaining an important guest tonight and I don't want anything to go wrong."

"Yes, Laoban," Jie answered, his thin voice quivering.

Laoban! LeAnn recognized the title, a term of great respect, or fear This new man was the boss, not just a boss, but *the* Boss.

The man smiled at her, exposing those big teeth, then put his hand on her knee, his soft cold fingers caressing her thigh. Bile rose in her throat as he touched one of her breasts, rubbing his finger across her nipple.

A red wad of mucus hung from his fingertip. The man's rich smile changed again as his lips tightened into a grimace. He studied his finger. His face was frightening; she had seen that look on her brother's face often enough, and even a few times on her mother's. Then the grimace faded and the smile returned.

God, his teeth were so white!

"No more of this, Jie," he said, showing Jie his fingertip, "and remember, a pretty dress for Brianne and have her at the house by seven—not one minute later."

"As you wish, Laoban." Jie's already reedy voice quivered.

He may have been smiling, but this new man was clearly furious. Pulling out his pocket square, he wiped the mucus off his finger and threw the fabric in a trashcan, then walked out of her view. His soft footsteps grew distant, then a metal door slammed, its heavy lock engaging. From outside, a car engine started. It was the deep, throaty growl of a powerful car; she imagined it being a big BMW or a Mercedes Benz, and she knew it was probably white, just like his gaudy suit.

"Dammit, Jie, I thought you were going to lose the rest of your finger today. Get the van inside while I clean this one," the big man said, pointing to Brianne.

Jie was disappointed, she saw it on his face as he walked away. He had wanted to watch Brianne shower and dress.

"You're a fucking pervert, Jie!" she screamed. The big man laughed and she realized he must understand English.

She looked over at Brianne as the bigger man unbound the girl and walked her out of the room, his heavy boots shuffling across the floor. Another door closed, then water began running. In two weeks, she could be the one in the shower, drug-addled and helpless.

She needed a name for this big man. Knowing a person's name made it easier for her to focus her hate, and not knowing left her with a gnawing, empty place inside.

Most of the drug had burned through her system, leaving her head clearer than it had been in days. Her ear still stung from the man's slap and there was a small cut inside her lip. The ability to feel pain again was refreshing. They could come back and dope her up at any time, and she wanted to look around.

First, she checked the bag on her IV pole—it was a clear bag of saline. Her bindings were thickly woven canvas straps with well-worn brass buckles, the kind used on prisoners and psychiatric patients. Each of her wrists was bound, and another single strap encircled her waist. She lifted her head as high as the bindings allowed and saw that four more straps held her by the ankles and thighs. Another strap encircled her chest below her breasts. Eight straps to hold a hundred and twenty pound woman. It was overkill for most women, but she was not ordinary. At the moment, though, she was helpless. She would need two hands to unbuckle just one of them.

The metal-tubed cot was old and flimsy. Its frame could be the weak point, but bound as she was now, it would be useless to try and get free. Her new mattress was cleaner than the last one and thankfully this one was still dry.

Behind her were the two metal chairs she had heard being moved earlier. A small wood-and-metal office desk that was at least fifty years old sat on the bare concrete floor. On top of the desk were a syringe and a small brown bottle. The lettering on the bottle looked like English, but it was too small to read.

Judging by the high open ceiling, she was in one section of a small warehouse. Rectangular windows high up on the far wall were screened with thick wire mesh and spaced evenly every ten feet. The glass was too dirty to see through and they were at least twelve feet from the floor. Even if she could reach them, she would never get past the heavy mesh. Several smaller rooms appeared to have been constructed recently. The block walls were newer and whiter while everything else looked old and cheap.

Inside one of those smaller rooms, the shower stopped, and the big man began yelling in Mandarin for Brianne to dress herself.

She doesn't speak Mandarin, you asshole, she wanted to yell, but she also didn't want him knowing she could understand him, at least not yet.

Eventually, Brianne walked back into the room wearing a simple sheer red sundress. The man opened a locker standing against the far wall and handed her a pair of shoes and a backpack.

The backpack must have been hers at one time. Brianne unzipped it and scavenged through it like she knew what she was looking for, pulled out a hairbrush and began brushing the knots out of her hair. She was a pretty girl and looked like every other young, innocent teenager, except for the dark circles under her vacant eyes.

The whine of an electric motor coming from outside startled the big man, and he walked over toward one of the smaller doors and waited. The hum of a small car's engine came from behind the door. Then a car door slammed.

"Khoo, it's Jie."

Khoo! She breathed a sigh of relief as another blank spot in her mind was now filled. His face and name were now permanently etched in her memory, along with that reedy voice. But there was still the new man, another blank that needed filling, and she named him *the Clean Man.* Calling him Laoban seemed wrong. It was a title of respect, and she had no respect for a bastard like him.

Whispering the three names over and over and hearing them comforted her somehow, and now she knew why her brother and sister had chanted their own list of names every night before they slept, and again each morning. *Knowing your enemy gives you strength and strength becomes a weapon,* Ramzi had said. She thought he was just crazy, but she was beginning to understand him now.

Khoo slid the heavy bolt aside and opened the door.

Shadows on the floor told her it was late afternoon and she felt her first pang of hunger.

"I'm hungry."

Neither man moved.

"I'm hungry!"

Khoo opened a desk drawer and threw two packs of orange crackers at her and put a lukewarm bottle of water on the cot, then released the strap on her right wrist so she could feed herself. The crackers were stale and soft, but she ate them all and licked the crumbs from her fingers.

Finishing the water, she handed the bottle to the big man and said, "Thank you," then brushed the crumbs off her chest.

"Where are my clothes?"

Khoo walked over and stared down at her, ignoring her question and then redid the straps, pulling at them until she felt pain biting through the drugs still in her system. Then he stared into her eyes, one at a time.

"What the fuck are you afraid of, you prick," she said, waiting for the slap.

In Mandarin, he said, "I'm going to dope this one again. There's something about her I don't like, and I don't want to listen to her shit while you're gone."

She watched him fill the syringe with a clear liquid and inject it into her IV.

He looked at her and smiled. "Fentanyl."

The fentanyl was quicker than the last drug and the numbness in her lips was immediate. The last thing she heard was Khoo, "Jie, Brianne is ready. Strap her into the van and make sure the straps are tight. The first trip is always the riskiest."

***

It was nighttime when LeAnn opened her eyes. The windows above her were black and six of the ten working light fixtures bathed the room in dull yellow light. How long this time? How many hours or even days?

"She's awake," Jie said.

"Take her to the shower, she stinks," Khoo said behind her.

Jie began unbuckling the straps, starting with her ankles and finishing with her wrists. When she sat up and almost fell off the cot as the blood rushed away from her brain, Jie cursed, but caught her before she fell.

Her head was still spinning, and she still felt like she was going to pass out or puke, but as the world settled, she let her feet touch the floor. The cold concrete felt good, but she was not ready to walk on her own. This was going to be the first time off the cot with a clear head and she wanted to see everything.

Jie rolled a wheelchair over to her and she got her first good look at the man. He was shorter than she expected, five feet, five inches at the most and not much taller than she was. Jie was a weak man with thin arms, and a neck that was too long for his frame. Khoo standing next to Jie, was the exact opposite—he was thick and muscular and probably six feet tall.

Both men set her in the chair. Khoo's grip was powerful, and she knew he was trying to hurt her, maybe sending a message not to try anything stupid. She could barely stand on her own, much less resist him. The thought made her laugh, and Khoo slapped the back of her head, the blow causing her to bite her tongue. She spit the blood out at his feet and tried to look him in the eye.

Khoo looked down at the spit near his boot. "You will pay for that, little girl."

Khoo speaking English surprised her, something she needed to remember. He pulled on her straps until they were so tight that pins and needles ran up her hands and feet.

"You're the one who's going to pay, Khoo."

Ignoring her, he pushed her toward the bathroom as she tried to memorize every part of the room.

In the smaller room, Brianne was sitting in front of a mirror, dabbing powder around her eyes. The young girl was back from wherever they had taken her the night before, and she was wearing a different dress.

"Hi," she said to the girl.

Brianne just looked at her, and the look told LeAnn she had lost all hope.

"I'm sorry," LeAnn whispered.

Jie rolled her past Brianne, started the shower, and pushed her into the freezing stream of water.

"You bastards," she said as both men laughed, watching her shiver in the ice-cold spray.

Using the chair's wheel, she turned herself around several times until the cold water was unbearable and then wheeled herself out. Khoo threw her an old, stained, and soured towel to dry herself. The smell nauseated her, and she let it drop to the floor.

"Can I use the toilet?" she said in English.

Jie hesitated and looked at Khoo. Khoo translated and Jie nodded.

Unstrapping her wrist, Jie lifted her off the chair, and she moved under her own power to the toilet. Both men watched.

"Can I piss without you staring?"

"No, you cannot," Khoo said in thickly accented English. "You can piss in your bed if you want. When was her last dose, Jie? I don't like her attitude."

"Four hours ago."

"Piss now or never, then it's back to bed until tomorrow morning," Khoo said. "And Jie, this time give her a full dose of the cheap stuff."

Thankfully, it was Jie who strapped her to the cot. He was gentler than Khoo, but he had to run his dirty and callused fingers all over her as he did the buckles. Then his face loomed over hers once again, his bloodshot eyes glancing over her body and then the sickening smile.

Jie began cooking a lump of black tar heroin. She couldn't see it, but she could smell it from six feet away, like the smell of vinegar and burning trash. It looked like old coffee in the syringe, and as he injected it into her IV, he grinned, showing her the red saliva in his mouth. Soon, she felt the warmth of a drug flowing up her arm and fought to stay conscious to listen in on the men's conversation.

The heroin left a sharp taste in her mouth as it made its way through her system. The effects were similar to fentanyl, and she felt her anger slip away, which was gratifying, but she had hoped for more time to think. She had to get out of this hellhole, and being doped up for twenty-four hours a day wasn't helping.

"The van needs fuel, Jie. Fill it up after you drop the girl off and I'll see you at seven in the morning. And be careful with her––the Laoban said she performed well last night, but he is not sure she is ready to meet the American. He also said he wants her unmarked so leave her alone. Don't touch her anymore."

Jie was angry, his fists clenched and the muscles in his jaw tightened as he glared at her. Then he smiled, ran his finger across his wet teeth and flicked it at her.

LeAnn was too drowsy to react or even care. Closing her eyes, she dismissed him, *"Let the bastard hate me,"* she thought. *"Let them all hate me."*

In two weeks, they expected her to be so addicted to the drugs that she would be compliant and fully under their control, but she was going to be neither. She was going to kill them all. Jie, Khoo, and the Clean Man. Then she thought of the man driving the van at the airport. She'd had only a brief glimpse of him when he turned and said, "Good one this time." That was the last thing she remembered. *Was it enough?* Yes, she could see his face clearly and added *the Driver* to her list of names.

"I need water," she croaked. Her mouth had been dry for as long as she could remember. If they brought her water, she never got the chance to drink it.

The drug began fogging her brain, the dirty room began spinning, and then Khoo, with his red-stained teeth, faded . . . and she found herself floating down the hall of a sorority house at New York University.

She opened the unlocked door of room six, where Christa Jurowski was sleeping under a white-and-pink floral bedspread. She sat at the edge of the bed and watched the girl; she saw the rise and fall of her small breasts under the matching sheet and listened to her softly snoring. She looked so peaceful, so calm and innocent, nothing like the bitch she was in Chemistry.

"You're such a freak, LeAnn, why don't you do us all a favor and kill yourself?" Christa had said. All LeAnn had done was refuse to give the girl a copy of her lab notes.

"Why don't you do us all a favor and kill yourself?" She whispered the girl's own words softly into her ear as she slid the thin music wire around her neck, and then pulled so tight not even her last breath could escape. LeAnn stared at those bulging blue eyes and saw recognition in them. Good, I want her last image to be my face.

She and Christa floated back outside the sorority house, and LeAnn sat her upright in the rear seat of the girl's car next to Olivia. Olivia would not mind; she and Christa were best friends.

LeAnn opened her eyes. The sunlight coming through the window told her it was now morning. She had slept, or was unconscious for almost a full day. Now the shadows and the sun were chasing each other across the floor toward Brianne's now-empty cot.

She felt pain between her legs again, and the sour smell of betel nut. *Which one had it been this time?* Khoo was the only man in the room. An electric motor whined, and LeAnn knew it was a garage door. Jie was back, so it had to be near seven in the morning.

Jie looked like shit, like he had been up all night or slept in the same clothes. Fresh stains covered the front of his shirt, and his hair was matted on one side.

Khoo said something to him, questioning his ability to stay alert through his shift, and Jie shrugged, ignoring him. There was tension between the two this morning she hadn't witnessed before.

Neither of the two men ever mentioned the time. The sun was all she needed, something Ramzi had taught her. She turned her head as far as she could and saw Khoo working on the desk. He had a Phillips screwdriver nearby and was using a wrench to tighten one of the legs. As he turned toward her, he smiled. The red saliva coating his teeth looked horrific, like a death mask from a movie, but she focused instead on the screwdriver. She could kill him with it if she could just get free.

The desk drawer slammed shut behind her and then Khoo was towering over her, his face expressionless.

"What now," she said.

Ignoring her, he turned, looked at Jie, then left, slamming the heavy metal door behind him. The garage door motor whined, the van's engine started and she listened as it accelerated, then faded. She hoped listening to it might give her some clues as to what was outside, but there were no clues, no hints of what lay behind the door. Now she was alone again with Jie.

She pulled on the straps to test her strength again; she was still weak but not as weak as yesterday. At least now she could pull hard enough to redden the skin around her wrists.

She would need to be free from these straps to get to Jie, which meant a trip to the bathroom, and not during Khoo's shift. Khoo was too strong, those huge arms could crush her and he also seemed the wiser of the two. It had to be Jie.

Jie was rolling her to the toilet twice each day now, usually just after injecting enough heroin into her veins to leave her helpless. She had even fallen off the seat once, and Jie had to lift her and put her back in the wheelchair. Another day, or maybe two, and she might have the strength to overpower him. Until then she would play the passive role they expected from her.

The Clean Man assumed she would be compliant enough to walk out of here on her own in two weeks he had said, maybe three, which now meant as little as nine days.

Brianne had walked like a lamb to the slaughterhouse. Another nine days of a drug-induced fog, and she could be just as willing as Brianne. Manila and New York were crawling with junkies, and LeAnn knew how powerful a motivator heroin was to an addict.

"I need another shot of that shit!" she begged the man. "Fentanyl this time."

Jie looked at her, confused, and she nodded her head at the bottle on the desk. He was happy to oblige, and this time she hoped to stay conscious. Asking for it was probably the first sign they looked for.

"Ah, the good shit," she said as the drug washed over her, and indeed, it did give her the feeling of euphoria. She was free from all her tormenting anxieties, the claustrophobia of captivity, of being helpless, and even her rage—and this time, she did stay conscious. It was a smaller dose now, she assumed.

"It's the bomb," she croaked.

"Yes, bomb," he said, imitating her.

That is how it will happen. Soon I will crave the absence of all my pain.

Jie stood over her and looked at her breasts, then his eyes went further down her body, and he cupped her vagina with his filthy right hand. Even through the fentanyl, her rage blossomed again. She forced it aside and watched his eyes. She even smiled, encouraging him on.

Compliance.

She wanted to vomit.

***

Sometime later, LeAnn woke in the darkness. All the lights were out and she was alone. There was just enough streetlight coming in through the windows to tell her both cots on either side of her were empty, and both Jie and Khoo were gone. She pulled uselessly at the straps until she could pull no more. Her captors were gone, and the door to freedom was just a few feet away. She could feel the freedom lingering on the other side of the door, teasing her.

"Help me," she screamed. Her shouts echoed in the empty warehouse. Over and over, she screamed until her throat was raw. As the echoes died, the silence was so profound, she yearned to hear Jie's voice . . . anything was better than this.

Something ran across the floor behind her. It was in one of the corners she couldn't see, its nails scratching the concrete as it raced across the barren floor.

For the first time in her life, LeAnn felt a profound hopelessness, and remembered that haunted look on Brianne's face.

CHAPTER 5

KWAN

Superintendent Kwan Kim Lai sat at his desk, stirring sugar into his morning coffee when his cell phone rang. "Are you sure, Chin?" he said.

Haron Chin, his assistant, was at the Tampines Mall, the scene of another abduction. This time it was a young mother on vacation with her husband and two small children.

Another one.

In the last year and a half, sixteen young girls, all tourists from as far away as Aruba, had been reported missing and three of them from this same mall. None had been found and the prime minister was coming down hard on the department. Soon, travel warnings would be issued advising tourists that Singapore was not a safe destination. The PM couldn't care less about the abductions, but tourism was a big part of Singapore's economy.

"I'm on my way, Chin."

Haron Chin was pacing between several uniformed officers and the mall's main entrance. The mall was a hot spot for tourists looking for souvenirs and authentic Asian goods before boarding their flights home, and at 9 a.m., the mall was already crowded.

The uniformed officers were talking to a middle-aged man speaking English, and Kwan listened in while examining the victim's photo. She was certainly attractive, but she was a mother in her early thirties and that did not fit the profile. Kwan's victims had all been young girls, some as young as fourteen, still, there were enough nagging similarities that Kwan couldn't dismiss it.

Modra Stargyl had left her husband and kids in a shoe store in search of a restroom in the mall's atrium . . . and vanished. It had been two hours now, and her husband was distraught and both kids looked as if they had cried until there were no more tears left. He had seen it before, and soon the husband would have that same look of despair. But for the moment, the man was clinging to some hope the police would find his wife.

"Chin, lets walk the route she would have used to get to the bathroom."

The most logical, and closest restroom the woman would have used was right outside the Hershey's Chocolate World and next to an employee service hallway that led to the parking lot. He could picture a man pulling a small woman down this deserted hall and into a waiting white van, not so different from the exit of Changi Airport's international terminal.

"No sign of a struggle inside the bathroom?" Kwan said.

"No sign of a struggle anywhere, no witnesses either."

"Dammit, Chin. Are they that good, or are they just lucky? Look at all these people." Kwan waved at the throng of men and women walking through the mall's interior. "What about all the cameras," he said, looking up at the one right above them.

"This is the last camera that would have a view of her, there are none in the service hallway, Chin said. "The next camera would be outside in the parking lot.

"It's going to be another late night, Chin."

***

At forty-five years of age, Kwan had hoped his promotions and advancements within the department would eventually offer a stable work schedule, but the opposite seemed true. He was missing more and more dinners at home with his wife, and this was going to be another one.

"Let's gather up all the camera feeds and have some of our people start going through them," Kwan said. "With any luck we'll find something worthwhile, and Chin, make a copy of her photo and get it out to all the patrol units as soon as possible."

For the next several hours Kwan and three of his inspectors looked at a dozen videos, some showing glimpses of the blonde woman walking through the mall with her family, and only one showing her near the restroom, but there was no sign of her abduction.

"Look at this Chin, these two kids just entering the camera's view, they're looking at her."

Kwan froze the video looking at the two teenagers in the top right of the screen, in the bottom left, the top of Modra Stargyl's head was still visible as she was about to walk out of the cameras view. In the next frame, the two men appeared to be arguing, and the larger of the two struck the second one in the face, knocking him down. Everyone around the two had stopped and were watching the confrontation. In the next frame, the Stargyl woman was missing, and the one teenager was helping the other one up off the floor, both looking in the direction of the victim.

"This isn't some random argument, Chin. They purposely distracted everyone around them while someone just out of view grabbed her."

"That's the last video of her in the mall, let's see what the ones in the parking lot have," Chin said.

Six cameras stationed around the exit showed several white vans moving through the lot near the exit, only two of them were a Toyota HiAce and the cameras view point stopped before either of them reached the exit. A seventh camera, one that would have shown the exit itself, was inoperable.

"How convenient, Chin, get with the mall, find out when that camera stopped working and why. I have a feeling it stopped working just as these women began disappearing.

"Yes, sir."

Frustrated, he left Chin, and drove back to the station and watched the video of the white van at the Changi Airport again.

The angle was wrong and the glare from the sun blocked some

of the image, but it was the only real bit of evidence so far, the only piece to his bizarre puzzle.

Again and again, the video showed the white Toyota HiAce pull to the curb, the cargo door slide open, and a man pushed— or did he just follow—the woman into the van? Kwan thought it looked like another person inside may have pulled the girl in, but the angle and the glare made it impossible to tell.

"Dammit!"

There were thousands, maybe ten thousand, similar vans in Singapore, and the van itself was a dead end. The witness, an old man, had said it was a young woman in a red jacket who was forced into the van. They had traced the woman back through the airport and her name was Leila Moran. Kwan knew the twenty-year-old Canadian woman had flown in from San Francisco, but little else.

Kwan had no doubt that she had been abducted, but it had been twelve days now and there were still no missing person reports matching this girl's description. Two cell phones captured the abduction: one a video and the other a photo of the back of the generic white van, the license plate unreadable, so both photos were useless.

The old man at the airport was certain he saw a tattoo on the man who pushed her, a skull inside a red circle on his neck. The description of the tattoo sounded familiar, something from years ago when he worked in the intelligence division.

He watched the video one more time. He couldn't see any tattoo. In frustration, he turned it off and called the woman in charge of the Airport Police Division, Kaili Min.

"Kaili, it's been almost two weeks since the Moran abduction, please tell me you have something."

"Yes, Kim. I do, but we still have several dozen cameras to check. I should have a report for you by morning."

"I could be out of a job by morning, Kaili."

"I'm doing everything I can, Kim."

Logging on to his computer, he searched the database using "skull tattoo," "neck," and "male" as key search words and seconds later had sixty-two hits with pictures and names. He went through each one and eliminated more than half of them. Some were in prison, some were dead, and some were the wrong age. Thirty men remained and he studied each one, trying to recall if he had ever dealt with them. Two looked familiar and a more detailed search listed every encounter those two had had with the Singapore Police Department.

One of them was Hui Jie. Kwan had arrested the man eight years ago for smoking marijuana in a park near the Geylang River. He remembered the tattoo, it was fresh with new ink, a fiery red sun with the gray skull in the middle. Jie himself was unremarkable, just a young kid in a crowd of other kids all smoking marijuana.

Kwan found Jie's old arrest form and winced each time he came across a misspelled word. Jie was short, 162 centimeters and thin, at least he was eight years ago. His mug shot showed two moles under his left eye, and the distinctive tattoo that covered most of his neck below the left ear.

Jie's most recent run-in with the police department was four years ago, a simple traffic ticket at the Pasir Panjang Ferry Terminal. Jie was a weak lead, but at the moment it was all he had.

He radioed his assistant, "Chin, anything new on the Stargyl woman?"

"Not a thing," Haron said. "But you were right, that camera has been out of order for sixteen months, two weeks before the first mall abduction. The camera's lens was shattered and a new one was ordered a few months ago. It's been sitting on a shelf in the security office ever since."

"Great! Meet me downstairs. I may have a lead on the guy from the airport."

***

Thirty minutes later they were knocking on the door of an apartment across the street from Tampines Central Park. As they waited for an answer, the roar of a private jet departing from

Changi reminded him how close they were to the airport. An elderly Chinese woman opened the door and bowed slightly, the smell of roasted pork following her outside.

Both men bowed deeply in return. "I'm sorry if we've interrupted your dinner, but I'm looking for Hui Jie, do you know him," Kwan said.

Looking at Jie's picture, she flinched and nodded. Frowning, she said, "My nephew. He's no good. His father was a sailor in the Taiwan Navy, he left my sister days after Jie was born. My sister died when he was seven and I raised him the best I could, but he was always trouble and I haven't seen him in years."

"Do you know where he lives now?" Kwan said.

"No, I heard he was working in the shipyard on Jurong Island, but that was two years ago. He was a welder, but he was involved in drugs and lost his job. I haven't heard anything since then."

"What about friends, do you know any of them?"

"He had two friends, old friends from school. One is dead and the other was in jail, last I heard. His last name is Khoo, that's all I know."

Kwan thanked the woman and wrote the name down in his notes. Except for the new name, he left empty-handed, but at least he had that.

"Let's go by the airport, I want to speak to Director Min and see what she has. This can't wait."

The Airport Police Division had an office in the air freight terminal, and Chin parked his Hyundai at the curb. The superintendent was behind her desk and was not surprised to see them.

"Kwan Kim and his faithful assistant, Haron Chin. How did I know you couldn't wait till morning?"

"Sorry, Kaili, there's been another abduction. Can you show us what you have so far?"

"Well, my report is not complete. You know we have hundreds of cameras, Kim."

"Tell me you have something, Kaili."

"I have two views of the van as it drives up and then away

36

from the international terminal," she said. "Here, take a look." Turning her computer screen toward the men, she ran the video. "It's definitely a Toyota HiAce, a new one and probably a rental. As it comes in from the main road, you can see two men through the windshield, not the best lighting but you can tell both men appear to be in their twenties or thirties. The first time we see it is seven in the morning as it drives past this camera, but it does not come up on the next camera until eight-forty when it pulls up to the curb. There's a blind spot between the two cameras, so it must have parked for an hour and forty minutes before the abduction."

"No doubt waiting for the inside guy to signal he was coming out with the victim," Kwan said.

The three of them watched the van's door open, a scene Kwan had already viewed a dozen times. "What's next?" Kwan said.

"This one. Here's the woman inside the terminal heading toward the exit. See how the guy in the black tee shirt starts following her? There's a bit of a tattoo exposed above his collar. He's calling someone on his cell phone, probably the van's driver. He stays ten meters behind until they reach the exit, then he gets really close as they're on the curb and he shoves her into the van," Kaili said. She pressed a few keys on the keyboard, and a different view came up. "Now, we're going backward in time as they pass through the previous camera near the gate."

This video was good, but not good enough to say the man was Hui Jie. "Kaili, are there any views of this guy from the front?"

"Of course."

In the next video was an older version of the Hui Jie he remembered. There was no doubt this was Jie walking toward the camera, the red sun tattoo prominently rising above the collar of his black tee shirt.

"I have you, Jie!" Kwan said, slamming his fist on the desk.

"Wait, there's more," Kaili said. "This morning we took another look at all the cameras at Ms. Moran's gate, and we almost missed this one. We didn't recognize the man at first. Look, it's the same man wearing a different shirt."

This last video showed Jie in a gray uniform with an airport ID tag hanging around his neck, emptying a trash can. He was emptying the can, but his eyes were watching someone on the other side of the terminal. The video continued, showing Jie as he disappeared into a bathroom, then came out a few minutes later in the black tee shirt.

"I have my people showing a still photo of him to the maintenance supervisors. Two employees working that terminal thought he looked familiar, but neither are sure. I know I've never seen him, but he could be new or a transfer from another department."

Kwan was trying to control his excitement. After one year and sixteen missing women, seventeen now, he had his first suspect. "Dammit, he was here all the time." He walked to the plate glass window and stared at the people waiting for their flights in the passenger terminal across the tarmac. *Jie could be right there, right now, staring back at me!*

"We need to get his picture out to all the units right away," Kwan said. "Chin, label him as a person of interest and if anyone comes across him, have them hold him for us."

"Thanks, Kaili. Please call me if you find anything new."

The sun was setting as Kwan and Chin drove westbound out of the airport, and the glare was intense.

"I arrested Jie eight years ago with three or four of his friends," Kwan said. "When we get back, I want you to look up all his associates and have the night crew start tracking them down. Hopefully, if we throw out a big enough net, we'll get a few good fish."

CHAPTER 6

LEANN

Jie and Khoo were moving around behind her, whispering. Awake now for several minutes, she listened with her eyes closed. Why whisper, unless it was about her.

"What are you talking about, Khoo?"

Silence, then the swishing sound of Jie sweeping the floor, while Khoo rocked in the metal chair behind her, it was their morning routine. It was early; the air was still cool and fresh, soon it would begin to warm and the stench would creep back in.

After waking up alone the night before, the sound of the two men was comforting, and the metallic taste in her mouth told her they had dosed her with fentanyl some time earlier. Then the throaty sound of a big engine announced the arrival of the Clean Man. The engine raced and then died and the metal door banged open with a crash as the man made his dramatic entrance.

The familiar rich smell of fresh leather mixed with something musky washed over her. As she opened her eyes, the man was staring down at her. This time, he wore a black wool suit, a gray shirt and a matching black tie with the same heavy gold chain keeping the tie in place.

By now she was used to Jie and Khoo staring at her naked helpless body, strapped down like a pathetic sheep. It was never pleasant, but she endured it. The Clean Man's leering examination was worse. His dark brown eyes traced every inch of her body, as if he were looking for flaws, or taking inventory of his wares, like a merchant going through his stock.

"You smell like a used car," she said.

The creepy smile on his face slipped for a second, then returned. Sucking in a deep breath through his clenched teeth, he made a whistling noise.

"Tsk-tsk, my little dove," he said as he walked around her, still scanning every inch of her skin. He grabbed her chin and turned her head, looking at her left ear. "I see our earlier discussion has left no permanent damage, but don't press your luck." He smiled again and patted her face like her father used to, feeling the softness of his skin, the smell of leather stronger now.

"Yes, yes . . . Ms. Moran will do well, Jie. I have a client already interested, and to be honest, I may have a go at her myself before we turn her loose." He walked slowly around until he was behind her and out of her sight.

At least he still thought she was Leila Moran. If he ran her fingerprints, things might be different.

"And who do we have here?" he said.

LeAnn turned and saw a new woman on the cot to her left. This woman looked pale and sickly, and LeAnn thought she was dead at first, only the slow rise and fall of her chest indicated she was still breathing. The once-empty IV pole now had a full bag of clear saline and another, smaller, white bottle hanging from the pole.

"Modra Stargyl," Khoo said. "We brought her in this morning."

Modra sounded like a foreign name, and with hair that was more silver than blonde, LeAnn guessed that she was Scandinavian.

"This morning, you say," the Clean Man said, walking around the woman. He stopped behind her head and his smile tightened. "Jie, I'm not so sure about this one. I think she is too old. Look at the wrinkles around her eyes, she has scars here too," he said, pointing to her abdomen. "At best we can use her for a month or two. Maybe she comes from money and we can ransom her off if the price is right. If not, we'll deal with her like the others. People pay for that as well."

The Clean Man turned to appraise his henchman. "I should promote you, Jie. You've been with me how long now, two years?

Just think, eight weeks ago I removed the end of your finger, and now I want to promote you."

"I made a grave error, sir. I deserved that and more."

"Yes, you did, Jie. One other thing, my friend, I want you to stop chewing that betel nut. The sight of it disgusts me. And you too, Khoo. I see its stains everywhere. Jie, I pay you enough that you should at least wear a clean shirt." He looked around the room and noticed the trash Jie had swept into a corner, "And clean this place up too."

The Clean Man glanced over at LeAnn, raking her with his eyes. "Neither of you are to touch Ms. Moran again. If you have to fuck someone, use this one," he said, pointing to the new woman. "And let Ms. Moran bathe herself from now on as well, as a reward for her cooperation." He winked at her and smiled, "I think she is ready for that, and leg chains only. Khoo, we need to fill that bed. Brianne did well again last night, so she will be staying with the others."

He came back around and stood at LeAnn's feet, and her neck ached as she tried to look him in the eyes. His smile faded and he looked angry now, less satisfied than when he had first walked in.

"But I think we need to step up her dosage, there is still a fire in her eyes that worries me. I want to put some of that fire out; not all of it, of course, just enough to keep her interesting. Another week, Jie, and I'll stop in again and check on your progress."

"Yes, Laoban."

"Keep a close eye on her—your eye, Jie, and nothing else, are we clear?"

"Yes, of course."

She heard the soft brush of leather soles as he walked away and then the big door slammed shut. *Another room, big enough to park a van inside and then a final door to the outside. Khoo, Jie, the Driver, and the Clean Man. How many more men were involved?*

***

Jie would be taking her to the shower soon, judging by the sunlight through the window. He bathed her each day as the light fell between two electrical outlets near the floor.

"Let her bathe herself," the Clean Man had said. Soon, she would need to make her move.

LeAnn looked again at the beam of sunlight on the floor, and guessed it was three hours past the 7 a.m. mark. Testing her strength again, she pulled the straps with both hands until they cut into her flesh. It was painful, but she was stronger.

Modra whimpered, and Jie grabbed the brown bottle and a syringe. The woman was hooked to an IV, and Jie injected the drug into its port. Soon the whimpering faded, and the woman was out. To test her, Jie pinched one of her nipples hard enough that Modra would have cried out if she wasn't completely under. LeAnn wondered if this was a test, or did it excite him, and had he pinched her that way too?

Jie turned to look at her. She smiled and closed her eyes, hoping he wasn't going to dose her before the shower. He moved around the room and then the squeal of the old wheelchair announced his presence as he rolled it up to her cot.

"Shower," he said in English.

She opened her eyes and nodded, hoping he mistook the acknowledgment as compliance.

Jie strapped her arms to the chair tight enough to cut off her circulation, and the skin on her hands turned bright red. Jie was afraid of her, afraid she would get loose, and . . . what? Run away? She could barely walk.

Rolling through the bathroom door, she examined a small vanity for anything she could use as a weapon. There was nothing there or anywhere in the room. Nothing but a bar of soap and a dirty towel.

How would she do it and when would she be ready? One more day, she promised herself, one more day to plan everything because it would be her only chance. If she failed, she would never have another one, if she lived through it at all.

"I want to pee first."

She could have gotten out of the chair and onto the toilet herself, but she was starting to see a pattern in the way Jie helped her. One more test.

"Help me up."

Leaning forward, he unstrapped her and lifted her with his left arm. As he did, he was off-balance and looking more toward the chair than at her. For just a few seconds, he was vulnerable.

If she could get behind Jie, she might have a chance at choking him in a headlock, but that would be too risky. As small as Jie was, he was still stronger and he would easily win any battle of strength.

Examining the room again, she noted that the toilet seat was firmly bolted to the bowl, but the ceramic tank lid was not. To test it, she leaned back as she sat and heard the lid shift on the tank, making a grating sound.

"I'm done," she said.

LeAnn stood and showered in hot water for the first time. The hot water was soothing, but she could feel her knees aching and nausea in her bowels, like she was coming down with the flu. Her first signs of an opioid withdrawal. How many hours ago had Jie injected her with whatever was in the bottle? She knew it wasn't always the same drug. She had never tried anything more than pot, but she had watched others shooting heroin and other opioids often enough in the streets of New York City and Manila. She had also watched some of them overdose and die right in front of her.

Jie stood in the doorway watching as she showered. He had a different look on his face now. His cheeks were mottled, red in some spots and pale white in others. He was angry. Poor Jie, the Clean Man had told him not to touch her again, and she thought that was what was bothering him. Would he obey the man? Jie wasn't smart, but his boss had smashed his finger with a hammer, so maybe he had learned something that day.

Clean and back on her cot, she observed Jie as he took a set of heavy chains from the desk drawer and attached them to her ankles, then looped them through the legs of the cot, securing it with a padlock. No more time-consuming straps, she supposed.

Brianne had been wearing these same chains for the last several days before they began using her, and that gave LeAnn chills. She knew exactly what they were doing with Brianne, and she was next. The chains gave her some mobility, but she would never be able to get off the cot without a key. It was an improvement, but just barely.

"Jie," she said in a voice she hoped sounded as weak as she felt, "I need a shot, and some water, please."

He turned to her, unsure if he understood what she had said.

She looked over at the syringe and nodded. "Fentanyl again?"

"No," was all he said. She watched him filling the syringe with something new. A clear liquid flowed into the IV port, and it took fifteen seconds for the rush to hit her. She was instantly warm. The aches she had felt seconds ago vanished and her arms and legs felt like they weighed hundreds of pounds. She tried to lift one arm but couldn't. She realized that she could never overpower Jie like this. Then she stopped caring, and it was one of the greatest feelings she could remember.

CHAPTER 7

KWAN

In the records section of the downtown police headquarters, Kwan pulled another file from the cabinet. In this room, the hard copies from the major crime units were stored, along with the inspectors' personal notes, cassette tapes, and in the newer cases, digital recordings of all interviews and interrogations.

The acrid, musty smell of the old files, some stored more than forty years, made his eyes water, and the yellowed report in his hand was dated January 4th 1979, when he was still wearing diapers.

Dates and case numbers were attached to each drawer, and in the far-right corner, he found what he was looking for, January-June, 2010.

The drawer slid forward, the papers inside less yellowed than the first and the smell was almost pleasant. Hopefully, in this cabinet he would find his old notes and a connection to someone named Khoo. Khoo was a common name, and without a birthdate, he had been unable to link anyone with that name to Jie. But he had arrested Jie and several of his friends eight years ago and hopefully Khoo was one of them. The arrest form didn't list any of Jie's co-defendants, but his original report and the notes attached to it might.

The cabinet was like a time capsule. As he held the papers, he was transported back in time. Homicides, robberies, thefts, and the file he held in his hands now was several pages thick. He thumbed through each page but there was no mention of anyone named Khoo.

The report he wanted was the second to the last in the stack. It was written the night he arrested Jie. It was short, only a page and a half. Khoo's name was not on it. It had been a long shot, but sometimes those long shots were money makers.

The last report in the stack was a thick one and was written in January 2010, with his signature scrawled on the last page. It had been cold that night, and he had worn his bulky, heavy coat as he and his six-member task force moved toward the old freighter tied up on the docks.

A tip had come in that the ship's cook was manufacturing black tar heroin onboard while the ship was out at sea. The freighter was called a 'feeder' for its small size; still, at 150 meters, and stacked high with steel containers, it was a formidable target for the assault squad.

A second team advanced on the ship's prow where a gangway was already in position. Both teams waited in the dark for the air-unit to illuminate the deck. Kwan heard the beating blades of a Sikorsky Seahawk flying in from the north, and as it came overhead and switched on its powerful spotlight, gunfire erupted.

Two men on the ship's bridge began firing AK-47s at the aircraft, then the sniper behind Kwan fired and one of the two went down. More shots were fired, and more men died.

Three of the ship's crew and one of Kwan's fellow officers were killed. There was no sign of heroin or any other narcotics on board. What they found were twenty-five Taiwanese women bound and held hostage in two of the cargo containers, all destined for the sex slave markets in the United States. The ship's captain and crew were all arrested and imprisoned.

And there it was—the name he'd been hunting, Tan Khoo.

He couldn't remember Khoo, or if he had ever interviewed him that night, but he remembered the slain officer, the youngest man on his team. He had been a bright officer, just twenty-one years old with a new bride and expecting their first child. Their daughter was twelve now, and each year he sent the girl a birthday card and her mother a note and a hundred-dollar bill, asking her to buy something nice for Jun Kai and tell her it was from her father's friends.

He held his notes, watching the pages tremble in his hands. It had been so many years ago, but the memories were still fresh, he could smell the salt air mixing with the stench of the cargo containers where the hostages had been held prisoner for weeks. He shivered, the room was cold, and perspiration still soaked his shirt.

Refiling the report along with the others, he looked at his watch. He had been reading reports for four hours. Reaching up for the files in the top cabinets and kneeling on the floor for the lower ones left his legs and back stiff and aching. He stretched for a moment, then wrote down the names of the other crewmen who were arrested that night along with Khoo. He asked the records clerk to run each of them for new history, and to do it as soon as possible.

Kwan needed addresses, phone numbers, anything that would help him find Jie and even Khoo. With luck, this new man Khoo might lead them to Jie. Moran and Stargyl might possibly be alive, and if he could save just one of them, all of this would be worth it. The clerk said the search would take hours, and Kwan needed to eat.

He pictured his wife sitting at home in front of the television, her feet up to take the weight off her swollen ankles, and called her.

"Honey, I feel like spoiling you. Can you meet me at Odette's?"

Kim had met Mei Lien ten years ago at Odette's, where she worked as a waitress to pay her way through college. They married six months later and finally, after eight years of trying, they were expecting their first child. Kim Hua "the prosperous" was due in another month, and Mei Lien's petite frame was now huge.

"Oh, Kim, you know how to steal a girl's heart. I was sitting alone feeling fat and ugly when you called."

Thirty minutes later, she walked into Odette's under her own power—a feat of sheer will, Kim thought, as he rose to kiss her.

"You look beautiful, so beautiful, and how is my little girl doing today?"

"She's been kicking me all day. She's going to be a professional dancer, I just know it. Any luck on your case?"

"Some, I went from nothing to having a suspect. I just need to find him."

"What about this latest girl, has her family come forward yet?"

"Leila Moran? No, it's been weeks, and nothing, I would have thought someone would be missing her by now. We've spoken to several of the passengers that sat near her, but only one woman remembers her. She had nothing nice to say about Ms. Moran, either. There's a record of the victim leaving San Francisco and arriving in Singapore, but the trail dies there. The name is too common for any other search, she's like a ghost."

"A loner in a foreign land, maybe," Mei Lien said.

"Maybe, but I'm afraid she's not the latest. Another woman was abducted this morning, in the middle of Tampines Mall. Chin and most of the team are still working the case, I don't feel lucky about this one either."

The two of them split the entrée, Hokkaido and toast, abalone with foie gras, and rosemary-smoked eggs. A flight of their favorite wines would have been appealing too, but Kim never drank on duty, and now, Mei Lien couldn't drink at all.

It was an expensive dinner, two days' pay at least, but he had neglected his suffering wife for the last few weeks, leaving her alone too long and coming home too late, often just in time to see her to bed. These missing girls were consuming him. The hope that they were out there and alive somewhere kept him going. Life as a police officer, his father would have said.

"I have a few more leads to run down tonight. I'll try not to be too late. Give your mother my love."

They lived in Singapore's northeast region of Serangoon, and his in-laws lived across the street. He was never quite sure if the woman cared for him. She wore a perpetual scowl on her weathered face, and the scowl deepened whenever he was around. "She always looks like that," Mei Lien often said. Maybe so, but he gave the woman a wide berth.

Kwan pulled into the station as the midnight shift officers were arriving, young kids mostly, fresh out of the academy.

He longed for those days.

CHAPTER 8

LEANN

The pale brown spider still worked above her, spinning its expanding web through the corroded wire cage of the light fixture. The spider was a welcomed guest, a distraction from the monotonous misery all around her.

"I will name you Speck," she mumbled.

She felt nauseous again and wondered if it was another symptom of withdrawal. Just moments ago, she had been dreaming, listening to the drone of her professor and scheming how she would kill Christa, sitting right next to her. She had been free inside that pleasant dream.

In reality, her legs were still chained to the frame of her cot. She lifted her legs, the chain's links rattling on the concrete, and the sensation of confinement worsened the nausea. She leaned over and tried to puke, but only gagged.

Khoo moved behind her and put a bucket next to her cot.

It was cloudy and without her sunbeam to mark the time, she didn't know if it was morning or afternoon, but Khoo was behind her, so it was early.

"Khoo," she said, but he didn't reply. The bastard would never speak to her. She almost wished he would. She needed something other than silence. "Khoo, I need water. I need to eat something."

"No."

"You prick!" she said, waiting for the slap.

The chair screeched on the concrete and the back of his hand struck her ear.

"Thank you," she mumbled. It was becoming a ritual between the two of them. She enjoyed annoying him, it was about the only thing she could do. Then her sunbeam appeared on the floor, right between the electrical outlets, and she knew it was seven in the morning. Shift change and shower time.

Please don't drug me now. Today may be my last chance.

She listened for Jie's arrival. Several cars or maybe trucks drove by, but there was no sound of the van's four-cylinder diesel engine. Despite the nausea, she felt ready, as clear-headed and strong as she was ever going to be. She began counting the seconds, then minutes, and twelve minutes later the familiar sound of the van and the whine of the garage door's motor announced his arrival.

Jie stepped inside and looked angry. First, he looked at her chains, then at her, and she thought he was going to slap her too, then he started yelling at Khoo. All she could make out was something about Brianne. The girl had been gone for several days and LeAnn had forgotten about her.

Khoo, still behind her, was ignoring him, then said, "Outside."

Both men went back outside through the metal door where she knew the van was parked. Exhaust flooded the room each time the men changed shifts. Outside, Jie was yelling but not Khoo, and finally Jie came back inside. The engine of the van revved up and then faded as Khoo left.

Jie's face was flushed, eyes wild, and for once, he kept his eyes off her and never even glanced at Modra. Pacing back and forth in front of her, his movements were rigid. This was a side of Jie she had never seen, and this Jie scared her.

He jerked to a stop as if he had forgotten what he was thinking, then pulled out a cloth bag of the betel nuts and began chewing. His lips were moving as well. He was talking to himself and twice pounded his fist in his palm.

"You're going to lose more fingers chewing that," she said.

Jie ignored her not understanding anything she said, and continued mumbling and pacing behind her. Twice she heard him say Brianne's name.

"What is the matter with you?" she said. "What about Brianne?"

He stopped, looking at her as if he had forgotten she was there. Something was wrong and she had to think fast.

"I need to pee," she mumbled.

Jie's face contorted as he chewed the wad in his mouth, and his eyes fixated on her. The man was having some type of breakdown, and she wished Khoo was back in the room.

"Bathroom," she said more forcibly, and nodded toward the toilet.

Finally, his face relaxed, his whole body slumped, and he moved toward the desk. Grabbing the key, he unlocked both chains and the heavy links clattered to the floor. She was free now and felt like she could probably walk but wanted to be sitting down. She needed to be in the chair if this was going to work. Motioning to the wheelchair, she did her best to look feeble.

"I feel sick," she said. "Sick!"

Jie pushed her as fast as he could, he understood what sick meant, and wanted no part in cleaning up the mess he thought could happen at any second. At the toilet, he hesitated, not wanting to help her on the seat and standing as far to her right as possible, just out of her reach—he wasn't entirely stupid.

"Sick," she repeated, holding her stomach as she rose from the chair, then stumbled and fell next to the toilet and cried out as if in pain, then tried to lift herself up onto the seat. Now Jie came forward to help. Her legs did feel rubbery and weak, and she began doubting whether she had the strength to carry out what was coming next.

Jie leaned in, and she swung the heel of her hand into the side of his neck with all the power and speed she had—the classic brachial stun—and Jie collapsed, his head smashing into the porcelain bowl of the toilet.

It was an excellent, simple move that causes unconsciousness by a shock to the nerves around the carotid artery, but it was temporary, and Jie would soon regain consciousness. She had only minutes to act.

Was she strong enough to choke the man to death with her bare hands? Another time and she knew she could, but just hitting him in the neck had left her too weak to stand. How long could she squeeze with fingers that were shaking so much? Her knees collapsed, and she sank to the cool tiled floor and watched the man breathe, then his leg moved. Any second, he would open his eyes and wonder what had happened.

Crawling to the toilet, she lifted the porcelain lid off the tank with both hands and smashed it into Jie's head. There was a satisfying crack as the lid disintegrated, and blood and bits of ceramic flew in all directions.

His body lay lifeless next to the toilet and she sat next to him hoping he was dead . . . then his eyes fluttered and he began trying to sit up. She didn't have the strength to hit him again, or even stand up. How was she going to kill him now? She needed a tool. Reaching up, she pulled open the vanity's single drawer and found two rubber bands and a plastic comb. *Useless.*

Jie was sitting upright now, blood pouring down his forehead and into his eyes and pooling in his lap. She needed that screwdriver, or something similar, and she needed it quick. She was going to pass out, and if she did, Jie would surely kill her despite the Clean Man's warning.

Small cuts and scratches from the shards of broken porcelain bloodied her hands and knees, leaving smears of red on the tile floor. Crawling into the main room, she staggered to the locker where Jie had found Brianne's dress. Two more dresses and a pair of pink shoes were inside. They were open-toe flats. If they had been spiked heels, she would have tried ramming one of them into Jie's eyes. Turning, she looked at the desk a few feet away and heard Jie wheeze in the bathroom.

Even those few feet to the wooden desk left her gasping for breath, but in the top drawer she found what she needed—the Phillips-head screwdriver. She had fantasized about killing Khoo with this same tool. It was old and rusty, but the shaft was four inches long. There was also a folding pocketknife with a dull, three-inch blade. The knife with its dull blade was the smarter choice; it could still cut Jie's throat, but it had to be the screwdriver. She had dreamed of killing either man with it, and now she was going to.

Her fastest speed was a shuffle. Her legs were like jelly from so many weeks of inactivity, even with her attempts to exercise.

If I could just stop and rest.

Jie moaned again, this time it sounded like he was cursing her. Jie could come through the door at any time, and she wouldn't be able to surprise him twice.

She found him still sitting upright, taking shallow breaths, his eyes were focused on her at first, then closed. The twitching in his hands and feet weren't as severe as they were minutes ago as the nerves in his neck began to function. As she watched the trembling stop, Jie slid down the wall, leaving an arc of crimson blood that looked like a red Japanese fan on the white tile.

He was on his side now, and all her dreams and fantasies of plunging the screwdriver into his chest and feeling it slide between his ribs and puncture his heart vanished. It was too awkward with him in this position, but his right temple was an easy target.

On her knees and using both hands, she slammed the screwdriver into the tender spot of his temple and watched his body convulse as his brain reacted to the intrusion.

It was too easy a death. He had raped her and fondled her, and he was not going to die so easily. She grabbed the handle and rotated it, like stirring paint in a bucket, feeling the steel shank mixing up the gray matter in his skull.

Finally, the convulsions stopped as Jie's last breath wheezed from his lungs, and she knew he would never draw another one. Sitting cross-legged in front of his body, she pulled the screwdriver from his temple. Watching his blood drip from the shank and onto the floor, she felt so alive and so empowered. She relished this quick moment, knowing it would fade.

How long she sat there she didn't know—the drugs were

playing tricks with her mind again. Had it been an hour or minutes? Khoo, or even the Clean Man, could return at any time — and she was still trapped in the building. She had a desperate need to get outside in the open air, fresh air without the smell of someone's piss in it.

That trapped feeling brought her out of her stupor, and she fought her old phobia, knowing she was far from finished.

She checked Jie's pockets and found an old flip phone, a roll of small bills, a set of keys, and his bulging billfold. The billfold was full of scraps of paper with handwritten notes and numbers, too much to go through, so she took it all.

She found her carry-on and her backpack in a second locker. Her wallet, ID and cash were missing. The carry-on was empty too, but the false bottom that supported the wheels hadn't been discovered. She flipped up the thin cardboard and saw her second passport, credit cards, cash, and her Canadian driver's license, all under the name LeAnn Aquino. The United States was looking for her under that alias, but it might come in handy.

Still nude, she needed her clothes, but there was no sign of her jeans, sweater, or rain jacket. That left the sundresses. She lifted one up to the light and could see through it, and she tossed it back into the locker.

Returning to the bathroom, she looked at Jie on the floor. He was a few inches taller than she was and just as thin.

She stripped him, leaving him in his stained boxer shorts — she would never let that cloth touch her bare skin. His dark blue shirt looked new, but still reeked of old sweat and was just as stained as his boxers, most of it from the red juice and his own blood.

The Clean Man would not have been happy.

Too weak to stand, she knelt in front of the sink and washed the shirt, getting most of the blood out, wrung it dry, and put it on and checked herself in the mirror. The shirt was baggy, the matching cargo pants were loose in the waist too, but with Jie's belt, she could pass herself off as a dock worker. She was tying up her hair with the two rubber bands when someone called out.

"Who's there," she said.

With the screwdriver in her hand, she stood and turned toward the door, ready to fight. But it was the woman's voice. LeAnn had forgotten about her fellow captive.

She looked back into the main room and told the wide-awake Modra Stargyl, "If you say another word, I will kill you. Do you understand?"

The woman nodded, eyes fixed on the bloody screwdriver. LeAnn relaxed, wiped Jie's blood from its shank, and put it in her back pocket.

"So, your name is Modra?" she said, studying the IV lines still in the woman's arm.

"Yes."

"Where are you from?"

"Switzerland."

There were small, spiderweb-like wrinkles in the corners of her eyes, but from ten feet, she could pass for a sixteen-year-old teenager. Jie was lucky, because up close, she looked at least thirty.

The IV bag strung on Modra's pole was empty. The writing on the bag was in Chinese, and the symbols meaningless to LeAnn, she had never wanted to read the language. She gripped the clear tube in one hand and pulled the IV out of the woman's wrist.

The woman was about to scream and LeAnn raised the screwdriver over her head and put a finger to her lips. "Hush," she said. "I really don't have the strength right now."

The woman froze, her lips still open, her eyes wide and fixed on LeAnn's, but she didn't make a sound.

"Were you at the airport?" LeAnn asked.

"No, I was at the mall with my husband and children."

"When was that?"

"Yesterday, maybe the day before. It was a Tuesday, I think. What day is it today?"

"I don't know," LeAnn said.

The woman was a complication to all her planning. She was weeping now, and LeAnn decided killing her quickly would solve the issue of a witness and end the woman's misery as well. She held the screwdriver in her hand, looked down at the mother of two—her captive companion—and knew she couldn't do it.

Jesus, what's wrong with me!

"Sorry, I don't have time for this," LeAnn said. "As soon as I can get out of here, I'll call the police."

There wasn't anything left to do. Her strength was returning, so she went back to the locker taking one last look hoping to find her shoes, but they were missing. The pair of flats lying on the floor of the locker probably belonged to Brianne. They were too big, but she would make them work because walking barefoot for miles might be a problem.

"No, please don't leave me here."

"I'm not your savior Modra, I'm really not a nice person either, but I won't kill you," LeAnn said, more to herself than to the woman. "Don't make me regret it."

She looked for the sunbeam, her only means of knowing the time, and it was gone. All she knew was that it was still daylight.

Modra whimpered as LeAnn checked the second door that led to the office. It was an old, heavy-gauge metal door, but the lock was new. Its steel bolt was meant to keep people out, which also meant someone was always inside, guarding the Clean Man's property.

The bolt opened easily and the door swung open into an empty garage bay. She could smell the fresh air already. There was a single overhead door on tracks and a smaller door next to it—her exit to the outside world.

With everything she could find of any use stuffed inside her carry-on, she pulled it across the concrete and reached for the doorknob, and as it turned, the overhead door's electric motor engaged, and the wooden door jerked in its tracks and began to open.

Khoo was back.

As the electric motor strained to lift the heavy door, the van's front bumper was visible. LeAnn shuffled back inside the main warehouse and slid the bolt closed, giving her time to think. She was safe for the moment, a few seconds at best, but also trapped.

Behind her, the woman on the cot was thrashing back and forth and then screamed, "Get me out of this fucking hellhole!"

"If you don't shut up, the man outside is going to kill us both in one minute."

LeAnn knew the woman was terrified and would probably start screaming again any second. She pulled the empty saline bag off the IV pole, folded it in two and gagged her with it, then put her finger to her lips and whispered.

"Shh."

The woman's eyes darted back and forth, she was still terrified but stopped pulling against the straps and lay still.

The overhead door stopped and the truck's engine revved up and then quit. It was right on the other side of the door now, and she waited, feeling the weakness in her legs, watching the screwdriver shake in her trembling hands, and her lungs gasping for more air. She was not going to survive if she couldn't get herself under control. "One thing at a time, breathe deep," she whispered.

Wearing a stranger's pink flats, Jie's baggy pants and stained shirt, she waited for Khoo, hoping he was alone. What if the Clean Man or someone else was with him? Would they be confused long enough for her to act? There were too many variables. Her prior kills had been planned out in great detail—and against defenseless victims.

"You're a sociopath," her psychiatrist had told her during one of their last sessions. "You can't feel emotions the way most people do."

She was feeling pretty emotional at the moment. What would that woman say right now? What advice would she give her?

Embrace the emotions you do have, LeAnn!

Holding the screwdriver in her right hand, she leaned against the wall, feeling her breathing finally slowing down. The truck's door opened and closed, and heavy footsteps thudded as someone approached the door.

Soaked in sweat, the cold damp shirt clinging to her chest, her skin on fire, and weak from hunger—she was going to have the fight for her life in seconds.

"Jie! I need help moving Brianne. Open the door." It was Khoo's voice. Was he coming in, or was he expecting Jie to go out?

She would never survive a fight with Khoo. He was three times her size and too strong. She slid the bolt back and waited, visualizing where his heart would be when he took his first step inside.

"Jie!"

"Tā mā de!" *Fuck!* She said in the lowest voice she could produce, trying to emulate Jie's high-pitched voice. It sounded nothing like Jie's, but it was all she had.

The door opened, and she saw the tip of his big leather boot in the doorway. She knew he was looking at the woman in the cot, and the empty one next to it—her cot.

Khoo stepped in and looked to his right. It was a mistake. From his left, LeAnn swung the screwdriver in an upward arc and hit him just below the ribs, feeling the steel sink deep, until her fingers and the handle hit him like an uppercut.

"Oooff," Khoo exhaled, but he didn't go down. Instead, he turned and looked at her. She saw the confusion in his eyes as he looked at Jie's shirt, and then he backhanded her with his left arm, knocking her to the floor.

The woman on the cot was wailing now. Even gagged, the unintelligible scream sounded like a fire alarm, and LeAnn knew she should have killed her. Getting to her knees was an effort and as Khoo bent down and grabbed her by the throat, she swung the screwdriver up into his abdomen, hoping to hit his liver.

The man seemed immune from the four-inch-long shank. Instead of releasing her, he squeezed so tightly that her tendons began popping against cartilage. Again and again, she swung the screwdriver, unable to aim at anything specific, feeling it sink deep into his flesh, but Khoo still hung on to her throat, his eyes bulging and full of rage.

Tunnel vision was blinding her, but with what little strength she had, LeAnn stabbed him in the chest until she lost consciousness, knowing she had failed. She collapsed onto the concrete floor—it still stank of old urine.

LeAnn knew she was dead. She had felt her death, seen the blackness and the empty void of hell all around her. But in this void, she found herself pushing a handcart down the aisle of NYU's Fine Arts auditorium.

The handcart was silent, its rubber wheels running smoothly along the carpeted runner, and Nicole was silent too.

LeAnn rolled the loaded cart up to the dark stage and cut through the duct tape that was keeping the girl upright.

She was not in hell; hell would never feel so good—and where was the fire and brimstone? No, this was not hell, this was purgatory, and she and her three friends were here to pay for their sins.

Dragging Nicole across the carpet, LeAnn propped her up in the seat next to Olivia. Either Olivia or Christa had already shit herself and the stink made LeAnn's stomach cramp. A fitting end for all three of them, she thought, pushing the hair off Nicole's ashen face. "I want you to look pretty when they find you, Nicole."

"And I'm sorry I didn't have time to dress you girls," she said, looking at the other two, "but you started this—and I did tell you I was going to kill you."

Christa's words that day in class were the final straw, her final sin. "You're such a freak, LeAnn, why don't you do us all a favor and kill yourself?"

"Fuck you!" she had said to the girl.

"You sure say 'fuck' a lot for a virgin, LeAnn," Nicole said, laughing.

And that was Nicole's undoing.

With the three girls posed properly, she sat next to Nicole and enjoyed the moment. If this was purgatory, she never wanted to leave.

Now LeAnn waited for the final chapter of her life. She knew she would not be dining with Jesus today. No, she would soon be meeting the Antichrist, the Angel of Darkness.

The faint sound of the devil's trumpets was coming from somewhere nearby, growing in intensity. Satan himself must be approaching. Odd that he would meet her in the school's auditorium.

The sound of trumpets changed to a warbling shriek, like the siren of a police car or a fire alarm—and she opened her eyes. Olivia, Christa, and Nicole were gone, and the auditorium began to fade like smoke caught in a stiff wind.

She was lying flat on her back, looking at the familiar light fixture above her, watching Speck hard at work harvesting a moth struggling fruitlessly in its web.

She was in hell after all.

The wailing was intense now. She turned to see where it was coming from but couldn't move. Khoo's leg was on top of her chest; she pushed it to one side and sat up.

The woman's mouth was wide-open, the skin stretched to its limits, and LeAnn thought the corners of her mouth might actually split apart. The wailing stopped for a second as the woman took a deep breath and then it started again.

LeAnn stood over Modra and reached for the screwdriver in her back pocket, but the pocket was empty. She looked at Khoo and saw the blue handle of the Phillip's-head screwdriver sticking out of his chest.

"Shut up!" she screamed, but if the woman heard her, she never even flinched.

LeAnn slapped her in the face as hard as she had driven the screwdriver into Jie's head, again and again until the woman finally stopped.

She had killed Khoo out of fear and Jie for revenge but she wanted to kill this woman for the anger and rage running through her right now.

How's that for emotions, doctor?

She thought of pulling the screwdriver out of Khoo's chest, or gouging the dull blade of the pocketknife through Modra's throat, but then slapped the woman again, putting every remaining ounce of strength she had into this last blow. The woman's head bounced on the mattress and her eyes rolled back.

That's better.

The blow had consumed her rage but now killing Modra felt wrong. Modra was a victim, just like she had been. She was a wife and a mother to some kids. LeAnn placed a finger on her throat and felt a strong pulse. Seconds later, Modra opened her eyes.

"Please don't kill me," she whispered.

"I will if you scream again. How long was I out?"

"Two minutes . . . ten maybe. I don't know, I thought you were both dead."

LeAnn looked back at Khoo. "He's dead, I'm not."

She checked him for a pulse and then pulled the screwdriver out.

She kicked him in the head as hard as she could, and her pink shoe flew across the warehouse.

"Fuck you, you crack bastard!"

The kick caused Khoo's head to bounce off his shoulder and roll back until he was facing her. His dead, dull eyes were half-open, and he stared up at her. Barefoot now, she kicked him again and punishing pain radiated up her calf.

There were a dozen small holes in Khoo's blue work shirt, some with big blossoms of fresh blood and others just ragged holes in the fabric. At least one of her blows had found his heart and killed him. She knew it had been close, and she also knew she had been lucky.

She rifled through his pockets, and like Jie, he had a cheap, ancient flip phone. She opened it and saw there were two missed calls. Someone was trying to get in touch with him. She smiled, knowing he was never going to answer.

Khoo had a lot more cash than Jie did, several thousand Singapore dollars, all in large bills rolled up and held with a thick red rubber band. His wallet was more organized than Jie's too. She found a Visa card with the name Tan Khoo and a platinum American Express card with the name "The Blue Room," issued last year. She took everything the man had, including a set of keys, and put it all in her pockets.

She checked the warehouse one last time for anything of value. There was nothing else she could use, and she looked at Modra again, who was naked and afraid.

"I'm leaving. There is nothing here to cover you with, and I'm not going to free you, but as soon as I get a block away, I will call the police. I don't want you anywhere near me. The police will free you."

"I won't tell them anything."

"Yes, you will, you will tell them everything, but it's okay, don't worry about me."

She had to roll Khoo away from the door to open it. The man was huge, and it took all her strength to get him out of the way.

The van inside the garage was a big one and looked new. It was white, with no side windows, possibly the same van that had pulled up in front of her at the airport. Once again, she replayed that brief moment; the cloth over her face, the smell, Khoo reaching out to her, and the driver.

He was Chinese, an older man in his forties, wearing the same blue shirt that Khoo and Jie wore every day. A work shirt worn by thousands all over the world, and one that would never stand out in a crowd. There was something about his nose, it was big, a bulbous thing bent to the side. He had turned toward her, looked her in the eyes and said something.

What was it he said?

The words wouldn't come to her, but that face, she would recognize him anywhere.

"You have a great memory for details," her psychiatrist had told her.

LeAnn had never driven a van and nothing nearing the size of this one. But she had the keys and it was less risky than walking. She opened the door and found Brianne's lifeless body inside. Now she knew what Jie and Khoo had argued over earlier.

The girl was dumped near the back door like a bag of garbage and she was flanked by two black plastic garbage bags, full of trash. Brianne was wearing nothing but the red sundress she was wearing the last time LeAnn saw her, ruined now by a stream of dried blood that ran down her now-misshapen forehead. Someone had hit her between the eyes with a blunt object, crushing and distorting the orbital bones of her right eye.

She'd been such a pretty girl. At one time she might have had a rich and beautiful life ahead of her. No longer, though, LeAnn thought, slamming the van's door shut. LeAnn walked through the smaller door and out into bright sunshine and blue sky.

The Clean Man was going to pay.

CHAPTER 9

KWAN

Kwan sipped his dark roast coffee and took a healthy bite out of his warm coconut egg tart when his desk phone rang. "Kwan here," he said, swallowing the last bit of the tart.

"Sir, dispatch is trying to raise you on the main channel."

He hated missing a radio call. He hung up the phone and keyed the mike on his radio.

"3107," he said and waited for the response.

"3107, units are requesting you respond to a homicide at Pandan Loop, near pier number seven."

"In route," he said.

Why would they want him at the scene of a homicide? He was detached from that unit and knew there were three homicide supervisors on duty . . . unless this involved one of his victims?

Mentally he braced himself for what he expected to see, some young girl not yet a woman, beaten to death, shot, stabbed, or drowned. Over the course of most investigations, he developed a bond with the victims, and their deaths were a source of his constant nightmares.

Grabbing his coffee, he made his way out into the parking lot. It was a crystal-clear morning with deep blue skies, not the kind of morning that made him think of homicide. He always pictured overcast skies and drizzling rain when dealing with death. Realistically, though, he knew the weather never plays a part when it comes to murder.

The scene wasn't difficult to find; it was the warehouse with all the police cars out front. He parked his assigned Subaru Impreza in the parking lot across the street. Standing between two uniformed officers and an inspector in a suit and tie, Kwan saw a young blonde woman wearing the top of a yellow rain suit with "Police" written in big block letters across the back. Fortunately, it was long enough that only her bare legs from mid-thigh down were exposed. He knew who she was, he had just seen her picture.

Modra Stargyl was trying to speak in English to a uniformed female officer who only spoke Mandarin.

"Officer," he said to the woman's partner. "Tell me what you know."

"Director Kwan," the officer said with a slight bow. "The responding patrol officer found this woman inside the warehouse. She was bound to a bed, nude, and is now wearing my rain suit. There are two dead men inside also, and a dead woman inside a van parked behind that door," he said, pointing to the closed roll-up.

"How did the call come in?"

"An anonymous call, sir. The dispatcher said it was a woman speaking Mandarin, but she was not fluent. The caller said there was a woman in trouble and gave this address. The call was made from an untraceable cell phone.

"Thank you," he said, and turned to the woman. "I speak English, madam. You are Modra Stargyl, correct?"

"Yes, my name is Modra Stargyl. I'm from Switzerland and was on vacation with my family. I woke up in there, and I've been here for I don't know how long. I . . . ."

"I know, I spoke with your husband at the mall. You are safe now. Can I get you anything?"

After eighteen months, he had found his first victim, and she was alive! He had so many questions.

Then the woman collapsed right in front of him, sobbing incoherently. Asking her questions now would be useless.

"Ms. Stargyl," he said, helping her up, "please sit in my car for a few minutes while I look inside. Try and relax, you're safe now — do you understand — you're safe. This officer will stay with you."

She nodded, and he helped her to the car.

Inside the warehouse's open door, crime scene technicians were going over a white Toyota HiAce, the same model and color of the van used at the Changi Airport. Two of the technicians were photographing it as a team, while the third was videotaping it from every angle.

The back doors of the van were partially open, and Kwan saw part of a red dress, and an elbow discolored with the purple and yellow signs of lividity.

Stepping around the technicians, he concentrated on the floor. It looked clean, no bodily fluids, no shell casing, no fibers, just old oil stains and dust. Inside the next door, the scene was bizarre. Three empty cots were lined up, each two meters apart. They reminded him of his early days as a conscript in the Singapore Army, only his cot never had straps like these did. These looked like they belonged in an old mental hospital, designed to hold a person against their will, to immobilize them, or to hold someone hostage.

A dead man was crumpled at the foot of the center cot. To Kwan, he looked like a big man, but it was hard to say as he was bent over at the waist. He must have been a weightlifter at one time; his biceps were huge, and his legs looked like tree trunks.

Kneeling down next to the dead man, he studied the small holes puncturing the man's shirt; some of them were clean, and others were saturated in large wet blood stains. He touched the man's forehead and he was still warm.

Behind each cot, a medical IV pole, complete with wheels, stood sentinel. One of the poles held a partially full bag of fluid and a small white bottle with a green label hooked in its retainer. An IV tube dangled down onto the floor, leaking a clear fluid onto the concrete. The larger bag was saline, used to hydrate hospital patients. The bottle was Diprivan, also known as propofol, or humorously referred to as Milk of Amnesia.

The hair on Kim's arms began to tingle, and the same feeling crept up the back of his neck. He looked at the three cots with their retaining straps, the IV lines, and thought of the dead girl in the van. This is what he had been searching for—how many girls had come through this hellish warehouse and what horrors had they experienced?

Three inspectors were conferring near a third closed door and taking notes.

"Who is in charge of the crime scene?" Kwan said.

"I am, sir, First Sergeant Chua," one of the two women said.

"Sergeant, I don't want to intrude or contaminate anything on your scene, but I'm sure this is all related to the missing tourists that my section is working. Can you tell me what you know?"

"Yes, sir. The unknown girl in the van, victim number one, was bludgeoned to death within the last twenty-four hours. We have no ID on her and we have left her undisturbed until the medical examiner arrives. This man," she said, pointing at the body by the cots, "was killed within the last hour."

She lifted a corner of the man's shirt and showed Kwan several of the small holes in the gut. Each had a rivulet of still-wet blood leaking toward the floor. "We have no ID on him, either."

"Have you printed him?"

"No, the technicians want to swab his hands first. There is a second man, victim number three, in the bathroom behind that door. He too is unidentified and his clothes are missing. The keys to the van are also missing."

"Can I see the other man?"

"Of course. You probably don't remember me, Superintendent Kwan, but you taught an interview and interrogation class while I was at the academy in 2012."

"I thought you looked familiar. I hope I didn't bore you."

"No sir," she said, opening the bathroom door. "This is victim number three, we haven't touched him yet. This is how the first officer found him."

The small bathroom's tile floor was covered in blood that had pooled underneath the victim. On the wall behind him, high velocity blood splatter sprayed out in a pattern beginning two feet above the man's head. Large pieces and smaller shards of the ceramic toilet tank lid littered the floor and pieces of ceramic were in the man's hair.

The dead man was lying on his side, his head at a forty-five-degree angle and resting on the ceramic base of the toilet. He was facing away, but Kwan could still see enough of the man's face. It was Hui Jie, and the sun and skull tattoo above his collar was just like he remembered. It was Jie's old gang sign, a gang that never fully materialized, leaving Jie with a useless tattoo.

"His name is Hui Jie. I arrested him years ago, and we have him on camera abducting a woman at the airport."

Kwan mentally replayed the video of the van coming to a stop in front of the small brunette woman and the muscular arm that had reached out and effortlessly pulled both the girl and Jie inside. Kwan was almost certain that the unknown man by the cot was that man.

CHAPTER 10

LeAnn

After using Jie's phone to call the police, she walked down the street next to the deserted pier until she came to the first warehouse open for business.

A dozen young men were stacking crates on a flatbed truck. One of them glanced at her, then turned his back and lifted another crate. She was near a seaport and she was dressed like all the dock workers, except for her shoes and the carry-on she dragged behind her.

The smell of food was coming from an open-air cafeteria just down the road and for the first time in weeks, the onset of withdrawals and hunger began to battle each other. Her need to eat won. A woman at the café window asked her what she wanted while casting a curious eye at the expensive leather carry-on.

Using Khoo's cash, she ordered a *char siu*, a spiced pork sandwich from the specials menu and sat at a table facing the street. From here she could look down the pier toward the crowd of officers several hundred yards away. It was too far away to see what they were doing, but that meant she was also too far away for them to notice her.

A couple of the dockworkers from the warehouse she had passed earlier sat at the next table and then a few more pulled up in a van. None paid her any attention and for the first time in weeks she was able to relax.

She listened to them talk, not caring what they were talking about but trying to get used to listening and understanding Mandarin again. It was a difficult language, and one that she would never speak fluently. There were so many different dialects of Chinese spoken in Singapore and most foreigners from all over the world never noticed.

Three bites of the sandwich and her stomach wanted to heave it back up. She asked the woman at the window for a bag to take it with her and saw a large black plastic sack on the counter.

"Can I buy that bag, please?" she said in her best Mandarin.

The woman gave it to her and refused the single dollar LeAnn left on the counter.

She dumped everything out of her carry-on into the empty bag and handed her expensive luggage to the surprised woman.

"Please, it's for you," LeAnn said.

Now she was truly just another worker, another face in the crowd. She sat back at the table, not feeling she could walk much farther.

The ache in her stomach began to ease, and she was contemplating trying more of the sandwich when a white van drove up and stopped across the street. It was identical to the van Khoo had driven—the one now with Brianne's body in the back. No one got out of the van. It sat there idling at the curb, its tinted windows keeping the driver hidden.

Feeling trapped again, she might as well have been strapped to the table, even her legs were shaking and nothing she could do would stop them. She wanted to run but running was not an option. She would not get far as weak as she was.

Fear and rage swept through her. Her instinct to run battled with wanting to kill the man inside that van. Forcing herself not to stare at it, she looked at the boy at the next table and tried to smile. He was a dockworker, probably just eighteen. He smiled and moved to her table with his lunch.

"Hello," he said. "My name is Jun Wei."

He was a few years younger than she was, with peach fuzz on

his lip, but he was blocking anyone in the van from seeing her face.

"My name is Lee," she said, hoping the words sounded truer than they felt.

They talked for thirty minutes; LeAnn struggling with her broken Mandarin and the young man laughing with her as she made mistakes . . . and still the van sat motionless across the street. It was close enough that she could hear the engine running.

Eventually the boy ran out of things to say and left. She thought of walking with him, but he was headed west, toward the police cars, and she wanted to put more distance between herself and the warehouse.

Two women at the table next to her finished eating and began to walk east. She joined them, and as she walked past the van, she glanced at the license plate, then took another quick look at the driver's window. The tint was too dark. She could tell someone was at the wheel but nothing more than that.

She turned the first corner and used Jie's phone again and called a Singapore MaxiCab, then waited in the shadows, fearing whoever was in the van would come for her. She held Jie's bloody screwdriver, her white-knuckled hand shivering, and vowed she would die there in the street before she would ever be taken captive again.

CHAPTER 11

KWAN

The fingerprint scanner identified the second man as Tan Khoo, the same Tan Khoo arrested years ago on the freighter. He was a petty criminal with an extensive history of mostly property crimes: burglary, theft, and fraud. But his crime trail had ceased two years earlier, like the man had found redemption.

But apparently Khoo had just moved on to bigger crimes. Murder and abductions were a giant leap for this criminal, and his last.

Armed with warrants for Khoo and Jie's apartments, Kwan and his men searched for hours and found little. Khoo lived modestly in a strangely clean one-bedroom apartment with little furnishings or personal property. No family photos, no computer, and except for utility bills, there was nothing to link him to anything or anyone. Most noticeably, there was no record of employment, yet somehow, he had paid his bills promptly each month.

Jie's one-bedroom apartment was over an auto garage that had been abandoned for months. There was no electricity and no running water. Every square foot of the room was filthy; old and dirty clothes hung everywhere, and the stench was unbearable. But like Khoo, there was no sign Jie worked for anyone. No banking information, no computer or phone records. A pile of unpaid bills dating back six months were all that tied Jie to the apartment.

Kwan and his team knocked on doors all around Jie's neighborhood, but none of those that answered could remember the man. There was so much useless evidence here to process, and so far, none of it was getting him closer to understanding what had happened in that warehouse.

Something was odd about both men's living arrangements. It was as if they had purposely scrubbed the last years of their lives clean. Jie and Khoo were obviously low-level thugs in a criminal operation. There was a third man, the abducted woman had said, but she couldn't describe him other than he was well dressed and spoke English.

Kwan thought of all the clothes and trash strewn around Jie's room and told one of the crime scene inspectors, "Collect it all. Go over everything, there has to be something here we can use."

CHAPTER 12

LEANN

The MaxiCab driver dropped off LeAnn three blocks from a condo, her brother and sister's safe house. At a strip mall across the street, she bought some decent clothes, two pairs of shoes, shampoo, and a bar of soap using Khoo's cash.

This neighborhood was cleaner than most she had seen since leaving the harbor and warehouses, and the smell of dead fish and machine oil were now absent. She had used the two-bedroom condo twice before when she felt the need to lay low, the last time after killing a man in a New York subway. She feared one of the surveillance cameras had caught her fleeing the scene and for days the paranoia of being caught consumed her. It was Ramzi who told her about the safe house.

"Everything you need is there. Madinah and I use it all the time."

They were both dead now. Lieutenant Trufant had killed her sister, and Ramzi, *well, I killed Ramzi.*

The condominium was right where she remembered it, a nondescript twelve story building in a nondescript, average neighborhood. It was perfect. She pressed the entry code at the building's main door and heard the satisfying click as the lock disengaged. Ramzi was brilliant at times, she had to admit as she rode the elevator to the top floor.

Would the spare key still be there? With the right tools, she knew she could pick the lock, another skill her brother had taught her as a child in Manila, but without tools she would need a key.

Anxiety was beginning to mix with the physical symptoms of withdrawal. The tiny elevator grew smaller and smaller as it bounced and jerked its way up, and she tasted the cheap sandwich trying to work its way to her throat and gag her again.

The elevator bumped to a stop, and the door slid open. Stepping out into the small bit of sunshine helped calm her stomach and her nerves, but it was darkness she craved, that and the solitude of an empty room.

The Butterfly Palm next to the elevator had grown a foot taller than the last time she had been to the condo and it took a few seconds to find the key. It was two inches deep in the rich black soil and its once shiny plating was dull and corroded. Will it still open the door?

She knocked softly, fearing someone would answer, but there was only silence from inside. She turned the key and the door opened.

Nothing had changed. There was a musty smell in the air of having been vacant for months, the same sparse furniture, bare cream-colored walls, and blackout shades. Her brother and sister had never changed anything since they bought the place six years ago.

Aching all over now, she felt her stomach cramp and raced to the bathroom, not knowing if she was going to puke or have diarrhea. Both, it seemed, as she heaved what little of the sandwich she'd consumed into a trash basket while sitting on the toilet.

The cramping eased, but the aches were getting worse by the minute. Her muscles, back, and even her scalp felt bruised. Was it food poisoning, the flu, or withdrawal from all the drugs? She knew it was the heroin and whatever else Jie and Khoo had been pumping into her for weeks.

"You fuckers!" she screamed.

Feeling relieved, she rinsed out the trash basket, stripped off Jie's filthy clothes, and collapsed on one of the beds. Sleep released her from the pain but not the nightmares that followed.

CHAPTER 13

KWAN

The next day Kwan drove himself back to the warehouse on the pier. Ignoring the crime scene tape and the warning posted in red letters, he opened the heavy steel door and walked inside.

The main section of the building smelled like ancient dust and urine. Even with the lights on, it was dim inside. The few tiny windows provided minimal light, and he tried to imagine being strapped to one of the cots he had seen earlier. Everything that had been here yesterday morning was gone now, impounded and being scrutinized by the department's crime technicians.

The mattresses on those cots held a variety of stains and they were covered in DNA. With luck and a lot of skill, the technicians could begin identifying which of his missing persons had been through this warehouse.

Blood stains in the grout marked where Jie had died. At first Kwan thought the man had been shot in the temple, but the technicians suspected it was a puncture wound from something like an ice pick. Nothing was found that could have caused the wound.

Khoo had similar wounds, twenty at least, ranging from his abdomen to the center of his chest. Some appeared superficial, the weapon hitting ribs had failed to do any real damage, but several apparently had been fatal, hitting his heart directly or possibly his aorta. Not that Kwan cared, but it would have been helpful to have found him alive. Khoo would never tell them anything useful now.

A cheap pine desk had sat behind the cots. It too was gone, but Kwan imagined sitting in the chair like Jie or Khoo, watching the captive girls. It was hard to imagine those two having the skills to keep the girls doped up and using IVs without killing them. Maybe they'd been given some type of medical training, something basic.

The narcotics inspectors had found heroin, crystal meth, Dilaudid, and morphine in the drawer along with used IV lines and syringes.

I would never be able to start an IV.

Most of his missing girls had no history of drug use, and Kwan could only imagine what had been done to them here. The sex trade in Southeast Asia and most other parts of the world depended on drug addiction to control their victims. The girls became willing subjects, wanting nothing but that next fix, that next dose of dope.

Standing over the spot where Khoo had died, Kwan wondered how one of the girls had overpowered him. Khoo was a big man and Kwan doubted his own ability to beat him. Even with all the skills he'd learned over the years, it would have been even odds at best.

Hopefully there was something still in this room that would help him find the rest of the girls. The woman from Switzerland hadn't been much help. She described Khoo as the man who abducted her, but she had no memory of anything until she woke up and Khoo was dead on the floor. Something wasn't right about the last part, though. She dropped her eyes each time she recounted waking up alone. She was afraid of something, and after hours of questioning, she suddenly said, "I woke up and saw a tiny girl stabbing the big man, like a machine. She said she was going to let me live, but I thought she was going to kill me anyway. She had that look in her eyes, like a crazy lunatic."

***

Her description of the girl could be the missing victim from the airport, Leila Moran, but it was so vague it could have been anyone.

That was all the investigators could get her to say. They had released her. She and her family were probably halfway to Europe by now, and he would never have another chance to talk to her.

Now he had one dead victim, Brianne Vasquez, seventeen years old. An autopsy would tell him little—what type of narcotics were in her blood, whether or not she had been raped, and what blunt object might have been the one that crushed her skull. Nothing that would help him find the rest of his victims— his girls. He pictured the petite brunette at the airport, Leila Moran. Was she the "machine" the Swiss woman had described, or was Leila dead as well?

CHAPTER 14

LeAnn

The pain was relentless, radiating from her spine in every direction. She was afraid to move, even her eyelids screamed as she stared at the ceiling. No part of her body was immune to the aches and spasms.

Where the hell am I?

She couldn't remember anything that made sense. *Was I at the airport yesterday, or am I still in New York? Am I in prison?*

Closing her eyes eased some of the pain, but then she felt like she was in a carnival ride, spinning in circles. She had thrown up, but how long ago was that? Probably not long, because she was still nauseous. She sat upright, trying to ignore muscles that felt as if they were tearing away from her bones.

Slowly, the room made sense. Jie's blood and betel nut-stained clothes were piled next to her, where she had stripped them off. She pictured the man in front of her, and when she did, the memories roared back into reality. She was going to vomit again, and the image of puking on the floor was a powerful motivator to stand or crawl to the bathroom.

Curled up on the shower floor, the tiles were cool and the nausea began to subside. She reached up and turned the water on. Hot water felt better than the cold, and she let the steam build, the heat sucking the aches out of her joints until the water began to cool.

The tiny space in the shower began to shrink before her eyes;

the wall and the glass door were now touching her elbows. Pulling her knees in tight to her chest, she began to sob as the dull aches returned.

How many times have I cried, once, twice?

Now she was bawling like a two-year-old. She felt vulnerable, defenseless, and small, like the night she woke up alone in the dark warehouse, listening to rats scurrying around her.

As the water evaporated, she thought back to the airport. She had been so careful and yet so careless. Some bastard had snuck up on her and gotten the best of her—Jie, a pathetic excuse for a man. The creep was dead now but the distaste in her mouth was like rancid milk.

Above her, the spiderweb of cracks in the plaster ceiling blurred and spun as her brain demanded a dose of opioids. She was beginning to doubt whether she could beat this unrelenting craving. The feelings of being weak and useless were new to her and were becoming unbearable.

How many hours had she been sitting on the shower floor? The clock had to be wrong, and the sun shining on the floor wasn't right either. Her head spun, reminding her of the time she had suffered seasickness. She realized she had slept all night and most of the next day; it was already late afternoon, more than twenty-four hours since she had escaped the Clean Man's hellhole.

Her new clothes smelled like chemicals and she dropped them in a pile to be laundered, then dressed in a clean pair of her sister's underwear and gray sweatpants. Madinah was dead now, killed in Chicago six months ago, but her clothes stacked neatly in the bedroom smelled like they had just been laundered. Madinah was taller, and heavier than LeAnn and so they fit loosely, but the feeling of wearing freshly cleaned clothes made her feel human again, despite the nagging aches.

"I need to eat something, maybe eating will help."

Hearing her own voice was a relief from the solitude and confinement, and she began talking to herself as she moved around the condo.

Pain flared with each step as she made her way into the kitchen. The cabinets were full of ramen noodles and little else, and their spice packet's chicken-flavor smell reminded her of what had happened to her sandwich earlier. The first spoonful of warm broth was bland and went down easy, but she decided half a bowl was enough for one day.

In one of the cupboards, she discovered a bottle of Advil and swallowed three of them. There was little else in the cabinets except the same ramen noodles. Forty or fifty bags were stacked neatly organized on each shelf, their labels all facing outwards. That was Ramzi's doing, so obsessive and so compulsive. She was aware of her own issues, but she was not a neat freak.

In the living room she found Madinah's laptop and plugged it in. Madinah's password had always been NasimHaddad, her father's full name. LeAnn never knew why and she never asked.

The computer logged on to the Wi-Fi, and her first search was for heroin withdrawal symptoms. Everything she was feeling was spelled out on the screen, and depression was one of them. Sweating, shaking, muscle spasms, and the worst was the never-ending need for another fix, another bag of dope.

'Your life will revolve around your never-ending need for the next fix,' the first sentence said.

"Never," she screamed at the silent laptop.

Tremors and spasms in her hands made it difficult to use the computer, and sitting in front of it caused her back to ache. Standing wasn't much better, so she sat in the corner of the bedroom and pulled her knees up to her chest as tight as she could, rocking back and forth.

She woke in the same position the next day. Twelve more hours gone in what seemed like minutes.

Her knees felt locked and brittle. As she tried to straighten them, she worried the joints might actually snap, but she pushed down on her knees, ignoring the pain until they were flat on the floor. Her arms were just as bad, she must have slept in that awkward position all night.

Closing her eyes, she tried to make a plan. She knew she needed a plan, she needed to act, because another day of sitting and weeping in the corner of this room would kill her as surely as the Clean Man would. But rational thought was impossible. As soon as she formed an idea, it would slip away and her mind returned to its own need, heroin.

"I'm a fucking drug addict now!"

Had she really just screamed that out loud in her empty apartment? Would the neighbors hear her?

"I can beat this. I have survived worse."

She found herself on the floor of the shower again but had no memory of how she got there. Still in her now damp sweatpants, the shower floor was dry and only the clock on the wall told her six hours had passed.

She remembered bits of a dream. It was the *Nutcracker* again, only this time the dancers were monsters, and as they spun around on the dance floor, she saw each was wearing a mask with the Clean Man's face. Its proportions were wildly distorted; his teeth took up most of his face, and his eyes bulged and stretched out toward her.

Tears streamed down her cheek, tears of weakness and shame. She had been kidnapped, fondled, and raped. Everything else that had happened to her blurred between reality and her nightmares. But the bruising on her wrists and the shades of yellow and purple on the back of her hand where the crude IV had been was all she needed to see.

She clung to the one part of her plan that never wavered as she began to nod off. The Clean Man needed to die.

The thought of that man's perfect teeth followed her into another nightmare. Leering down at her, his saliva tinged red, his dead, dark eyes taking in every inch of her body, and then he touched her, his moist palm touching her cheek…

She woke screaming and this time she knew it was loud, because someone was pounding on the wall.

"You will burn in hell," she whispered to her unseen neighbor. The dream had been so vivid, the colors so bright, but the images were fading, the bright colors on his face turning to shades of gray. The last thing he said was, "I own you now, soon you will want to please me."

The memory of killing Jie and Khoo satisfied some part of her need. She replayed their deaths over and over, relishing the sounds, and the sensual feelings of their deaths were almost erotic.

The hallucinations started that night. They were dreamlike at first, similar to all the rest of her nightmares, but she knew she was awake. She was lying on the floor in a fetal position in the corner of the bedroom, the only place in the apartment she felt safe, and secure. From here she faced the bedroom door, and through it could see the condo's front door.

At first, Jie was standing over her, the screwdriver protruding from the side of his head, and he was speaking in English. "You think this is over?" he said. Then his face blurred and he became Ramzi. She stood up and heard traffic from the street below. Ramzi was ten years old now and holding a soccer ball. "Leila, why?" Ramzi never called her Leila.

Still standing in the corner, her legs were shaking and she knew she was close to falling. But she stumbled her way through his image and into the kitchen where her older sister was sitting at the table drinking tea. "LeAnn," Araya said. "I need you to call me." Then Araya faded away and she was standing alone in the kitchen with Jie's phone in her hand.

Now, her mother reached out and grabbed the phone, "I'm still waiting for your call Leila, why didn't you come to the funeral. I'm still waiting for you."

Another day came and went. She had been free for three and a half days and still no sign the withdrawal was easing.

How can I sleep in so much pain?

She thought of how peaceful it would be to fall asleep and never wake up. She would be free from all this pain, all the anxieties she had suffered her entire life. Who would grieve for her if she died in this room right now? Her sister Araya was now her only living family.

She remembered watching Ramzi slide Madinah's ashes into the crypt and wondered, "What about my ashes?" And then the strangest dream followed her into the dark . . .

She was walking into a church wearing white. A tall man stood next to her. He was her father one minute and then a stranger. In a pew next to her, her mother sat holding a tissue under a blinded eye, wearing a black funeral dress and sitting with the Clean Man, his perfect teeth and lips still covered in red saliva.

Church bells pealed nearby, shaking the walls with each note. She was at an altar now and the room shimmered around her. Thunder shook the building. She looked up at the Clean Man dressed in his fancy white suit standing next to her and said, "I do."

Bam! Bam! Bam! The sound of gunfire startled her awake and it sounded like it was happening right outside her door. Bam! Bam! Just two this time and then someone called her name. LeAnn!

It wasn't gun shots; it was someone knocking on her door. She cried out, knowing it was Jie or Khoo coming for her. Sitting in the corner, unarmed, and wearing only a cheap shirt and sweatpants, she frantically tried to remember where she had put the screwdriver.

Frozen in fear, her brain refused to process a plan.

"Think, think, think," she whispered hitting the side of her head with her palm.

It can't be Jie. The bastard's cold dead body was miles away somewhere.

The knock was louder the next time and she stood up, trembling and teeth chattering like a cartoon character's. The screwdriver was right there on top of Jie's dirty shirt. She picked it up, holding it in a death grip for fear it might fall out of her hand. She was so weak, so vulnerable. She would never survive another attack — she just didn't have the strength.

Through the peephole she could see the back of a woman's head, and she moved away, hoping the woman hadn't seen movement through her side of the hole. She remained silent, not even breathing, hoping the woman would leave.

Looking through the tiny hole again she heard the woman say, "LeAnn, open the door." Was she hallucinating again, or still sitting in the corner dreaming?

This didn't feel like a dream, or a hallucination, so she opened the door, just a crack clutching the screwdriver.

"Oh my God, LeAnn, what has happened to you?"

Her oldest and now only sister stared back at her. Araya, who she hadn't seen in years, brushed past her and into the apartment.

"You look horrible and I couldn't understand anything you said. Who did this to you?"

"Why are you here, how did you find me?"

"You called me twice, and I flew in on the first flight I could get out of Manila. You said on the phone you were attacked and needed me. Tell me what happened. Are we safe here?"

LeAnn stumbled into the kitchen and sat at the table trying to remember making a phone call. What else had she done she couldn't remember?

"I don't remember calling you. I think I've been hallucinating and I'm not sure—I'm not sure we are safe here. I don't know, Araya."

She had never wanted anyone to touch her, even as a child in Iraq, her family knew not to hug her. Touching another person, even her own mother, was somehow repulsive. But now she leaned in and wrapped her arms around her shocked sister and held her as tight as she could.

"Please help me."

"I'm here, LeAnn. I won't leave you."

"It started in San Francisco."

They sat in the kitchen, and she told Araya how she was afraid Trufant was following her at the airport, and an hour later she finished with how she left the Swiss woman bound to the cot and made her way to the safe house.

"I think they kept me doped on heroin or maybe fentanyl for weeks. I heard them say fentanyl once but I know they were giving us heroin too. It's really hard to remember anything for sure. The bastards raped me, Araya, and they killed one of the other girls."

She collapsed into her sister's arms again and sobbed uncontrollably. Weeks' worth of rage and humility poured out, and for the first time in her life, she felt a connection with another human.

"You look emaciated, LeAnn, and your skin—it looks like you have jaundice. When was the last time you ate?"

"I ate some ramen noodles yesterday, or maybe it was the day before. I can't remember, but I'm not hungry right now."

"Okay, LeAnn. What is all this?" Araya said pointing to the blood encrusted screwdriver laying on top of Jie's clothes.

Also on the table, both men's belongings were spread out in two piles: their driver's licenses, a few credit cards, the remaining cash, two cell phones, and Jie's old knife.

Araya picked up one of the phones and stared at the screen.

"LeAnn, there are a dozen missed calls on this phone, and one of them was just a few minutes ago. They can track you with this."

LeAnn grabbed the phone, took the back off and removed the SIM card and battery, and then did the same for the other phone.

"How close can they be?"

"I'm not an expert, LeAnn, this block probably, maybe even this building. Have you been outside at all?"

"No."

"Good. LeAnn, when was the last time they gave you anything, can you remember?"

"Three days ago, I think, but I'm so fucked up Araya, I'm not sure of anything, why?"

"You should have gotten through the worst of withdrawal then. Another four or five days and you should be okay."

"How do you know that?"

"I did volunteer work at my church when I lived in Chicago. Part of what I did was referrals for the homeless to drug treatment centers. What's in here you can eat?"

Araya opened the cabinets one after another, then turned and looked at her.

"This is too weird, is this all those two ate?"

"I think so. Ramzi and Madinah were preppers. I think they wanted to be able to hole up for a month without ever going outside."

LeAnn looked at the disabled phones on the table.

"Araya, I'm going to need some of the information on these phones soon."

"Why?"

"I need to find him, I need to find the Clean Man, and maybe his driver, yes, definitely his driver."

"You should let this go, LeAnn. You almost died and look at yourself—you are in no shape to do anything. Go to the police and let them take care of it."

"I can't go to the police, and I can't let someone else do what needs to be done. You know I can't."

"Okay, well, I'm going to the market I saw down the street and get some real food. I'll stay with you until you're ready to travel, or whatever it is you're going to do. I know they need to pay for what they did. But I want no part of that. I don't want you to tell me about it either. I wonder how many girls they did this to. Maybe I can find out something while I'm at the market."

"Thanks, I'll look on the internet while you're out. Can you do me a favor, though? Go far enough away from here, turn the phones on and copy everything you can: pictures, numbers, texts, anything you think I can use. Somehow, I have to make them pay. Maybe I will tell the police."

"I'm not sure if I believe you, LeAnn, but I want them to pay for what they did to you. Crazy or not, you are the last of my family. I love you, and I'm going to help you through this."

Somehow, hearing her sister say that felt odd. Love, friendship, those emotions had been lost on LeAnn, but she felt something stirring in her now, a twinge of regret, remorse, or maybe it *was* love.

Araya picked up the phone parts and opened the door.

"Araya, be careful and look for a white van. The driver is an ugly man with a big nose. He was older than the others, maybe forty or forty-five. I'm sure they are looking for me."

"I will."

Alone again. She held out her hand and watched as her fingers twitched on their own. She opened and closed her fist several times, watching the tendons in her wrist tighten. The fingers still twitched and each knuckle felt stiff, and bruised, but at least her strength was returning.

With Google Maps, she found Jie's and Khoo's addresses. Jie's was just a few blocks away, and Khoo's was farther, but still within walking distance. She tried a search for the Blue Room, the name on Khoo's credit card, but found nothing but pictures of rooms painted blue.

She emailed a friend in New York, an IT major who called himself "The Deacon." Christopher Dashiva was known as a decent hacker, and she asked him to try a search for the Blue Room in Singapore. He had helped her find people who didn't want to be found; maybe he could figure out what the Blue Room was and where she could find it.

Next, she typed in "missing women in Singapore and scanned through the search results until she found one with a picture of Brianne. The photo was probably from a school yearbook and showed a pretty, young girl with bright shining eyes.

"Not so pretty now, Brianne," she said aloud and then regretted it. The girl had been raped, abused, and murdered, and she hated herself for making a joke about it.

"God, I'm feeling remorse now too!"

It's the drugs, she told herself, that and the trauma of the last three weeks had done something to her head, and she did not like it. Life was so much simpler without the baggage of emotions. Anger and violence had always been her companions, but all these new emotions complicated her ability to think straight.

She read about Brianne and several more posts related to missing women. One of the posts asked for information about a possible victim, and LeAnn saw a blurry CCTV picture of herself as she walked through the airport. In the frame, there was a man's pants leg and arm, and she knew it was Jie. There was no face to go with the arm and leg, but she knew.

"You died like a pathetic sheep, Jie. I hope you knew that in the end."

None of the other search results helped, but each one mentioned the same police officer, Kwan Kim Lai.

CHAPTER 15

ARAYA

Brilliant sunlight and unseasonably humid air greeted Araya as she walked out of the condo. This was her first visit to Singapore, and it reminded her of Manila; same climate and the same crowded streets. The condo was on the outskirts of the business district and owned by Lucretia Investments, one of several shell companies her mother had put together years ago.

In 2011, she and her surviving family moved from Iraq to Manila. It was good to get away from those horrible memories, still, the brutal death of her father and sister was something she thought of everyday. The move helped, but soon the killings began.

Today, ten years later and fourteen hundred miles away, she could still remember her mother's face as Ramzi described killing an American tourist. Her mother was euphoric, and two weeks later Ramzi's twin sister Madinah killed another man. That was more than she could bare. She and her fiancé immigrated to Chicago and she broke off contact with them all, except LeAnn. There was something different about her and she held out hope that LeAnn could still be saved. She was so young then, but already so damaged. And now, here she was in Singapore still holding out hope.

Turning left on a dirty sidewalk, she was in the middle of the block when she saw a white van with a gold decal on the front bumper moving slowly toward her. Through the windshield, the driver was looking left and right at women walking on the sidewalk, then he looked right at her, stared briefly, and looked away, focusing on another woman walking ahead of her. As he drove by, she caught a glimpse of "an ugly man with a big nose." There was no doubt this was the man LeAnn had described. He was looking for someone, definitely a woman. The van made a right turn and disappeared behind the building.

The market was two blocks farther down the street and as she walked, she kept looking for the van. There were lots of them in this part of town, most were making deliveries to the markets up and down the street, but she didn't see the one with the decal again.

The crowded market was tiny, but she found everything she needed to make enough meals for her and LeAnn to last several days.

Trying to walk casually with a shopping bag in each hand was harder than she thought. Am I walking too fast? Heading down the street got her farther away from the condo and with each block, she felt safer. The next block was a public park lined with shade trees, benches, and most importantly, plenty of people. Sitting on a bench, she assembled the phone LeAnn said belonged to Jie, one of her captors.

As the old phone powered up, there were two missed calls from the same number. Each call had been made two days ago and there were no voice mails. There were several dozen outgoing calls, all to the same number, each one lasting less than a minute. He had received just as many calls from that same number as well. That's strange, she thought, unless he wasn't allowed to use it for any other purpose other than staying in contact with his employer. But there was a single picture on the phone, a naked, unconscious woman strapped to a cot.

LeAnn.

The image shocked her and the phone slipped from her fingers, bounced off the bench and onto the concrete sidewalk next to her shoe. She closed her eyes trying to flush that image from her memory. It worked, but only for a moment, then a flash of anger, something close to rage overcame the shock. She opened her eyes and scanned the streets again looking for the van.

Grief and anger wouldn't help LeAnn right now. She brushed dirt off the phone and went to work. With her own phone, Araya began snapping pictures of each outgoing and incoming call, showing the times the calls were made and received. There were no text messages and just one number on the contact list, the number that belonged to the second phone LeAnn had taken.

After taking Jie's phone apart, she put the other one together and noticed a missed call and a new voicemail that had just been left. She played the message; it was a man's voice speaking perfect English with a British accent.

"I know you are listening, Ms. Moran. I will see you soon so you can make amends. You have much to answer for."

Araya made a recording of the voice mail using her own phone, then opened the contact list. This phone had many and she took a screenshot of each one. There were also several text messages she couldn't read, and she took photos of them as well. Pictures of nude women filled the photo library; some were bound to a cot like LeAnn, and others were of smiling women dressed like strippers and prostitutes.

When she finished, she took the SIM card and battery out of this phone as well, looked at her watch, and then looked for the van. It was 10:35.

An outdoor café was just down the street and from where she stood, she saw a dozen tables filled with men and women her age eating lunch. It was a perfect spot.

Hidden behind a cup of hot tea and the local newspaper, she observed the passersby and traffic. Twenty-two minutes later, the same white van appeared, driving slowly toward her. Through the tinted glass, the driver was again scanning the crowd, focusing on the youngest women and clearly ignoring the older ones.

As the van neared the café she adjusted her newspaper, peering over the top until the van passed. It parked at the end of the block and the driver got out and walked toward her.

She was wearing a distinctive bright blue, long sleeve wrap, it was one of her favorites but it stood out like a flashing neon light. Would he remember seeing her on the sidewalk thirty minutes ago? How could anyone not.

The man was three shops away now and walking fast. Pulling the wrap off, she stuffed it deep inside one of the bags at her feet. Now in a simple white sleeveless blouse, she hoped he wouldn't remember her.

He was two tables away now and she understood why LeAnn had noticed his nose. His face was unusually thin and his nose wasn't that large, but it had probably been broken and never reset. It was bent far to one side; the odd angle making it hard to forget.

Just feet from her table now, the man stopped a young couple on the sidewalk and asked them something in what she assumed was Chinese, and then showed them a picture. They shook their heads no. He glanced directly at her, and then continued down the sidewalk. She exhaled and took a deep breath, realizing she had stopped breathing.

Eventually he made a complete circle of the park, returned to the van and drove away.

The trip back to the apartment was uneventful, although she felt a little paranoid walking alone. Several white vans passed her, but none caught her attention. Still, the paranoia kept her head on a swivel, checking the alleyways and shadows of the taller buildings. Returning to LeAnn's building, Araya waited for the elevator as it made its way down from the seventh floor, the chime announcing each floor growing louder as it approached.

The chime startled her as the door jerked open and a middle-aged man rushed out. For that split second, he was the Driver and she started to scream—but it was not the same man.

She trembled as the elevator began to rise, holding her breath as it passed each floor, and praying that it wouldn't stop. Finally, the doors opened on the top floor. She brushed away a tear and walked down the hall, still feeling like she was being watched.

"LeAnn, it's me," she said. "Open the door, please."

CHAPTER 16

LEANN

"You saw him, didn't you?" LeAnn said. There was something in her sister's wide eyes that looked like panic.

"Yes, twice. The last three numbers of the license plate are 676, and there was a gold decal on the front bumper. That's all I could memorize. Jesus Christ, I need to sit down."

"Did he see you?"

"He looked right at me but dismissed me. He was definitely looking for someone. LeAnn, I turned on those phones at a park four blocks from here, and twenty-two minutes later he was right there. Twenty-two minutes, LeAnn. Who can do that?"

"People who know what they're doing. What did you find on the phones?"

"Look," Araya said, showing her everything, ending with the photo of LeAnn, drugged, unconscious, and bound to a cot.

"Araya, do you get it now? Look at me," she said stabbing at the picture on the phone with her finger. "You understand why I can't let them live?"

"LeAnn, I get it, I don't like it, but I get it." Araya said, "There was a voice mail and I think it was for you, listen." She started the recording and LeAnn's face turned ashen.

"That's him—that's the Clean Man."

"LeAnn, you need to call the police. You're in something bigger than you think."

"The police? Araya, you know I can't get anywhere near the

police. I just can't do that. This bastard has to pay. They all have to pay!"

"LeAnn, he called you Ms. Moran. I'm guessing that's the name you were traveling under, and I suppose that's a good thing. At least he can't link you to Ramzi and the mess you two left in San Francisco. I really think you should just leave here. Come with me to Manila for a few weeks."

"I can't. Not yet anyway."

"LeAnn, I can't be involved in someone's death, you know I can't. I'm sorry this happened to you, but . . ."

"I know. You would just get in my way anyhow, Araya, and I don't want you to get hurt or involved. Let's not talk about it anymore. The less you know, the better."

The two of them made grilled ham and cheese sandwiches and tomato soup. A simple lunch, but for LeAnn, who was tired of ramen noodles, it was a gourmet meal.

She held out her hand to Araya. Her fingers still twitched, but less than they had the day before.

"Look, it's already better, Araya. I can see it. Once I stop shaking, you should probably go home."

***

Two days later there was no sign of a twitch.

"Araya, it's time for you to go."

"LeAnn, you will never really beat addiction. You know that, right? You will struggle with it for years, if not the rest of your life."

"I know what they say, Araya, but I'm not like everyone else, and it's all the more reason I'm going after them. But you're right, I'm going to mail the phones, the SIM cards, and all this other crap to a cop named Kwan Kim Lai. Remember that name in case something happens to me. I think he's in charge of all this shit. I'll let him handle it, but I'm still going after both of them."

CHAPTER 17

KWAN

"Superintendent Kwan, I have an ID on another print from the van," the technician said, handing Kwan a three-page printout. A photo of a middle-aged man identified the print as belonging to Tommy Fong, a forty-two-year-old Chinese national with a modest criminal history. Kwan read through the report and then read it a second time.

Fong was once the number two man in a small-time crime ring in Taiwan. There were numerous arrests for drugs and organized prostitution. He had two more arrests in Singapore, one for a drunken brawl in 2010 and another for possession of pornography in 2012. He spent two years in prison for the pornography.

Fong had been clean for eight years now, or had he, Kwan wondered. Maybe like Jie and Khoo, he had moved on to something bigger, something more professional, and it was paramount that they stay out of the eyes of law enforcement.

The prison booking photo was seven years old, but the picture on his driver's license was current, taken eight months ago. Fong was noticeably older and had longer hair. His height and weight appeared average, an unremarkable man — except for a grotesque broken nose. Kwan put a copy of the printout on a junior inspector's desk and made a note for the woman to check Fong out thoroughly in the morning.

The fingerprint was a partial thumbprint on the outside of the van's rear door. Any passerby could have touched it and left a similar print. It was not enough evidence for a warrant, but it was more than he had yesterday.

Fong's last known address was just off the East Coast Parkway. It was already late, so Kwan decided to do a quick drive-by of the man's house on his way home. As he drove, the afternoon sun dipped behind the high-rises along the port. He took the next exit.

Traffic was heavy even on the back streets and then thinned out in the suburbs. If Fong still lived here, he was in a single-family home surrounded by similar homes in a middle-class residential neighborhood.

Over-grown landscaping obscured most of the house except for the front door, which faced the street. Kwan slowed and looked for any sign that Fong was home, then stopped right in front of the house.

Even from the street the surveillance camera was visible. Kwan took his foot off the brake and coasted until he was out of its range. If there was one camera there could be another hidden anywhere, and most likely they had already captured his unmarked car. Enough for one day, he thought, driving back to the parkway.

Tommy Fong's doorbell camera signaled movement in front of the house. The resolution was excellent, and Fong watched the white Subaru Impreza on his cell phone as it slowed and then stopped, then moved slowly out of the camera's view. It was difficult to see the driver, but it appeared to be a man and it was clear that the driver was looking right at his house.

Fong punched the numbers into the phone and waited.

"Yes, Tommy?"

"Laoban, I believe the police just drove past my house."

"Keep an eye out, Tommy. I will know when you need to worry. I will see you tomorrow."

CHAPTER 18

THE CLEAN MAN

James Soong, the Laoban, sat behind his dead father's desk and stared at the stain in the ancient Persian rug in front of him. The stain was the color of dried blood. Brianne's blood. She had shamed him, and she had paid the price. But those few seconds of rage had put two months' worth of work down the drain. A wasted effort, an investment that would never produce a return, and now he had lost three girls. Two of them would have been listed as prime inventory. But the act of killing the girl also had its benefits. Violence was a powerful motivator for his employees, and he made sure that they all knew of Brianne's demise.

Such is life, his father would have said.

A knock at the door interrupted his thoughts of Brianne's untimely death.

"Yes?"

Tommy Fong stepped through the crack of the door and bowed deeply, staring at the floor.

Soong enjoyed seeing the fear in his employees' eyes, even those who had been with him as long as Tommy. Tommy was afraid and rightfully so. The man remained motionless, waiting for permission to speak—and Soong let him wait.

Finally, in an almost-whisper, he said, "Speak, Tommy."

"Laoban, I haven't heard anything new about Jie or Khoo. The blonde woman is back in Europe and the second woman is still missing, sir."

"That is old news, Tommy, and Tommy, I asked that you have this carpet cleaned. I can still see the bitch's blood."

"I will have it cleaned again, sir."

"Do that, Tommy. Have you spoken to my associate at the police department?"

"Yes, he was able to read a few of the reports. The blonde woman first lied and told them she woke and found herself alone, and Jie and Khoo were already dead. Then she recanted and said a small woman was stabbing one of them, probably Khoo, 'like a monster,' her words, sir. Her description was vague and the inspector thought she was afraid of the woman. It was probably the Moran girl, sir."

"Any link to us yet? I know they searched their homes. Did they find anything?"

"No, nothing of value, sir."

"Well, I have to give them credit for that, at least. This girl still has their phones. Is she baiting us or is she a fool?"

"She's an ignorant bitch, Laoban," Tommy said.

"I think you're wrong, Tommy, remember she killed Khoo. Jie was a weak man, my mother could overpower him, but Khoo? I want you to be careful with this Moran girl. I saw something in her. Tell the rest of your men to do the same. My source with the phone company says both phones have been off-line now for twelve hours, but I don't think she is done with them yet. Be ready should she use them again.

"Yes, Laoban."

"Tell me about this new site, how is it working out?"

"As well as can be expected," Fong said. "I want to put more security on the building though, cameras at least."

"Tommy, do whatever you think, but no visible cameras outside. Anyone driving by must think it is nothing but the dump it has always been. No more than two cars outside, ever, and make sure you wear the old uniforms. Too many prying eyes these days."

"Yes, sir."

"Tommy, we need to replace Jie and Khoo as quickly as possible.

What do you think about taking the two Ng cousins off the street and training them? I know the younger one is not the brightest, but we need two people we can control, and I use their mother as a courier."

"Simon will do well. I can train him to pick out the girls, but his younger cousin is immature. I think he will eventually be useful, though."

"Do it, Tommy. I want those two other cots filled as soon as possible."

"Yes, Laoban."

Fong began rolling up the stained carpet when Soong stopped him.

"Before you go, Tommy, there is one more thing about our new girl. I don't have to tell you how important she is—the American is going to pay big money for her—more than I made all last year. It's a one-time deal, so no mistakes—am I clear?"

"Yes, Laoban. I have Gerard Sen watching her at night. He is also inexperienced, but I can train him. I dope her during the day and just before I leave at night. Tonight, I will have him start with the fentanyl. Gemma has been drugged for three straight days now, and everything is going as planned. Four more days and we will stop the sedation."

"Tommy," Soong hissed, his oversized white teeth bared. "Don't use her name—ever. Does your man know who she is?"

Tommy bowed low, his head touching the stain left by Brianne's blood, his fingers trembling. "Only her name."

"That's not good. I expect her disappearance to be on the news any day now. Watch your man closely and start calling her something else. Important people will be looking for her and it's best no one knows who she is. The charade won't last long, but it doesn't need to. Once she is ready, I'll call the American and it will be done. There will be a bonus for you and your man. Let him know that and maybe he will keep his mouth shut. If he doesn't, he will die, right here where Brianne did."

"Yes, sir."

"Violence," Soong said, "is an important tool, and it's meant to be used. You may leave now, Tommy."

"Yes, Laoban."

"Be vigilant, Tommy, my man hasn't heard any mention of you yet. And yes, the car you saw could have been someone from the police department. Keep me informed."

Soong was amused watching Tommy bow while holding the rug in both hands. But it was good that he was humbling himself. Anything less was unacceptable, and he was in a mood.

As the door closed, Soong opened his laptop and watched the video of Brianne on her knees, those big brown eyes pleading for mercy. She had disappointed an important client, and that infuriated him. He turned up the volume as the bat crushed her face. That sound eased his anger, and he backed it up and listened a few more times. She was twitching now, and not quite the beauty she had been. He closed the file and selected another video. A blonde this time.

CHAPTER 19

LeAnn

Ten days after her sister's sudden appearance, LeAnn watched her vanish into a throng of international travelers at the Changi Airport. LeAnn assembled Jie's phone and made a call to the local American Airlines desk. She asked the agent about the seat status of several outbound flights, making sure they repeated her name, and then hung up and took the phone apart. If the Clean Man was still tracking this phone, she could play that game as well. Let him believe she was trying to leave the country. Her plan was in motion and the first step was changing her image.

At a kiosk in the airport's food court, she used more of Khoo's cash to buy two Samsung pre-paid smart phones and searched for a beauty salon near the airport. Then she set up an Uber account and waited for it at the same exit where Jie had grabbed her weeks ago. Turning, she checked the doors behind her and scanned the crowd of travelers. No one was following her.

The Tokyo Beauty Salon was a short ride outside the airport's perimeter. She used her new phone now, for the next few days she wanted the Clean Man to believe she had vanished, but she would need Jie and Khoo's phones one more time before sending them to the police station.

A fourteen-inch-long section of dark brown hair fell on her lap, then another. "Shorter," she told the beautician in Mandarin, and several more inches of her hair dropped to the floor. She thought of dying the ends another color, dark red perhaps, but changed her mind. She wanted to blend in now, not stand out. Now, it was all about the hunt.

"That's perfect," she said looking in the mirror.

Outside the salon, several Ubers were lined up outside a coffee shop, each with the recognizable decal on the rear window. She stopped at the first one, asking the driver, "Can you take me to Avis?" in Mandarin. The woman nodded, and an hour later LeAnn was sitting behind the wheel of a silver Honda four-door compact sedan. Most of the Avis fleet appeared to be this exact car, and she wanted to blend in with as much of the traffic as possible, an invisible driver in an equally invisible car.

Driving in the left lane while sitting in the right seat was challenging, and it was harder than she imagined. Just backing the car out of its parking space was difficult. Circling the parking lot several times helped and gave her the courage to pull out onto the street.

Screeching tires and an air horn blast from a delivery truck were the only warnings she had. Jerking the wheel to the right, the truck missed her driver's door by inches. In a panic, she pulled off the road and sat in the idling car until she could breathe again.

Shaking all over, but afraid to sit on the side of the road any longer, she pulled back onto the street and took side roads all the way back to the condo. Tomorrow, she would venture out again, and again if necessary, until she was sure she could handle the next step without killing herself or wrecking the rental.

That night, and for the first time in days, she slept without seeing her captors in her dreams. In the morning, she spooned down a Chinese version of Cheerios and milk, with only a few honking horns on the street below breaking the silence.

Footsteps outside her door startled her, and she dropped the spoon, grabbed a steak knife off the counter and waited, but the sound faded, and she saw the shadow of someone walking by the kitchen window.

The milk in her cereal was warm, and her watch told her thirty minutes had slipped by since she heard the footsteps. Time lapses in her memory weren't new, but she had not had one like this in years. Gaps of twenty or thirty minutes, sometimes as long as an hour, would pass, and she could not explain it; it was as if time was simply running along without her. Bloated cereal floated in the warm milk. She threw it all in the sink.

Dressed in her black T-shirt and gray sweatpants, she took two steps at a time down to the first floor and then tried running back up. The run lasted just two floors, and she collapsed between the second and third, her chest heaving. "You're so pathetic, LeAnn!" she said aloud. Still gasping for air, she walked the remaining steps, having doubts whether she could climb one more floor, much less make it all the way to the twelfth floor.

When she finally returned to the condo, panting and soaked in sweat, she rested on the kitchen's cool tile floor until her heart stopped pounding, then the cramping in her legs began. *My God, I'm only twenty-one, and I can't walk up a fricking flight of stairs!*

Slowly, she forced her legs straight out, one at a time, trying to ease the pain in her thighs. Nothing worked. As soon as the cramp in one leg relaxed, the other one cramped again. She watched her thigh muscle spasm, quivering like a bowl of Jell-O. Standing helped some, and walking cured the last of the cramping.

"I'm not ready for this," she said to her reflection in the mirror. "I'm so thin."

She had always been thin, but she looked anorexic now. "I look like an emaciated boy," she said, critiquing her profile. The black T-shirt hid her breasts. They had always been small, but the drastic weight loss had made them even smaller. She nodded to herself, as if coming to an important decision.

"I've got to do this now."

She took the elevator to the garage. Behind the wheel, she eased the Honda out into the afternoon traffic, remembering to check for oncoming cars in the opposite lane, then accelerated and drove to the same park Araya mentioned days ago.

Passing several white vans along the way, she felt a rush,

hoping it was him, but was disappointed when it was someone else. Had it been the Driver, her plans would have to change, though, and she didn't like changes. This afternoon she wanted to draw the man out using Jie's phone and follow him, learn his habits—study her prey. It was all part of the hunt, she told herself.

The big public park was surrounded by tall, ornate wrought iron fencing; gates on each side gave access to a grassy area, huge oak trees, and public benches. Outside the fence were small mom-and-pop stores frequented by the locals.

Joggers and walkers were everywhere, both inside the park on trails, or on the sidewalk outside. Most were young, her age, but there were a few older people and even a few young mothers pushing strollers. It was the perfect place to hide in plain sight.

Circling twice to get a feel of the place, she parked and got out, walking with the crowd and then into a convenience store. Picking out a box of latex gloves and a dozen black N95 respirator masks, she handed the cashier Khoo's Visa card. *Let the Blue Room pay for it all*. The woman tried the card twice and gave LeAnn a look of concern.

"What?" LeAnn said in English.

"Card no good."

"I'm sorry, my father must have canceled it," she said, and handed the woman a wad of cash. It must have been the last of Jie's money; red stains were on a few of the bills.

Wearing one of the N95s, she walked outside and joined the pedestrians on the sidewalk, half of them wearing similar versions of her mask. In one of the glass storefronts, she checked her reflection. The mask covered most of her face, adding one more layer of concealment.

She tripped on a buckled section of the sidewalk and almost fell. Huge cracks and whole sections of the concrete were an inch higher in some places as roots from oak trees forced their way underneath. The uneven sidewalk made it difficult to scan the crowd and walk at the same time. She didn't expect anyone to recognize her yet, but she knew they would come. She hoped it would be the Driver, but the Clean Man could send anyone.

Cool breezes carried the aroma of a nearby bakery. The scent was intoxicating, and she followed it down to the intersection of two side streets. Pastries of all sorts and colors, stacked in trays, were displayed in the glass window. The look of them, along with the smell, was irresistible. *I could use the calories too.*

LeAnn ordered four croissants, or some Asian version of them, and began eating the first one as she made her way to an empty park bench.

It's peaceful here; something I could get used to, and that feeling was odd. *I've never felt anything peaceful.*

As she ate, she checked her watch to make sure she hadn't lost track of time. Only fifteen minutes had passed since she parked.

A strange-looking dark gray squirrel jumped on the bench next to her. There was something different about it.

It has small ears, and it's smaller than the squirrels in New York City. Or maybe it's just young.

It was a nervous creature, unable to stay still and chittering at her, but never taking its eyes off the croissant. She tossed a big crumb on the sidewalk, and the squirrel ran off with it as if it were a priceless treasure.

Brushing crumbs off her sweatpants didn't bring the animal back. She waited for it and then remembered why she was there.

I'm not here to feed a stupid squirrel. Time to focus.

She had survived by listening to her instincts, trusting her strange obsessive-compulsive need to stay on task, so she checked the time again and made her way through the throng of pedestrians and got back in her Honda.

Behind the wheel she had a perfect view of all four intersections surrounding the park. LeAnn pulled out Khoo's phone and inserted the battery and SIM card. Only 10 percent battery remained, but this would be the last call she would make on his phone. It connected to the system, and this time there were no new missed calls or texts. Dialing the number for her friend in New York City, she checked her watch again, not worrying about her memory this time, but to start the twenty-minute countdown.

"Hello?" She heard confusion in her friend's voice, knowing he was looking at an international number on his caller ID.

"Christopher, it's LeAnn. Any luck on the name I sent you?"

"The Blue Room? Some bits and pieces, but some really weird stuff linked to a similar name came up. I think if I poke any further, I might start some real shit."

"What do you mean?"

"First, the Blue Room isn't actually a place. It's the name of a chat room and it's invitation only. I found a way to get in and shadowed the conversation a few nights ago. Three people were on, no names were used, and it was all very cryptic. It sounds like a prostitution ring with people bidding on a product. There were some really big players and some huge bank accounts. LeAnn, one of them mentioned 250K, and I'm pretty sure he was referring to US dollars, so I'm not sure it's just prostitution."

"I think that's exactly what it is, but maybe they are into other stuff as well; they seem to have easy access to drugs and pharmaceuticals. Email everything you can to me. Christopher, I have two more names I want you to look at: Hui Jie, birthdate October 9, 1992, and Tan Khoo, birthdate June 25, 1988. Mostly I need to know what they have been doing, who they hang out with, and if there's a link between them and the Blue Room. Christopher, they're both dead now, but I still want to know."

"They're dead? Jesus, LeAnn!"

"Nothing I did," she said, hoping he believed her. "But there is one more thing. I'm using one of their phones so you may want to get rid of yours now, and Christopher, be extremely careful."

"LeAnn, one guy sounded like the seller and the other two the buyers. The seller mentioned having new stock soon and referred to it as fresh. Whatever deal they were discussing is happening soon."

"Yeah, fresh as in very young. Thanks, I owe you, and again, be careful and get rid of that phone."

She hung up, took Khoo's phone apart, put the pieces in her backpack, and waited.

"Eight minutes," she whispered.

***

Tommy Fong was six blocks from the park when his phone rang.

"Yes, Laoban," he said.

"The phone is on again and it's in the same park. Someone is calling a New York City number right now, and I'm trying to track that down. Get over there and look for her. Don't fuck around this time, Tommy."

***

"Twenty minutes," she said, looking at her watch.

There were three white work vans on the park's perimeter, but she was only interested in one of them. She knew it was him the minute she saw him turn toward her. Someone driving a little slower than everyone else, someone looking at more than just the traffic around them. A single predator among hundreds of sheep.

"Twenty-four minutes — right on time, you bastard."

She put her mask back on just as the van passed her. The tinted windows were down now and she could see his face . . . and the memories of being pulled into the van blinded her. *She could smell the chloroform on the rag, and smell Jie behind her.*

"Please, not again," she whispered.

Looking in the rear-view mirror, she imagined what he could have seen of her, part of her shirt and maybe a bit of her masked face, just enough, she hoped, that he would dismiss her.

The van's engine's rpms never varied, slowly but steadily cruising away from her, its tone diminishing until it was gone.

Only then did she turn and look through the side mirror. It circled the park, pulled into an empty spot farther up the street, and the Driver stepped out.

That face! Chills racked her, she shivered even in the warm outside air. It was like facing the nightmare of Jie and Khoo all over again.

Impulsively, she began planning how she could kill him right here in the park. But she had no weapon. Except for the car's manual and registration, the glove box was empty and there was nothing in the console. Something in the trunk, maybe?

"Shit, shit, shit."

The Driver was on the opposite side of the street, looking back and forth at the people in the park and then turned to look behind him at the lot where she was parked.

Forty feet away and closing.

She thought of a tire iron in the trunk, surely this rental would have one.

How does the trunk open?

The dashboard had so many unfamiliar buttons and knobs and panic was setting in.

Thirty feet away now.

"Too close," she whispered closing her eyes.

Voices were all around her now, and one of them could be him, but she feared if she opened her eyes, he would be staring at her through the open window. Fear was overpowering her need to defend herself . . . she was paralyzed. She could sense him, right there, a sick grin on his face.

She had to look. Pushing the feeling of dread aside, she opened her eyes. There he stood, still twenty-five feet away, looking at a young couple on a bench inside the fence. He was comparing a picture to the girl, then shook his head and turned toward LeAnn's Honda.

There was not a single thing inside this car she could use as a weapon, not even a ballpoint pen. If she lived through this, she would always have something with her. Even Jie's knife in her hand would give her a chance, but it and the screwdriver were back at the condo. Now unarmed, she would never be able to kill a man twice her size, and in a public park. This man was smaller than Khoo, less muscular, but she caught Khoo off guard that day and surprised him. She had been lucky, and she knew luck was not going to help her now.

Her breathing now was erratic and she could hear herself wheezing.

"Give it up, LeAnn, you can't kill him here," she told herself. "Be patient."

Twenty feet away now, crossing the street and walking right towards her. She put both hands on the wheel and closed her eyes again. In her mind, a beautiful ballerina spun on her toes across the stage . . . and the last of her fears left her, her grip on the wheel eased, her breathing slowed, and she opened her eyes.

Through her open window, she could reach out and touch him. He was talking to another man in fluent English, an older man walking a small dog.

"No, I don't think so," the new man said. "I think I would recognize her if I had seen her. You say she's your daughter, have you called the authorities?"

"Yes she is, but I don't want to involve the police, thank you."

Fong was so close to the window that his chest was at eye level. LeAnn put the window up. He turned toward the sound, and she knew he was looking at her now through the closed window.

How much of me can he see?

She had been holding her breath so long, spots floated across her vision., She was about to pass out.

Breathe, LeAnn, breathe.

Her vision cleared, enough that she could see him right next to her, the front of his blue shirt inches from her locked door.

Will he break the glass to get to me? No, he'll try and get me to lower the window and maybe use chloroform like Jie did. He'd have to be crazy to try that with so many people around! No, he'll do something else. If I were him, I would follow me as I drove out, fake a car crash, rear-end me somewhere private, or force me off the road and then use the chloroform.

Pushing the engine start button, she put the car in gear and waited. Her fingers and forearms ached as she gripped the steering wheel. Fear was not an easy emotion to deal with; it was a weakness she had tried to master all her life, and today it was a raging battle

There was just enough room between her car and the one in front of it. If she had to, she could hit the accelerator and pull out onto the street if he recognized her. She took two deep breaths and held them, then exhaled.

In the side mirror, she watched him turn away and walk farther down the sidewalk, a lumbering gate, almost limping . . . a weakness maybe. Dressed just like Khoo in dark blue work pants, the lighter blue collared shirt and heavy work boots, he shuffled farther down the street and stopped another couple, showing them the photo.

He was ten feet behind her now and never looked back, walking casually down the sidewalk. "Phew, that was close," she whispered, then put the car back in park and watched him in the mirror.

For half an hour, he walked around the park's perimeter, talking to some people and watching others. Several times he disappeared inside the shops, only to come out minutes later and scan up and down the sidewalks.

He was angry, she could see it on his face. Standing next to the bench where she had seen the squirrel, he kicked a trash can, startling the couple sitting next to it.

"Yes, you're a loser, old man."

Amused, she thought of taunting him, maybe getting out of the car and following him on foot to see if he recognized her. "Who am I kidding? Just minutes ago, I was scared shitless." She had sat right next to Lieutenant Trufant in San Francisco and even talked to him. That was different, though, Trufant was a cop. Still, her craving for revenge was powerful.

"No, LeAnn, stick to the plan."

The Driver made the final turn and walked back to his van, took one long look in her direction, opened the door, and began driving east and away from her. Putting the car in gear, she pulled out and drove east, accelerating until she had his van right in front of her.

Traffic was light, which made following him along the Tampines Expressway difficult. Too close and he would know he was being followed. He might even recognize her Honda from the park. Too far away would be just as bad. She could lose him and he might never fall for the phone trick again.

The Honda's cramped interior was beginning to trigger her claustrophobia. The phobia could cripple her if she allowed it. Opening all the windows, the rush of warm, humid air and even the stench of exhaust refreshed her, and the sensation of being crushed in the tiny car vanished as quickly as it had begun.

The temperature outside was thirty-four degrees Celsius, according to the Honda. "Ninety-four frigging Fahrenheit degrees," she mumbled. Sweat dripping in her eyes burned and blurred her vision. She needed the windows down, though. Dealing with sweat was better than the alternative.

Keeping two cars and a pick-up truck between her and the van now, she relaxed, cruising at the speed limit and safe distance behind. Then the van signaled a right turn and began to slow. She was going to be exposed as soon as he made the turn. Staying out of its rearview mirror and moving closer to the center line kept the pick-up truck between them, and fortunately, that truck and one of the cars made the same turn.

Side streets dotted with small shops, open-air restaurants, and used car lots gave way to a run-down warehouse district. Buildings on both sides of the street were similar to those near the port where she had been held captive. The smell of rotting garbage, sucked in by the Honda's air conditioner, filled the car as she passed a row of green dumpsters. Several bloated flies came in with the stench.

Only the truck remained between her and the van and then it too pulled off the road. The hair rose on her arms and neck—she was too exposed. The van was right in front of her, the only two cars on the now deserted street. Braking hard, she parked next to a seafood warehouse and watched the van continue on down the street and out of sight. She had been so close, and now she had lost him.

Shooing the flies out, she waited ten minutes, and then another ten, then pulled back out onto the street following the van's last direction of travel. There was no sign of it anywhere. The road continued for several blocks, then came to a three-way intersection. Left or right? She turned left, and in the middle of the next block, the van was right in front of her. It and a similar but older van were parked in front of a small white building. Above its steel roll-up door, a logo of a sewing machine was crudely painted in black.

A quick glance as she drove by told her both vans were unoccupied and there was no sign of him. Continuing down the road, she turned at the next cross street, then looped back around and parked under a shade tree. From a block away, she watched the building and waited.

An hour later, the door opened and a man and a young woman came out. The man was short and stocky. Even from this far away, she knew right away it was not the Driver. Her breath caught in her throat as she looked at the woman, or girl. She was young, tall, and thin with strawberry blonde hair—and she was wearing a dress just like the one Brianne had worn.

"You poor bitch!"

The Clean Man was back in business.

The older van backed out and drove away, hopefully leaving The Driver inside the building. Not knowing if he was still inside, ate at her. In the twenty minutes she had sat on the side of the road, he could have left with someone else, leaving the van. She would wait as long as it took.

This far away and under the tree, LeAnn would be difficult to spot unless someone was looking for her. She wanted to be closer, but there was nothing but empty parking lots between her and the warehouse. The risk was too great.

I need a good pair of binoculars. Until then, I'll just wait here.

She didn't wait long. The Driver walked out from an alley between the building and the one next to it carrying a box. He looked like a different man, taller and he no longer limped. The shuffling old man appearance had been a ruse. "Very clever, you bastard."

The van backed out and headed away from her, eastbound just like the other one, and as he turned the first corner, she put the Honda in gear and drove past the building.

How many more girls are in there? How many men does the Clean Man have?

Far in front of her now, the van cruised on. He was obeying all the speed limits and even using his turn signals to change lanes, driving like a professional, not some lacky like Jie or even Khoo. This man was a hunter, a smart one too.

Are you hunting me right now? Probably not, it's just in your blood, isn't it?

Well, she was hunting too. LeAnn loved the exhilarating rush of adrenaline, and she was feeling it now—studying her target, looking for weaknesses, anything to use against him. This piqued all her senses. It was a better high, or at least a different kind, than all the drugs the Clean Man had forced on her. She learned from her victim's mistakes too, and so far, this man hadn't made any, except that he had been right next to her in the park.

She changed lanes, still trying to keep as many cars as possible between her and the van, until he turned into a residential area. It was a two-lane road and without another car to conceal her, she pulled into the grassy swale in front of someone's home and watched as the van continued down the street.

Then his brake lights flashed twice.

What was that, did he see me?

"No," she screamed, slamming her fist into the padded dashboard.

A block away, the van was stopped at a stop sign, waiting for something. If he had seen her, he would come for her, circle the block, or just put it in reverse and come back. Then the van rolled slowly across the intersection and pulled into the driveway of a house.

With the same box in one hand, he opened the front door with a key, and went inside.

"It's got to be my lucky day."

His house was painted a pale yellow and surrounded by overgrown landscaping. Hedges obscured most of the windows on the two sides she could see and there was a side door facing her.

For thirty minutes she waited, and then pulled out and drove past the house, eyes straight ahead, and just fast enough not to draw his attention if he was looking through the windows.

Enough for one day.

On her way back to the condo, she stopped at a sporting goods store and bought a powerful pair of Nikon binoculars, a spool of 150 lb. stainless steel leader wire, wire cutters, and a crimping tool. At a locksmith's shop, she used the last of Khoo's cash and purchased tools that included everything she needed to pick most locks.

CHAPTER 20

KWAN

Kwan held the missing persons report in his hand, reading it for the second time. Was this a new victim? He had almost dismissed it as a runaway, the teenage daughter of a wealthy politician. Gemma Balakrishnan was fifteen with a history of running away from a life of prosperity; a rebel, her father had called her, and she'd disappeared from an outdoor concert three days ago.

All of it sounded plausible, but something nagged him, something didn't fit, so he searched the previous reports and found the three missing persons cases, all filed in the previous year.

In the first report, Gemma had argued with her father and ran away while her family slept and returned before noon the next day. In the second report, she'd had another argument, this time with her mother over a boy, and again she returned the next day.

Three days ago, the girl went missing again, but there was no argument—quite the opposite, her mother had said. Gemma had been in good spirits and had left with two of her girlfriends to see a local band play at a nearby park.

When the concert ended, Gemma was gone. Her friends had last seen her near the park's restrooms an hour earlier, and she seemed excited about watching the band's final songs.

So, what happened to the girl? The following day, inspectors had done the usual search and even carried it further once they realized she was the daughter of Parliament's Deputy Speaker.

There were two links to CCTV video showing limited views of the park, but the inspectors reported there were too many blind spots, and with the heavy crowd of teenagers, they could easily have missed her.

One video did show Gemma's friends speaking with a uniformed officer hours after the concert ended. It was a high-resolution camera and it was obvious the two friends were concerned.

His desk phone rang as he closed the file.

"Kwan," he said.

"Kwan." He recognized Commissioner Arul's voice instantly, and he knew this was not going to go well.

"I just got off the phone with Prime Minister Hsien," the commissioner said. "He is not happy, Kwan, and so I'm not happy either. He wants to know what we are doing to find the Deputy Speaker's daughter. So, what do I tell him, what are we doing?"

"Sir, I have the report in my hand. The first officer dismissed it as a possible runaway. There is no link to this girl and the tourists, but there are a few similarities. Do you want me to add her to that list?"

"No," the commissioner said after thinking about it. "Let's not panic the man yet, but can you eliminate her as being another abducted victim?"

"I can try, sir."

"Do it. I told the PM I would get back to him tomorrow."

"Great," Kwan said, after hanging up the phone.

He reopened the first video link and watched three hours of pedestrians and traffic crossing through the camera's limited view and then started the second link from a camera on the opposite end of the park.

The first vehicle to enter the frame was a white Toyota HiAce van. He paused the video and zoomed in on the driver, a middle-aged man looking through the passenger window toward the throng of teenagers on the sidewalk.

He knew in his gut—something primal told him this was the same man and the same van involved in the abduction from the airport almost two months ago. He had asked First Sergeant Jiawei to check on the print taken off the van recovered at the warehouse, and he hadn't heard back from her yet.

"Jiawei," he said, calling her on his cell phone.

"Yes, sir?"

"The print on the white van, have you checked on that guy yet?"

"Tommy Fong, yes, I've tried several times, sir, including this morning, and I've never found him at home. I'll check again tomorrow."

"Thank you. And Jiawei—make sure you have someone with you."

"Yes, sir."

He ended the call and fast-forwarded through the video and spotted the van several more times. Chills raced up his spine; he knew what he was watching. This man was searching for a victim, and not just any victim, he was searching for Gemma.

CHAPTER 21

LEANN

Pale moonlight reflected off the hood of her Honda. Parked in front of a vacant house, she was five houses north of the Driver's home. This home was for sale, and from the outside, looked like an exact copy of his.

The side door lock was new, and with her picks, it was easy to open. Walking through the unfurnished house, she memorized every room, every light switch, until she could walk through it with her eyes closed. What did she hope to find in his house? What were her goals? Answers, to the hundreds of questions she asked herself each night. What were his weaknesses, his habits, and most important, what was his name. Repeating "the Driver" each night and each morning had become an obsession and one she wanted to be rid of.

Back in the Honda with her 7x50 binoculars, she studied every detail of his house. There was no fence, or any other sign of a security system other than a fixed camera facing away from the front door. It was pointed at the driveway, and she would not be going through the front door. There were no other cameras and sensors she could see in the dark, but they were so small now, she knew she could easily miss one.

This was the third night of her surveillance and the second step of her plan. The Driver was home, the van parked nose first in the driveway. If he was on schedule, he would leave at 6:30 sharp as he had done the last two mornings, and he would return soon after 7 p.m. Shift work, and the schedule Jie and Khoo had used.

The two previous days, he parked his van at the warehouse with the sewing machine logo and he never left. Bored now and knowing he wasn't leaving home anytime soon, she drove back to the warehouse twenty minutes away and parked on the next block with a clear view of the front and east side of the building. An older, Toyota white van was parked in the front.

Dressed in dark gray leggings, a long-sleeve Henley, and black Skechers running shoes, she walked along the darkened street until she was close enough to see the details of the building. Up close it looked abandoned, except for the old van. She turned into the alley and approached it from the rear; light leaking from a back window helped her avoid wooden pallets stacked against the back wall. The glass panes were cracked, and at one time had been painted black, but sections of the paint near the cracks had flaked off enough that she could see inside.

Dim yellow light turned everything inside to shades of black and white, devoid of color. Sitting at a metal table, a man sat with his back to the window, reading a magazine. More magazines were stacked on the table, along with an open laptop and a coffee machine. The man turned his chair and she could see some of his face.

This wasn't the same man she had seen with the girl three days ago. This man was younger, and as she watched, he nodded off. He was about Jie's age, thin, with an acne-scarred face and long hair. It was too dark to see much more of him, but right behind him she saw a toilet and a sink that looked new, like they had been installed recently, in contrast to the gray, dirty floor.

The sound of a car approaching made her duck down next to the stack of old pallets. She listened to the car's engine getting louder until a gray four-door sedan passed between this building and the next, its taillights giving the alley a red tint. The sound of the engine never varied, and she listened to make sure it didn't stop somewhere down the street.

Her knees ached from kneeling and popped loudly as she stood up. Peeping through a different crack in the glass, she saw more of the room. Two unused IV poles, their chrome stands glistening, stood next to an empty cot. A shadow moved inside as the man at the desk walked over to the toilet and pissed. He looked to his right and smiled at something.

Moving closer to the stacked pallets, she could see to his right and what she saw made her step back, knocking the top pallet off the stack, then the entire stack fell with a crash. It was loud and she saw the man turn toward the window, the smile on his face now a contorted look of fear.

Backing away as quietly as possible, she reached the alley between the buildings as the sound of squealing hinges from a door she hadn't noticed swung open. A shaft of yellow light illuminated the crushed weeds where she had just been standing.

She froze, then crouched down below the weeds. Using her hands, she felt the dirt in front of her, feeling for anything that would make noise, and began inching her way deeper into the alley. Something warm crawled over her fingers, and she jerked her hand back as a white beam from a flashlight swept the weeds above her.

"Who's out there?" he said in thick Mandarin.

The man stepped outside, causing shadows to move across the white wall behind her.

"I see you," he said, but his flashlight was pointed away from her.

"Come out!"

His voice sounded pinched and the flashlight beam shook as it swept across the weeds. As the beam neared her, she noticed that several piles of broken pallets were mixed in with the weeds, and most of them were taller than she was. He would have to move out and away from the building to see her.

On all fours, she crawled deeper into the alley and then around the side of the second building and hid between several oil barrels. The beam made another slow pass, illuminating the tops of the weeds and the oil barrels and then winked out. The door closed and the alley was dark again.

Checking her watch, she waited thirty minutes, enough time for a tired man to get complacent and whatever adrenaline rush his fear had given him had probably run its course. Still, she avoided the main street when she walked to the Honda, then drove back to the condo.

That was too close. I was careless and almost blew it.

She wanted to believe she was invincible but knew it wasn't true. All her previous victims had been weak-minded losers, like the three bitches who thought they were cool because they could pick on her. They were only tough when they sat together at the dining hall, and she proved them wrong. And the pervert on the bus in Manhattan—he could not have been more pathetic—crying like a babe before she had the wire around his neck. And the wino on the subway platform? "Gimme some coochie, sweet thing." She had warned him twice to shut up. He had been the easiest of them all. But the Clean Man and his accomplices—these men were different. All their lives, they had been the ones inflicting pain.

It was a vendetta now, and she was bringing the pain to them. She just needed to distance herself from what they had done. It was clouding her vision and affecting her decisions.

"It's all in the prep work," Ramzi often told her. "Being smarter than your victim is not enough. Be more meticulous than the people who will be looking for you." Ramzi was brilliant at times, but he was also obsessive. She was too, but Ramzi let it get personal at the end, and it cost him his life.

In bed, the sheets and blankets pulled up tight to her chin, the monstrous image of the Clean Man's face hovered just above her. His presence was sharp and realistic, so real that his cologne, the cloying smell of new leather, invaded the room.

"So, you're back in business," she said to the specter. "I thought killing Jie and Khoo would have cost you more, but they were amateurs, weren't they?" The image smiled, she could count his massive white teeth, then he winked and the image was gone.

"I'm not an amateur," she said, "and I'm coming for you."

Brianne had been held at least three weeks that LeAnn knew

of before they took her out. The girl she had seen in the sundress must have been several weeks into her addiction also, and maybe even longer, which meant he had at least two warehouses in operation while she was captive. How many more were there? She would let Kwan worry about them. She had her list, she would cross off each name and be done with them, let Kwan clean up the leftovers.

Dawn was creeping in around the blackout curtains, and she thought of the girl she had seen through the crack in the glass. Was it the same girl or a new one? She had only seen the girl's foot and the steel tube frame of a cot, just like the one she'd been bound to. LeAnn could almost smell the urine. The image enraged her, and she couldn't understand why.

Because I want to save her!

As she drifted off, her mother spoke to her, "Never let your emotions affect you, LeAnn." The woman had been an emotional wreck, but her advice was sound.

Eight hours of restless sleep felt like two—the bastard was in her dreams again. "Get out!" she screamed at the image in her head. Each day, though, she felt a little stronger and her mind a little sharper. She still had aches and pains in her joints that she assumed were a residual effect of withdrawal. Something she'd read mentioned those pains might be psychosomatic and might never go away. "I can live with them, if that's the worst I'll suffer."

Afternoon sunshine spilling through the curtains crept up the wall as the sun made its way toward the horizon. Tonight, she'd take another step with her plan. She wanted to know more about this new warehouse, the girl inside, and the guy watching her.

The shift change would be at seven. She arrived at 6:15, and the Driver's new van was parked in front of the closed roll-up door. The older van was gone, so she waited. At 6:45, the sun began to cast long shadows on the front of the building, and the light began to fade—the "gloaming," as her Lit teacher called it, that eerie period between day and night.

At 7 p.m., a rattling sound broke her reverie. An old red motor scooter belching blue smoke turned toward her at the far end of the street. The driver shut the engine off, coasted to a stop next to the van, and leaned the scooter against the wall. His red helmet covered most of his face, and in the low light she couldn't see much of him.

This was someone new, not the guy she had seen the night before. Studying him through the binoculars, he looked young, maybe twenty. So, there were three men now, not including the Driver and the Clean Man. The new guy knocked twice and the door opened.

As she waited for the Driver to come out, headlights lit up the interior of the Honda. A car was coming up behind her. It was a gray, four-door sedan with tinted windows. Inching down in the seat, she watched it pass her, then slow as it neared the warehouse. It was the same gray sedan from the night before, she was sure of it. The car accelerated and turned right at the end of the street.

It looked like an ubiquitous rental, but it also looked like an unmarked police car. Was someone else interested in this warehouse? Was it the police, or was it just someone who worked nearby going home for the night? Now she had one more thing to worry about.

None of the streetlights worked on this block. It was pitch-black and most of the boarded-up businesses were vacant. Except for the van and the scooter leaning against the wall, the entire block now looked like an abandoned slum. Half an hour later, the Driver came out. He glanced in her direction, got in the van and drove away.

The familiar dim light leaking from gaps in the window frames and cracked glass shed a weak glow on the dead grass as she walked through the alley to the back door.

Tonight, she wanted to memorize every inch of the alley and the back of the building. One of her many plans included an escape through the back door at night, and running into a stack of pallets might cost her. Mistakes are fine, she thought, as long as you live to learn from them. Last night she had been lucky, the man inside might have thought a stray cat had knocked something over. If he had spotted her, the Clean Man and this operation would have disappeared, and she would have to start all over.

In the waist-deep weeds, she could see the pallets had been restacked near the back door, camouflaged in the dim light. Moving slowly, she edged up to the window.

I need to see this girl, to see her face, to see if she is awake. Or is she drugged out of her mind while heroin slowly consumes her like I was?

The questions nagged her, and the dim light bulb inside was little help. All she could see was that the girl's toenails were painted with a dark polish.

Moving closer to the door provided a slightly better vantage point. LeAnn could see the girl's body from the waist down; she was naked and strapped to the cot. An IV line was taped to her wrist; the pole held a full saline bag and a smaller white bag that LeAnn thought was propofol. Anger raged and her nerves felt like her skin was on fire. From what little she could see, the girl looked young, thirteen, maybe even younger. The age of innocence . . . LeAnn was just ten when her father and sister had been murdered right in front of her.

As that horrible memory flooded over her, LeAnn sat down in the grass, her back to the wall.

I know what you're going through, my little friend.

Over the years, the memories of that day had become tangled with the nightmares, and she was never sure what was real. This girl was going to suffer a similar childhood.

Not if I can help it.

Her new-found compassion confused her, but it also helped her focus. She stood up and peered through the window. There were two more empty cots next to the girl, cots she knew the Clean Man wanted filled—and the younger the victim, the better. The pricks in the Blue Room would probably pay even more for a child.

I can walk back to the car right now and call the police, I can call Kwan. I can save this girl tonight. But I could lose the Clean Man and the Driver if I do . . . and they had to pay. And will Kwan do his job? Who was he anyway? Sorry, Kwan, I can't trust you with this.

There was nothing else visible, the man inside had his back to her again, flipping through one of the magazines. He looked like a younger version of Jie, so much so, that she had an urge to knock on the front door and lure him outside.

"You're going to have to endure at least one more night, my dear," she whispered. She felt wrong leaving and the emotion surprised her.

What's happening to me, what is this, guilt?

Empathy and guilt were weaknesses, no better or worse than fear. The girl was a stranger, a nobody in LeAnn's life. She had killed her three classmates for insulting her; this girl could be just as much of a bitch as they had been.

"Bitches," she whispered in the dark. Saying it aloud eliminated any trace of empathy.

Stay focused, LeAnn!

Three, six, nine . . . she walked off the distance between the back door, the stacked pallets, and the alley and guessed it was thirty feet, and another thirty feet to the wall of the warehouse behind it. If she needed to run, to rescue the girl and escape, she had a clear path and could do it in the dark now. Satisfied, she returned to the Honda and drove back to the safe house, checking her mirror and circling the building twice. When she was certain no one was following her, she pulled into the underground parking lot.

When she returned to the condo, she focused on the next step of her plan. Working with the braided stainless-steel wire was easier than music wire. Twice in New York, she had used piano wire as a garrote. The wire was difficult to twist, and buying it at a music store could have left an easy trail, especially after one of the detectives working the case had referred to her as the "B-Flat Killer."

"No more piano wire," she said, twisting the loop big enough for her gloved hand. Three garrotes, each thirty inches long, sat on the kitchen table next to a bowl of cold ramen noodles. The meal was easy to fix, required no real thought, and she knew that was Ramzi's style. Nothing to distract him while he ate, sitting in seclusion and planning his next adventure, and the taste wasn't that bad. She was beginning to appreciate his style.

Six hours now until dawn. Closing her eyes, she fell asleep in seconds and slept, dream-free, until the sun rose.

Since killing Jie and Khoo at the warehouse, her morning routine started as soon as her eyes opened. Stretching her hands out in front of her, palms up, then palms down, she eyed her fingers, looking for the slightest shake or tremor that would tell her she was still and always would be a junkie, but her hands were steady this morning. "Like a rock," she said. Then she repeated the nicknames of both criminals as she visualized their faces, and the reason she was going to make them suffer.

The route back to the Driver's house took twenty minutes in the light pre-rush hour traffic. She parked in front of the vacant house, put two of the coiled garrotes and the leather gloves in her pockets, then scanned the Driver's house with the binoculars.

The front door CCTV camera looked like a cheap one, even through the binoculars. The camera was fixed and centered on the driveway. If it was as old as it looked, it probably didn't have Wi-Fi, and was a simple camera wired to a recording unit somewhere inside.

I hope.

Even if not, she was prepared for the worst. Thirty minutes, maybe, and the Driver could be back at the house. Who would watch the girl, though? Would he leave her alone, or would he have someone else check his house?

Either way, she was ready.

Right on time, he came out, checked up and down the street, never giving her a second glance, and then drove away. It was another mistake. He should have recognized a strange car in his neighborhood and checked it out. A half hour from now, he would be parking at the warehouse and start his twelve-hour shift; unless, of course, the Clean Man had hired another flunky to replace him. She had a feeling the Driver was higher up on the food chain than either of the other two. He was older and maybe smarter and would soon be back to his old job of being the wheel man.

The walk to the house was easy. Few of the residents on this block were even awake. She slipped into the shrubbery around his side door and waited silently, listening for anything unusual, noises on the inside, a dog barking, an alarm beeping, a neighbor outside, anything. What if he has a dog? The possibility had never occurred to her.

I'll deal with the dog if I have to.

Hidden from passersby, she studied the door. A white vinyl shade blocked her view through the window. The bottom half of the door had been neglected for years. Several shades of peeling paint covered old and splintered wood. Spiderwebs and two empty wasps' nests hung from the corners. There were no signs of an alarm; no wires in the screen and no magnetic contacts visible. A simple keyed doorknob, its brass finish dulled by patina and corrosion, held the only lock.

Bending down, she peered into the keyhole. It was full of dried mud. Some insect had built a nest inside. It would take time to clean it out if she wanted to use the lockpicks. She stood up and tried to turn the knob. It was locked, but there was a quarter-inch wide gap between the door and its frame. She could open it using Jie's pocketknife.

The knife, now honed razor sharp, slid easily between the door and the jamb. Twisting it back and forth, the blade cut in to the soft brass bolt and she inched it backward until it cleared the jamb. She pulled gently on the knob until the door cracked open wide enough to trigger a contact switch. Pressing her ear into the opening, she listened for the telltale beeping of an alarm system, but the house was quiet.

A rusty hinge screamed as she pulled the door open wider still. *Christ! The neighbors across the street could have heard that.* But the opening was wide enough now to fit her head inside and look for motion detectors. It was too dark. Waiting for her eyes to adjust, she listened again for any sign of an alarm, a pet, or even someone in the house. All she heard was ticking; it sounded like a clock in another room. When her eyes adjusted, the bare walls were visible. Installers always put motion detectors near the ceiling and in the corners for maximum coverage. There were none in this room. Moving as slowly and as quietly as possible, she stepped inside and relocked the door.

Now it was really dark. A thick blackout curtain covered the roller shade in the door's window. She knew she was in the laundry room, a front-loading washer and matching dryer stood side by side like one-eyed sentinels. The clock was louder now, still the only sound. Her pulse kept time with it, the tempo slow and steady.

LeAnn flipped the light switch and bright light blinded her as a buzzing fluorescent tube flickered like a strobe light, giving a ghostly image of the two white appliances. Three blue uniform shirts and two pairs of pants hung on wire hangers above the dryer. The rest of the room was bare. She turned the switch off and waited again until she could see.

From this angle the living room was visible. Next to the front door, there was an alarm key pad, its steady red LED light signaling that the alarm was on. She had not tripped any sensors yet or the LED would be flashing.

She crept into the kitchen, inching her way to the counter. It was agonizingly slow. Three years earlier when Ramzi was living in Chicago, she watched him practice walking through his apartment, creeping through a motion detector's field of view without setting it off. LeAnn had failed each time she tried.

The red light remained steady though. Opening the drawers and cabinets one at a time, she found silverware, measuring cups, coffee filters, a box of rubber bands, and in the last drawer, an unloaded Glock 19, a 9mm semi-automatic pistol.

Inside the Glock's plastic case was an empty 9mm magazine and a list of handwritten phone numbers. There were six with no names, but a seventh was underlined. the Clean Man's number perhaps. She took a screenshot of the list, and put the magazine and the gun back in the drawer, unloaded, it was useless.

In the last cabinet, she found cereal, bags of rice, plates, a glass jar full of bolts and screws, but still, no bullets. Was this guy as competent as she thought? Why keep an unloaded gun?

Finding nothing else useful in the kitchen, she moved into the hallway, looking along the ceiling for that telltale sensor. On her left was the master bedroom, on her right was the living room. *Left, or right?* She turned left.

Blackout shades and curtains covered the two windows, leaving the bedroom as dark as the laundry room. He was obviously used to working nights and sleeping during the day. Ramzi had the same type of curtains in the condo. A brass floor lamp next to a king-sized bed provided the only light. It was enough to see a magnetic sensor attached to the window screen, the first sensor she'd found. The 1980s-style sensor would only trigger if someone removed the screen to crawl through the window.

You're a lucky girl, LeAnn.

His bed was unmade. The bright red comforter and black satin sheets were balled up on one side of the mattress. The headboard was covered in dark red velvet. Two ornate antique chairs, upholstered in red tufted leather, sat on each side of the bed. Picturing the man from the park in the black sheets, bile rose in her throat, and she thought she was going to vomit. The eclectic décor gave her the impression of sleazy renaissance whore house.

On the dresser, a computer monitor flashed a compilation of photos acting as a screen saver. LeAnn stared at a picture of herself, stretched out nude on the cot with her eyes half closed. This was taken in the first few days after they had grabbed her from the airport. There was a man's hand in the photo resting on her thigh, someone's left hand and a large ring was on the middle finger. The ring was gold, with a large red stone surrounded by smaller white ones, diamonds maybe, it was similar, but smaller to the ring the Clean Man was so proud of. Neither Jie or Khoo had worn a ring, then a similar photo of Brianne replaced hers. The same hand was in the bottom right corner of the picture.

The monitor shattered as it hit the wall behind the bed's headboard, and bits and pieces of gray plastic covered the black sheets. Sweat or maybe tears burned her eyes, her knuckles ached as she gripped the footboard of the bed; she wanted to scream, she wanted to kill him, but the bastard was miles away. Instead, she collapsed, shaking, and gasping for breath.

Minutes or hours later she forced herself to sit up and then stand. How long had she been in the bastard's house, and she still didn't know his name? She needed that name now more than ever. She could curse a name but calling him the Driver was so weak, she felt shame just thinking of it now.

In the dim light, she opened the chest of drawers and rummaged through his clothing.

Men's black bikini underwear, how fitting.

In the next drawer, she found a stained-glass jewelry box. Inside were several gold rings, some so small they must have belonged to small women, or young girls. Underneath them was an ID card, something official with the Driver's picture staring at her. Chinese characters covered the front and back of the card but written in English was the name Tommy Fong. This was an old ID, taken before his nose was broken.

Tommy Fong.

"His name is Tommy Fong," she said squeezing the rings in her fist. Saying his name aloud brought an immense measure of relief. She screamed the name over and over, until her dry throat ached.

Rage helped her focus. She opened her hand, two of the thin rings were now crushed and their bent images etched in her flesh would be bruises tomorrow. She put the rings and Fong's ID card in her pocket and pulled on the next drawer. It opened with a loud squeal as dry wood rubbed against old metal rollers.

Without touching it, she knew she had found something more useful than an unloaded gun.

Guns make a lot of noise and attract immediate attention from everybody for blocks around. This was something she could use, something quiet, and her plan of getting the Clean Man to pay for violating her was now one step closer.

It was a yellow-and-black heavy-duty stun gun. She took it, along with the charging cord.

In the last drawer, she found the 9mm ammunition, three dozen brass bullets in a Styrofoam tray. She went back for the gun and loaded the empty magazine. Now this heavy weapon felt useful, it had a purpose, and it felt good in her hand.

LeAnn felt invulnerable now. She had the man's name, a stun gun, and a loaded Glock 9mm. If he was standing in front of her, she would kill him, not with the gun though—she wanted him to suffer.

With nothing left to see in the bedroom, she slowly stepped into the hallway and began searching for sensors again.

Peeking around the corner and into the living room, she saw the steady red light on the alarm panel was now flashing. Somewhere, somehow, she had tripped a sensor. Her watch told her she had been inside the house now for forty minutes. Fong could already be on his way home; he could be pulling into the driveway any minute.

I should leave now, she thought, but I want to know what's in the rest of the house. With the alarm tripped, there was no need to be stealthy, and she ran to the alarm panel.

A car door slammed just outside the front door, and then another. Two cars meant at least two men and maybe more. She was trapped. Running to the side door, she turned off the lights in the kitchen and stood at the door, one hand on the knob and the other holding the stun gun.

She felt the weight of the Glock in her waistband and thought about loading it. The magazine was full, but the chamber was still empty. "Shit, I don't know anything about Glocks and I don't want to accidentally shoot myself," she whispered. "But I don't know much about stun guns either."

I'll never make it to the car.

One of them was probably already coming around to this side of the house. They knew someone had been inside. "They aren't stupid, LeAnn." Taking her hand off the knob, she folded her petite frame between the washer and dryer. In the dark, they might miss her. She pushed the dryer away from the wall enough that she could hide behind it.

Cobwebs touched her face, and she was breathing in lint from the dryer. She was going to sneeze. Taking a few deep breaths, she held her nose and closed her eyes. The dancers tiptoed all around, and Tchaikovsky's Arabian Dance filled the auditorium. This time, the images didn't help her at all, she was shaking . . . and she was still going to sneeze.

She couldn't see a thing. The light was too dim, and the dryer blocked most of her view.

I'm dead if I stay in here.

Terrified and trembling like a child on Halloween, she pushed the dryer out farther, stood up, and walked to the door leading into the kitchen.

I would rather die fighting than be back at that warehouse—nobody is going to touch me again, and I'm not going to die hiding behind a fucking dryer. I'll shock the first one I see, then worry about the next one.

Opening Jie's pocketknife, she held it in her left hand and the stun gun in her right, then waited.

What's taking them so long? The front door still hadn't opened.

A man's voice. Someone was talking just outside the closed front door. His silhouette was visible through the door's glass window. Now another voice, a woman's maybe, both speaking in Mandarin.

I can't hear what they're saying.

Yes, the second voice was definitely a woman. Something was wrong. LeAnn moved closer, between the kitchen and the living room, so she could hear.

"Yes, inspector, I remember trying to open the door of a van I thought was mine. You see, mine looks just like the one in your picture."

The woman was soft-spoken and hard to hear, but LeAnn heard the word "investigation."

"Would you like to come in for a moment?" the man said. "I came home to use the restroom and I need to go right now, if you know what I mean."

The sound of his keys in the lock forced her back into the laundry room. The front door opened, and a beeping sound told her he was using the alarm's keypad.

"Come in and make yourself comfortable, Sergeant Jiawei. I'll just be a moment."

"I just need to see your identification and the van's registration, Mr. Fong, and I can be on my way."

"Okay, one second, please."

From the laundry room, she could hear him walk into the master bedroom and pause. He was looking at the shattered monitor and the open drawer.

Now he knows for sure.

His heavy boots came out of the bedroom and into the kitchen and then a final cabinet opening.

Would he search the house first or get rid of the woman?

She waited for the sounds of his boots again and could picture his hesitation. Someone had taken his weapons, and that person could still be in the house. Finally, she heard him walk back into the living room and say, "Here you are, inspector."

Breaking glass and a woman screaming made her jump, then something heavy fell in the living room.

"You lying bitch," the man screamed. Then she heard his boots walking through the kitchen again. Crouched between the washer and dryer with the stun gun in one hand, and Jie's knife in the other, she waited for the lights to come on. In the dim light she could see her fingers were steady and her breathing had slowed. Her earlier fear was gone; she was in "the Zone," as Ramzi would say. Tommy Fong was going to die in a few minutes, she just didn't know how yet.

The heavy sound of his boots came toward her. She stopped breathing as he entered the laundry room. He looked huge through the gap between the appliances. The side door opened and bright sunlight lit up the room now like a spotlight.

I'm going to jump up and stick him in the gut with the knife and tase him in the groin at the same time. I'll deal with the woman later. It was a plan. Not perfect but it would have to do.

Fong closed the door, and the room was plunged into darkness again, even darker now that the sunlight had ruined her night vision. But if she couldn't see, neither could he.

Fong was breathing hard, panting like he had just gotten off a treadmill. Either he was out of shape or feeling a little fear of his own. Hopefully both. Walking past the dryer, he never looked down, he would not have missed her if he did. Drawers and cabinets were opening and closing, their doors banging shut. Fong was in a fury trying to find what else might be missing.

Bootsteps again, and then she heard him speaking.

"Yes, Laoban," Fong said.

The Clean Man! He's on the phone with him now!

Easing out from behind the appliances, she crept into the kitchen, not wanting to miss a single word.

He was talking too fast. Speaking and understanding Mandarin was hard enough, and she was only hearing half the conversation.

"Yes, it could have been the police, maybe they had a warrant, but I think it was the Moran girl. Why would the police leave everything else? The alarm was triggered almost an hour ago, and only my stun gun and the Glock are missing. All the drugs are still here."

Drugs?

There was a long pause as he listened. She moved in closer and saw him standing near the front door. At his feet, a body lay crumpled on the floor, a woman wearing a pantsuit. A plain clothes detective, Sergeant Jiawei, Fong had called her.

"Yes, Laoban, she is breathing, and I think she is coming around now. Who is coming to pick her up?"

Another long pause and the shape on the floor moved.

"Yes, I need their help in sanitizing the house."

The woman was trying to sit up now, and Fong put his boot on her chest.

"Thank you, I will," Fong said and ended the call.

With his foot still holding the woman down, he screamed, "Did you take my gun? Where is it?"

The inspector moaned, and Fong kicked her in the ribs. The crack was terrible, and LeAnn heard the woman grunt in pain.

"Tell me!" Fong screamed again.

Backing deeper into the kitchen and into the laundry room, she gave up the idea of killing him. There were too many variables now with more people and maybe even the police on the way. Open the side door and sneak out. An easy escape, the Honda was only three houses away. It would take her less than a minute to reach it, and another few seconds to start it and back out. She turned the knob and remembered the squealing hinges. He would hear it, and she would never make it to the car. Then she heard the ripping sound of duct tape.

"One last chance, are you going to tell me?"

The sound of his boot hitting the woman again froze LeAnn in her tracks. Her hand was still on the knob, a crack of daylight now visible through the opening. Guilt, that same sickening feeling she'd had with the Swiss woman. She'd let that woman live, and it had done something to her, something emotional that felt . . . pleasant.

She closed the door and locked it. He was not going to kill this woman, not today.

Fong had his back to her and was binding the woman's legs with black tape. She had to act quickly; she did not want this woman executed right in front of her. Killing the woman herself was one thing, watching this bastard do it was another.

She was no match to physically fight him, and she would never be able to load the Glock without him hearing it.

The stun gun felt huge and awkward. She had never used one, never held one either, but had seen them work. Was it even charged? She would only have one chance.

She put the stun gun on the floor, then put the gun next to it, and took the leather gloves and one of the garrotes out of her pocket. With a loop of stainless-steel leader wire through each glove, she crept into the living room.

Committed now, she took a slow breath, and saw the woman's eyes shift, she was looking at LeAnn now, and Fong saw it too, he began to turn his head.

"Tommy Fong," she screamed.

Then it all happened too fast. He saw her coming, stood, and began to turn toward her.

Fong was taller than she expected—she hesitated, then ran straight at him. It must have shocked him—and now he was the one to hesitate. She got the garrote around his neck, then pulled with every ounce of muscle she had, lifting herself off the ground. Wrapping her legs around his back, she squeezed them tight, still pulling on the wire. Fong should have dropped to his knees immediately, but he began to turn in circles, trying to grab her hair with his left hand.

Somehow Fong had gotten two fingers of his right hand under the wire, and the garrote had not cut off the blood to his brain as she intended, but he hadn't been able to breathe either. She relaxed the tension on the wire, and he pulled his fingers free, then she pulled the garrote with her entire body, fearing the wires would snap. Something popped in his neck, and a torrent of blood shot out in all directions, covering her and the woman on the floor.

Fong's knees finally buckled, and the two of them crashed into the living room wall before hitting the floor. Somewhere during that fall, she heard several of her ribs crack, and an explosion of pain shot through her chest. The pain was incapacitating, and she was struggling just to remain conscious.

Taking a simple breath was impossible. Her ribs screamed in

pain, no matter how shallow a breath, each new breath reignited a new wave of white-hot pain. Fong was lying right next to her, inches away, his dead listless eyes staring back at her. Seeing him like that gave her a moment of relief, until she took the next breath—and screamed out loud.

Sergeant Jiawei flinched at the sound and began whimpering like a child. She was staring at LeAnn with her one good eye, the other was swollen shut and that side of her face was covered in blood: some of it was hers, some of it was Fong's.

The woman appeared to be in her forties, dark hair with a touch of gray near her temples, and crow's-feet around her brown eyes. Even on the floor, LeAnn could tell she was tall, almost as tall as Fong and probably weighed as much too. She was terrified, shaking uncontrollably, and her lips were moving as if she wanted to say something. LeAnn had seen this type of fear before, a paralyzing fear survivors felt after a traumatic event.

"Where is your radio?" LeAnn said, wincing with each word. Talking proved just as painful as breathing. The police woman was still bound with duct tape, but LeAnn needed to know if the dispatcher was sending anyone else to Fong's house.

"Do you speak English?"

"Some," the woman said, then her teeth began to chatter as she quivered on the floor. "I can't leave you here like this," LeAnn said in Mandarin.

She pointed to Fong and said, "His people will kill you if they get here first. Do you understand that?" The woman's lips were still quivering, and LeAnn couldn't tell if she understood at all. "And where is your gun?"

She was barely able to stand and it hurt to breathe, but she needed to get out of Fong's house. The entire police department, or a dozen of the Clean Man's men could be racing to the house right now.

The woman finally moved, she was trying to sit up and LeAnn helped her. God, her face was a bloody mess, with her right eye wide-open, she stared at Fong's body laying right in front of her.

"It's okay, it's all over and he can't hurt you now," LeAnn said. "Just get a grip on yourself. I know my Mandarin is no good, but pay attention. Do you understand me?"

The woman nodded yes.

LeAnn bent over Fong to check his pockets and another fresh wave of pain made her gasp. She could feel the ribs sliding against each other in her chest. Both sides hurt, but her left side was much sharper. She took Fong's key ring, wallet, and a roll of cash bound with a rubber band. Next to his feet, she found a bright orange battery, it was square with "Motorola" labeled in black. The radio had to be close by.

Leaning next to a broken end table, was a two-foot-long metal pry bar, covered in blood and bits of flesh, and next to it was the sergeant's radio. LeAnn picked up the pry bar and the woman screamed.

"Relax, I'm not going to hurt you," LeAnn said, dropping it. A few weeks ago, she would have finished the woman off, put her out of her misery, but like with the Swiss woman, it didn't feel right.

"Where is your gun?" she asked the woman again. Seeing the woman's blank stare, LeAnn repeated it in Mandarin. But the woman was looking at a painting behind LeAnn.

She had thought it was a cheap painting of a sleeping nude woman, but now, up close, she realized it wasn't a painting at all; it was a photograph of a young girl lying on a red-and-blue striped mattress. Stepping over Fong's body, she looked closer. A man's fingers were in the girl's hair, a huge gold ring with a red stone on the ring finger. This picture, like the ones on his monitor and the rings in the jewelry box, were his trophies. She looked at the ring on Fong's hand—and kicked him in the ribs. Both LeAnn and the inspector screamed and LeAnn collapsed next to her.

I can't pass out, not here and not now.

Fong's face was inches away from hers. *Oh, I wish I could bring you back to life and make you suffer more, you bastard.*

As the pain eased, she rolled over, knelt next to him and pulled the ring off his bloody finger. "I think I'll keep yours, Tommy, this is my trophy."

She ignored the whimpering sergeant and limped into the kitchen. Each step felt like an electric cattle prod, pressed into her ribcage, but she had to get out of the house. She put the stun gun in her back pocket and carried the Glock back into the living room.

"Please don't, please don't, please don't," Jiawei repeated in Mandarin.

"It hurts me to talk, so shut up. I'm leaving," she told the woman. "His friends are coming, do you understand? Nod if you understand me, Jiawei. Is that your name?"

"Yes, First Sergeant Jiawei."

"Remember, Jiawei, they want you dead, and they could be here any minute."

The woman nodded and sat upright, looking around the room as if seeing it for the first time. "My radio," she said.

"I have it. I'm going to give it to you and this too," she said, dropping the Glock in front of her. Popping the live rounds out of the magazine, she laid them all out in front of the woman. The radio chirped as soon as she put the battery in. The dispatcher sounded calm, sending officers out on a routine traffic accident near the airport. No one was looking for First Sergeant Jiawei.

LeAnn put the radio in the woman's hand. "Call for help, and then I want you to load this gun when you hear the door close behind me. Be ready for his friends. I don't think you're fast enough to load this and shoot me in the back, but if you try, I will kill you. Are we clear?"

"You want me to call now?"

"Yes, yes, right now. Go ahead, I want to make sure they hear you before I leave."

The woman keyed the radio and began screaming. "Help me," was all LeAnn could understand, but that was enough. Hopefully police would get there before Fong's friends showed up.

"I don't want to see you again, do you understand," LeAnn said.

Jiawei nodded furiously, desperation in her one good eye, knowing she was going to live. LeAnn turned her back. Bloodied and limping, she walked out the front door and across five lawns to her Honda, and drove away.

CHAPTER 22

KWAN

The station was in chaos, someone's radio was at full volume and Jiawei's screams were echoing up and down the hallway. Kwan leaped from his chair and ran to the parking lot as dozens of police cars raced out of the station, each with their blue lights and sirens wailing.

Jiawei was still screaming on her radio, slurring her speech and making it difficult to understand her, "Calm down, calm down. Help is on the way," the dispatcher repeated. "We can't understand what you are saying."

Fortunately for Jiawei, she had given the dispatcher Fong's address before getting out of her car, and now the first of the units were arriving at the scene.

***

A sea of police cars lined the small residential street, and Kwan had to run the last hundred meters to reach the house.

Jiawei was on her back in the front lawn being tended to by paramedics. The left side of her head and her hair were covered in blood and her left eye was swollen shut.

"She is a devil! She is a devil, the devil, I say!" the woman kept repeating, ignoring all attempts to question her. It was useless trying to talk to her now, the woman was hysterical, but at least she would live. Parked in front of the wounded woman's car was a Toyota HiAce van, a twin to the one found in the warehouse on Pandan Loop and the one seen on video during the Moran girl's abduction.

"Superintendent Kwan," a patrol officer yelled to him from the front door. "They need you in here."

Kwan went through the front door. It was dark inside; a single table lamp illuminated the crime scene. A dead man partially blocked the front door, and a roll of black duct tape lay on his chest. Blood covered everything in a five-meter circle.

The living room looked like a battle zone. Most of the furniture was damaged or overturned; broken glass and ceramic shards covered the floor, and a large section of drywall was crushed inward, exposing the studs and wiring inside the wall. Someone, either the dead man or his killer, had been slammed into the wall with enough force to tear the wall open.

Kwan knelt next to the man's body, trying to match the old picture of Fong to this man's bloody face. His eyes bulged, his nose had been broken at least once, and several recent scars ran through both eyebrows. This man had been a fighter at one time, Kwan thought, maybe a boxer or martial artist.

The shoulders of the dead man's dark blue shirt were covered in white powder that matched the drywall. It would have taken a big person to throw a man this size into a wall and do that type of damage, but Jiawei kept saying *she*, could a woman have done all this? Then he remembered the Swiss woman's description of the Moran girl and what she had done to Jie and Khoo. Yes, she could have done this, he thought.

Kwan looked at the wound on the man's neck. It was covered in thick arterial blood, making it difficult to see, but still it looked too perfect, like a straight-line incision encircling his throat and disappearing at the back of his neck. There were no signs of a weapon in the living room. What could have caused this type of wound?

The man's eyes were bulging and bloodshot and tiny red dots covered the whites of his eyes. Those were petechiae, broken capillary blood vessels and a possible sign of strangulation. But there was too much blood.

"He bled out, I think," Kwan said. "Look for a wire, she might have used a garrote."

If it was a garrote, it had to be thin enough to cut through the skin until it severed the carotid artery or the jugular vein. Death would have been quick once that happened, thirty seconds or maybe a minute, Kwan estimated.

On the floor next to the sofa was a metal pry bar. Fresh blood and strands of dark brown hair stuck to it, Jiawei's hair.

Could the petit Moran girl do all this? 'Like a machine,' the Swiss woman had said. And now Jiawei's description. 'Like a devil.'

Fong's living room reminded him of his own apartment when he worked the midnight shift, blackout drapes on every window, soft white lightbulbs, dark carpet and furniture. But it also reminded him of the whorehouses by the docks that sprang up as fast as the police could shut them down. It looked like a bachelor's place but not in a good way. Dark red-and-black vinyl chairs, leopard fur lampshades, and a painting of a nude woman adorned the main wall.

Kwan examined the painting and realized that it was a photo altered to look like a painting. The girl's hands and everything from the waist down had been cropped out of the picture, but enough of the mattress was visible—the same type of mattress that was in the warehouse where the Swiss woman had been found.

His assistant came through the door breathing hard, "Sorry I'm late, I was on the other side of town," he said.

"Chin, I've seen this girl before," Kwan said. "She was one of the first victims, maybe the very first. Her name was Victoria. She was sixteen years old when she vanished and has never been seen since."

"I remember her too, look at this," Chin said, "look at the hand, it's the focal point of the picture."

In the photograph, a man's fingers were entwined in Victoria's brown hair. A large gold ring with a red stone surrounded by small diamonds was on the man's left ring finger. Kwan looked at the body on the floor. Blood smears and streaks covered some of the man's left hand, but there was a tan line on the fourth finger, right where a big ring would have been.

"She took his ring," Kwan said.

Kwan phoned the station and soon every inspector on his task force was in route to the scene along with the major crime's forensic team, the best technicians the department had.

"I want everyone out now," he ordered. "Don't touch anything else until the techs get here."

Kwan waited an agonizing thirty minutes. Something in this house could break his case wide-open. Seventeen young women had been abducted, eighteen if he counted the Swiss woman. If he could recover just one of them, maybe he would sleep better than he had in months.

Pacing back and forth between the front door and the sidewalk, he tried to picture the petite Moran girl he had watched walking through the airport overpowering and killing men like Khoo, Jie, and now this guy, Tommy Fong—a career criminal.

How does she do it, and why would she try and kill Jiawei, and then leave her alive? None of it made any sense.

Finally, everyone he needed was assembled in the front yard. The chief prosecutor of the Coroner's Court, a senior level medical examiner, a photographer, and another tech with a video camera all paused in the doorway. Tommy Fong's body was still blocking the entrance.

The technician with the video camera walked in first. Stepping over Fong, his shoes covered with disposable booties, he panned the room in one slow 360-degree circle. Careful not to step in the pool of blood or the footprints around it, he knelt next to the body and videoed the man from head to foot.

One by one the rest of them came in, each of them studying the wound on Fong's neck.

"A garrote of some type." Claire Heng Chee, the chief medical examiner said. "He didn't suffocate. I think we will find he bled to death when the garrote cut through the jugular vein." She looked at the blood spray on the walls, the damaged drywall, and all the bloody shoe prints and said, "He lived a minute, maybe two, before he collapsed here. Those are probably his handprints on the wall, and his footprints. This is his boot print, and you can see this much smaller one. It looks like some type of athletic shoe, a cross-trainer or a running shoe. You can see they were both turning in circles—your subject was probably behind him with the garrote."

Kwan left the examiner as she began directing her photographer and walked in to Fong's bedroom. The tawdry, dark furnishings mirrored the living room. Kwan looked at the destroyed monitor and the shattered bits of plastic covering the sheets.

"Chin, I think Moran was in the house, saw something on the screen that enraged her and she threw it against the wall, then Fong came home. Jiawei must have shown up then as well. It's the only scenario that makes sense. Hopefully we can talk to Jiawei soon. Have someone take this computer to forensics right away. I want to know what's on it as soon as possible."

A technician brought in bright lights and set them up in each corner of the living room and began marking evidence. The blood was brighter now but looked right at home with Fong's lewd furniture. Faded and threadbare curtains hid newer, heavier shades covering the two windows, his black suede leather couch was stained and ripped in some places near the seams. Most of the furnishings were cheap and old but surprisingly clean—at least they were before Fong was murdered.

Kwan found the empty case for a Glock automatic pistol and the list of phone numbers. One of them looked familiar. It was the same exchange number as his office phone. He dialed it and waited.

"Sergeant Goh," a familiar voice answered.

Goh! The hair on Kwan's arms stood up.

Goh worked in the fraud unit and had never impressed Kwan.

He was intelligent but seemed satisfied doing as little as possible to avoid standing out. Someone had once described him as "an empty suit."

"I'm sorry, Sergeant, I've got the wrong number," Kwan said and ended the call.

Kwan took a photo of the list and left it where he found it. He wanted to have his men thoroughly check the rest of the numbers.

"Superintendent Kwan, come see this," someone yelled from the master bedroom.

A technician on his knees pointed a flashlight at a small gold ring on the carpet. "It's a woman's ring, and there is an engraving inside the band, but I can't read it. It looks like Spanish, and I can see the name Francisca."

Kwan sighed. "It's probably Portuguese. There was a victim with that name, Francisca Mora, she was Brazilian." Francisca's high school graduation picture was in a file at the station. "She was nineteen and a beautiful young woman. Last July she was with two college friends on spring break. She stepped off a cruise ship and disappeared. Her parents still call me."

Francisca Mora's case file was as thin as all the others. One after another, the cases had gone cold. In the next day or two, Kwan would add another single page to her file.

Kwan slammed his fist onto Fong's dresser.

The sun set, and by the time the technicians finished collecting and processing everything, it was well after midnight. There were no other surprises in the house. Fong lived frugally, no fancy or expensive clothing, no jewelry other than the missing ring, and Kwan feared that even with all the evidence, they were still at a dead end.

The sun rose as Kwan drove to the hospital, twenty hours now since Jiawei was beaten and all they had was a dead man. Maybe the list of phone numbers and something on the computer would lead them to an arrest.

And then he remembered First Sergeant Goh! How was this loser of an officer involved?

In the hospital's lobby, Kwan looked at the crowd of Jiawei's coworkers huddled in one corner, each of them eyeing everyone coming through the doors. One of the senior inspectors walked his way.

"She is in surgery again, Sir. They are trying to repair the bone around her eye, which is crushed, but they think she will be okay," the inspector said. "I talked to her some last night. She was sedated and not everything she said made sense, but she said she went by the man's house just as he came home. She said the guy was unusually cooperative, and she never thought of asking for a backup. She doesn't remember what happened, except that when she came to, a woman was on the man's back screaming, "like the devil" and there was blood everywhere.

"Fong dying like that had to be pretty gruesome," Kwan said.

"Who was he, do you think he was the boss?"

Kwan considered it for a second, trying to picture someone capable of running a sex trafficking ring, abducting and drugging so many women over a two-year period.

"No, I don't think so. Fong was involved, no doubt, but I don't think he had the skills to pull this off. He wasn't the brains, and that's who we need to find."

***

Sergeant Goh. Why would Fong have his phone number? The question hounded Kwan all the way back to the station. It could be nothing more than an old case Goh was involved in, or maybe Fong was an informant or even a victim at one time. Still, Kwan had his doubts, a gut feeling that Goh was somehow involved with these girls.

The department's internal affairs office was on the fifth floor of the main station, and Superintendent Halim Hazlina, was waiting for him.

"Hello, Kim, come in, how is Jiawei?"

Kwan sat on a sofa across from her desk. Hazlina had graduated from the academy with him and had climbed the ranks to deputy superintendent. She was an intelligent woman who took her position seriously. "She is going to be okay, thank you. Hazlina, I really need a break on this case, and I think we are getting close. Do you know the name Tommy Fong?"

"No, I don't think I do. Is that your subject?"

"I think Fong hit Jiawei, but it was one of my missing victims who killed the man."

"That's an unusual twist."

"Yes, it's the Moran girl, she's also the one who killed the first two guys, and somehow, she found Tommy Fong and killed him too. I don't think she's responsible for Jiawei, but who knows. Jiawei has a concussion, and she's sedated, so I haven't been able to talk to her yet. I'm hoping that forensics can piece together what happened in that house in the next few days. Fong is a low-level thug; nothing tells me he is anything more than that. But there's something odd, Hazlina. Fong had Goh's office number in a drawer along with a few other numbers. I'm going to have my people go over each one, but tell me, what do you know about him?"

"Goh! He's an odd one for sure. He's been on the force twenty years, a decent street cop at one time I hear, made it into investigations and did well as a narcotics officer, but something happened when he went undercover working the shipyards. I heard it might have been a mental breakdown, or got too close to the drugs, and then he was suddenly back in uniform patrol. There's nothing in his file about it, though, which tells me someone above us must have owed him a favor."

"You think someone's covering for him?" Kwan said.

"I'm saying there should have been something in his file, but there's not," she said. "Once he was back on the streets, complaints started coming in, mostly for excessive force. His supervisors said he was a discipline problem, and he was calling in sick too often. Two consecutive evaluations said his performance was unsatisfactory—and then he was transferred back into investigations."

"That's odd," Kwan said.

"Yes, it is. He could have been put on probation or even fired, but someone took care of him. You want his file?"

"Yes, thank you."

"It's digital. I can email it to you tonight if that's soon enough."

CHAPTER 23

LEANN

Several of her ribs were definitely broken. Breathing caused excruciating pain and just touching the skin around those ribs hurt like hell. "I was lucky again," she said. "I could have been the one lying in a puddle of my own blood, not Tommy Fong, but that's another name off my list."

Twelve hours and the pain was worse now. Sleep had been impossible, every breath had felt like someone was jabbing an ice pick in her side, and she could still feel her dam ribs moving. She was dead tired, not as dead as Fong, the bastard, she wanted to laugh at that, but that would hurt too.

Coming back to the condo yesterday afternoon, she had parked in the garage while two women were walking toward the elevator. Her clothes were covered in blood, and she had nothing to change into. She had to stay in the car. She had nowhere else to go. So she sat in the Honda—for six hours. At one in the morning, she opened the door and listened. It had been hours since the last car had parked, and all the spaces on this floor of the garage were full. There were no sounds, not even the sound of traffic in the street, just a deafening silence.

That was last night, today the apartment was dark and safe. Her bloody clothes were in a black plastic bag by the door, and as soon as she felt she could drive, she would put the bag in a dumpster down the street. She also had Jie's clothes in a box, along with his and Khoo's wallets. "I'm going to mail them to

Kwan," she told herself. "But I'll need to find an appropriate quote to go with it. Something intriguing, something other than Shakespeare." She loved playing that part of the game. The Zodiac Killer had sent coded messages the FBI was still trying to read. Shakespeare had been her mother's idea.

***

Another day came and went and the pain was just as intense. Lying flat on her back on the carpeted floor was the least painful position. "Three dead, at least one to go," she said, staring at the ceiling. "I need to free the new girl too, but the pain . . . I can't . . . not yet."

As the sun set, she rolled over onto her stomach and pushed herself up into a sitting position. It was the only way to get up off the floor without that rib moving.

A quick search on WebMD told her broken ribs could cause a punctured lung. She had most of the symptoms already: pain when taking a deep breath, shortness of breath, abnormal breathing, and fatigue. At least she wasn't coughing up blood. It also told her the ribs could heal on their own but to avoid strenuous activity for at least four weeks.

I can't wait four weeks!

***

She called "The Deacon," in New York City using one of her Samsung pre-paid phones; it was past midnight there, but her dark-web geek friend always said he did his best work before dawn. Christopher's voice told her to leave a message.

"Christopher, it's me. I need some new information; this number will be good for twenty-four hours."

She hung up and hoped he would call before she had to ditch this phone. She preferred these cheap phones when she was "in the thick of things," an expression her brother used whenever he was hunting. A decent pre-paid phone was twenty bucks, and the battery would last a week. Once you felt it was compromised, or burned, you destroyed it. Throwing them in a river had always been her preferred method, but who knew what the cops could do with them now.

Seconds later the phone rang, a New York area code, but not Christopher's number.

"Hello," she said.

A woman's voice asked, "Who is this?"

"I'm not saying."

"Did you just call my husband?"

"I called Christopher."

There was a long pause, but she could hear the woman breathing.

"Christopher did a search for me. I need another one," she said, hoping the woman wouldn't hang up.

"Christopher is dead, murdered three days ago."

"What happened?"

"Some Asian motherfucker shot him is what happened."

"I'm so sorry." How had anyone in Singapore connected her to Christopher, or was it a coincidence? Christopher had warned her though, and now he was dead. She hung up the phone, already planning to toss it in the bay as soon as she got dressed, but the phone rang again.

"Are you LeAnn?"

"Yes."

"He mentioned you. He said he trusted you—but now he's dead—so I want to know what he was looking for. Someone has to pay. Do you understand? Some mother fucker is going to pay."

"Someone did pay, and soon, a few more will pay as well," LeAnn said.

After a long silence, the woman said, "The last time he talked to you, Christopher said he had stirred up some serious shit, that's how he said it. He was definitely afraid of something, I could tell. He spent the afternoon wiping some of his hard drives and that's not like him, he's never that careless What was it you asked him to do?"

"How did it happen?"

"I'm not answering any more questions. I want some answers," the woman said.

"I asked him to check on a place in Singapore. If I tell you, they may come after you too."

More heavy breathing, and then, "He was at the Dotcom. It's a cybercafé in Manhattan. He said he needed to work away from home; he does that whenever he's doing deep shit, "going dark" he calls it, where no one can track him, or so he thought. He told me he would be right back, that he had something for you, but he never came home. The Asian bastards came in and shot three people. The video is all over the news, Christopher and his friend were killed, the other guy is going to live. So tell me, what was he doing for you?"

"It was computer stuff. I don't know if you would understand."

There was a long pause again, she was shuffling papers and typing on a keyboard.

"I taught Christopher everything he knew about computers, tell me, goddammit," the woman said.

"What do I call you?"

"You don't need my name, and no more phone calls until I find out what's going on. Reach me at this address, it's a secure drop box. Hang up, toss that phone you're using, and send me everything you have. Give me twenty-four hours."

LeAnn wrote down the address, memorized it, flushed the paper down the toilet, and took the battery out of the burner.

"Shit."

They killed Christopher, which meant they had a pretty wide network to trace a phone call. They found him and killed him in just a few short weeks.

She opened the laptop, logged on to the site and sent the woman everything she had sent Christopher and added what she knew about Fong, including the list of numbers she found in his kitchen.

***

The next morning, LeAnn eased the Honda over a series of railroad tracks, trying to avoid the worst of the uneven roadway. Each steel rail made her cry out in pain. She was on her way to the post office with the box she was sending to Kwan. Part of her wanted Kwan to finish what she had started, which would mean that he would arrest the Clean Man and every bastard working for him. She was still in too much pain to do it herself and four weeks was a long time.

On a bridge near the wharf, she lowered the window and the afternoon heat and humidity were waiting for her. Halfway across, hopefully over the deepest part of the bay's inlet, she threw the burner phone out the window and watched it splash into water that looked like brewed tea.

She had underestimated the Clean Man. Thinking of him as a small-time crime boss wearing fancy clothes was a mistake. He was more than that. He had employed someone with great computer skills, someone who could track phones instantly. He could track someone and have them killed thousands of miles away. He'd found and killed Christopher, a competent and careful hacker who she'd thought of as a friend. All that and the Clean Man was able to organize a team of criminals to abduct, drug, and traffic young girls. Letting Kwan finish what she had started was going to push her anxieties to their limits.

CHAPTER 24

KWAN

Haron Chin set a brown cardboard box on Kwan's desk. "This just came for you. We sent it through the scanner, nothing explosive and the x-rays show two phones, some jewelry, and what looks like clothing."

"Thank you, Chin," he said, turning the sealed box around.

Kwan Kim Lai was written in bold letters, along with the station's address, and in smaller print, a return address.

"Chin, isn't this return address in the old commercial district near the Kallang River?"

"Yishun Avenue, yes, it is. I used to patrol that district years ago. Most of the businesses have folded or moved closer to the port."

"You smell that? Something in this box stinks," Kwan said. "It looks like it's been in transit for two days. Let's open it."

Kwan cut the packing tape wearing a pair of purple nitrile gloves. The rank smell of decomposing flesh was worse now. "Yes, something definitely stinks. I hope it's not part of one of our victims."

Two cell phones, two wallets, and a clear plastic bag full of gold rings sat on top of a blue uniform shirt and a darker pair of pants. The shirt was neatly folded, and most of the blue fabric was covered in dried blood stains. "There's where the stink is coming from," Chin said.

One of the phones chirped and both men jumped. They were

cheap phones with limited capability, good for texting and making calls; you could take pictures with them, but they would be poor quality. The screen on one of them was lit, and an address scrolled across it. Kwan gently lifted them out and set them on his desk.

"This text was sent this morning. It's the same return address, 140 Yishun Avenue #7. Who's our best person with cell phones?"

"Aiden Vikram, I'll call him."

Kwan opened the first wallet, and Jie's face stared back at him. It was his driver's license, issued two months ago, then he looked at the bloody shirt and he knew why Jie was wearing only boxers when he was killed. "Chin, the Moran girl sent this. I don't want to touch anything else but look under the pants. It's a note."

Written in English and in beautiful cursive, Kwan read the message out loud. "Revenge, the sweetest morsel to the mouth that ever was cooked in hell."

"What does this mean?"

"I have no idea, let me run it on the computer."

"And look at this," Kwan said, holding the clear bag. "Look at the big ring. That's Fong's ring, the one in the picture on his wall. Is she threatening me, sending me a message?"

"Well, she did a number on Tommy Fong," Chin said.

"Yes, she did, I'd like to know how she found him."

"Something on one of the phones, maybe, she must have tracked him down or followed him home"

"But from where, Chin?"

Both men looked at the return address on the box, another old run-down warehouse district and the image of Gemma Balakrishnan, his latest victim, bound on one of those horrible cots flashed in his head. "Chin, I want two officers sent to that address ASAP and tell them to use caution."

"What kind of woman is capable of killing three men? She's twenty-one, a young woman according to her passport, if we can believe that, forensics still thinks it's a forgery."

"Kim, that quote is from a novel written by Walter Scott, *The Heart of Mid-Lothian*. I'm printing a section of it out now."

"Thanks, Chin. Maybe I should read that book. My gut tells me she wants to help us, just a feeling, but I'm not going to bet my life on it."

Kwan sat at his desk as the forensic technicians bagged everything including the box and took it all downstairs for processing.

Who are you, Leila Moran?

Sergeant Jiawei had called her a devil, a small, boyish-looking devil. Kwan remembered the video of her walking through the airport terminal, a small woman with long brown hair almost to her waist. There was nothing boyish about that image . . . and this woman was a victim of a violent abduction and probably much worse.

"Chin, what would keep her from coming to us for help?"

"Perhaps she isn't the woman we think she is," Chin said. "Maybe she's more afraid of us than she is of them."

"Afraid of us?" Kwan thought about that, it was the only thing that made sense. "Perhaps you're right," he said.

Now, Sergeant Jiawei's wild story was beginning to make sense. The crazy woman killing Fong wasn't so crazy after all. What was it Jiawei had said the woman kept screaming? "Die you mother fucker!" The Moran girl, if that was her real name, might be more than just crazy.

That was the only way any of this made sense. Leila Moran was a ghost. They had tracked her down to her inbound flight from San Francisco, the name, had to be an alias, her passport probably a forgery. A woman on the run from something and now she was truly a ghost, or the devil according to Jiawei.

"But," Kwan said aloud, "devil or not, so far, she has accomplished more than any of us at cracking this case. A vigilante bent on revenge, and now a homicide suspect herself."

Is she taunting me?

Kwan shivered, picturing Fong's death. He had studied serial killers and knew that they often toyed with the police, usually the lead officer. Who was going to be her next victim? Maybe Chin was right, something off the two phones could help them

Victim or not, killing Jie and Khoo while escaping that hellhole was one thing, but she had tracked down Fong and committed a homicide.

"Let's go, Chin. I want to see what's at this address."

CHAPTER 25

LEANN

Through the powerful binoculars, LeAnn studied every piece of trash and every weed growing around the front door. From two blocks away, the building looked deserted. The old motor scooter should have been leaning against the wall, but it wasn't. Worse, she hadn't seen anyone go in or out since she arrived at dawn. That was six hours ago. Killing Fong must have changed the Clean Man's schedule—but someone had to be watching the girl inside. Maybe the man inside was on a twenty-four-hour shift.

I'm not sitting here for twenty-four hours.

Twice she thought she heard the rattling sound of the motor scooter on the next block and drove up and down the street looking for it, but this street was also deserted. The next block over had two open businesses, a catering service and a bakery. Dozens of cars were parked in front of each, but there was no sign of the scooter. This was all wrong, these two warehouses were active, too many people coming and going, and she knew the Clean Man would never have his girls on this street.

She parked under the tree near the sewing factory again and waited. One more hour, she decided. Killing Fong had seemed like a good idea at the time. She'd crossed his name off her list and felt the tension and anxiety he'd caused begin to ebb. She was freer now. Now she worried about the girl inside and felt connected, somehow. What was different about this girl?

She put the binoculars on the seat and thought about Modra.

She'd wanted to kill the woman just to shut her up. The screams had grated on her nerves, like nails on a chalkboard. She had leaned in, ready to strangle the woman, to choke the life out of her—and stopped. She had felt connected to Modra. Modra was a fellow victim, but not just any type of victim. Modra had been raped. Now she was connected to this new girl too.

I want to know her name. Is she alone in there?

It was almost noon now, and LeAnn wasn't going to sneak through the alley in broad daylight to find out. The box she sent Kwan should have arrived at the police station, and he could be racing here right now. She lowered her window and listened for sirens, but there were none, just the sounds of a jet passing overhead and a few sparrows chirping in the tree above her.

The thought of the girl inside and alone, possibly dying right now, began to eat at her, gnawing at her insides.

"Dammit!"

Her ribs felt a little better today, and she considered knocking on the front door and taking her chances.

"Who am I kidding," she said to herself. I can't even tie my shoes without wanting to scream."

She touched the skin on her left side, and it still felt like a hot knife was jammed between her ribs. It had been four days since she killed Fong; they would be expecting her. Four days, hopefully Fong's body was rotting in some dark morgue.

Sitting in the car with the engine idling, the air conditioner battling the oppressive summer heat, she found herself longing for the warm comfort of heroin. It had been seven weeks since she had flown in from San Francisco, and four weeks since she had escaped. The drugs had done their job for the Clean Man; she was, in a way, addicted, and maybe she always would be. Everything she read said most addicts would relapse.

She shivered at the thought of being that vulnerable again. This morning she felt alive and ready to take on the last name on her list. These new people she would leave for Kwan. But the Clean Man, he was going to suffer, maybe not today, but soon.

A speeding police car raced past her, rocking the little Honda, and then another. Scooting down in the seat as far as she could, she watched them through the binoculars.

Those two were joined by two more that had come from the opposite direction. Several officers in uniform raced into the alley as others huddled around the front door, their backs hugging the concrete wall.

"I told you I would come for you," she whispered.

Two more unmarked cars pulled up next to the others, and two men and a woman in civilian clothes joined the others behind the cars blocking the street. Someone was using a bullhorn, and even from this distance she could hear them asking for anyone inside to come out.

She hoped to see the door open and the skinny guy with the acne scars surrender, but she also wanted to see them smash the door, to hear gunfire and see ambulances arrive. She wanted that man inside to be dead—but nothing happened—for twenty frustrating minutes. Her eyes were hurting; the strain of looking through the binoculars was blurring her vision, but she was too afraid she would miss something.

Finally, one of the uniformed officers used a battering ram, a long pipe with handles, to smash open the door, and she watched all of them rush inside. How long had this girl been bound to that cot. "Please be alive," she whispered again.

***

Another twenty frustrating minutes passed until finally one of the men wearing a suit stepped outside. The man looked down to the far end of the street, then turned and looked right at her. *Is that Kwan?* How had he known she was here? She was stuck like a rat in a trap, to move now would expose her. Kwan would see a car leaving the area and have someone stop it. Then she put the binoculars down and saw how small the man looked.

He can't see me this far away.

The man turned again and went back inside. Taking a deep breath, she held it in and then exhaled. That was too close.

Rolling the window down again, she hoped to hear the wailing of an ambulance or a rescue truck, but it was quiet. Surely, they would call for paramedics. Something was wrong. Was she dead, or was she even in there?

The Clean Man must have moved her once Fong was killed.

He was smart. He was a quick learner and knew that she wasn't finished with him yet. She had promised him after all: "I'm going to kill you, old man!" He knew she had hunted Fong down and killed him, and he wasn't taking any chances. This warehouse was a link, and it was better to move the girl and start somewhere fresh.

That's what I would do. I need to start thinking like him. I would relocate to another city and get as far away as possible.

His business was more than likely conducted over the internet anyway. Except for his crew—he would need loyal people to manage the girls—someone he could trust, someone local, like Tommy Fong or Khoo.

No, relocating wouldn't work. He would need to stay close. His entire infrastructure was right here in Singapore.

Three officers in uniform came out of the building, got in two of the marked cars, and drove away. The emergency was over, and with it, her last lead. She had traced Fong from this building, and now she had nothing to find the last name on her list.

Two white vans drove past her and parked down the street next to the last marked police car. Crime scene technicians, probably. She had streamed enough cop shows to know what they were and what they did.

Time to leave, she thought, backing out of the parking lot. Turning the steering wheel sent another jolt of pain through her chest and reminded her how vulnerable she was.

CHAPTER 26

KWAN

The battering ram struck the deadbolt and the door exploded, showering all of them with rotten wood and splinters. The first of the four Special Tactics and Rescue, or STAR officers, rushed inside and all too soon Kwan heard him announce, "All clear."

If Gemma had been here, she was long gone.

It was a small warehouse, half the size of the one on Pandan Loop and probably a sewing shop, Kwan assumed with the sewing machine painted above the door. The building was empty, not even a trash can left behind. Kwan could smell bleach. In several places, the concrete floor was still damp and cleaner than everything else inside. He and his two inspectors fanned out looking for anything, some simple clue he could use.

Kwan pushed open the rear door. Years of old paint and weather had corroded the steel hinges, exposing the weeded lot behind the building. The weeds told him no one had used this door in years, much less days, but he noticed the weeds under the window next to the door, and a path to the alley, had been crushed; their stiff stems broken off as if someone had walked through the alley and stood next to the window. He pictured Leila Moran on her tiptoes, peering in.

What did you see, my friend, did you see little Gemma in here?

Back inside, his forensic technicians were on their hands and knees, scouring the floor for anything of value. He suspected that this time, the criminals had done a thorough job of cleaning up after themselves.

"Superintendent Kwan, look at this."

The technician was pointing to a crevasse between the brick wall and the floor. Wedged in tight was a piece of clear plastic, the protective cover of a syringe. Like the new plastic dental floss picks, they were everywhere in Singapore. Once used, they were thrown out car windows and dropped on the sidewalks by drug addicts. But this one, he knew, wasn't left behind by a junkie. This one was brand-new and had only been there a day or two at most. They had been here.

He stood up and looked around, visualizing a half dozen cheap cots, a young woman or girl bound in each one. He could feel them in the air. Leila Moran had waited too long.

**

Back at the station, Kwan stepped out of the elevator in time to see Sergeant Goh Gan Kim coming out of his division's office.

"Sergeant Goh, can I help you?"

Goh looked relaxed, not like a man sneaking around where he shouldn't be, but he had also been a skilled covert narcotics officer. Kwan could feel something out of place. Had he ever seen this man on his floor? All this just after finding his phone number in Fong's kitchen. Too much of a coincidence.

"I was dropping off a supplement for Inspector Dian, sir."

"Sergeant," Kwan said. "Did you know Tommy Fong?"

"It doesn't sound familiar. Why do you ask?"

"Nothing, thank you."

Kwan walked past the man and into his office and closed the door. Looking at his desk, he pictured how it looked before he had rushed out. Was anything different, anything missing, or was he being paranoid?

Kwan felt like he had been one step behind this case for months, then just as he thought things were coming together, everything changed. They rescued a victim, the first known survivor, but she couldn't t help them. The only person she could describe had killed and effectively silenced two of her abductors. Four dead bodies now, hundreds of pieces of evidence and DNA, and he was no closer to stopping whoever was behind so many still-missing girls.

And now, a politician's daughter was missing, and one of the department's own might be somehow involved.

All he had now was Goh.

Well, that's better than nothing.

Lee Dian was a Direct-Entry Inspector, and a good one. Kwan found him at his desk working on a report.

"Lee, were you just speaking with Goh?"

"Yes sir, he dropped off a supplement to a case I'm working, a domestic violence arrest we made weeks ago."

"Can I see it?"

"Sure, anything important?"

"How well do you know Goh?"

"Not at all, this is the first time I've ever spoken to him."

Kwan looked at the single page report, it all appeared normal and routine.

Goh was reporting that some woman had contacted him, one of his old informants offering information about the husband Dian had arrested. The information was vague but plausible. The woman was a neighbor who wanted to remain anonymous but wanted the police to know the wife was seeing other men.

"What do you make of this supplement, Lee?"

"Not much to it, sir, I was just going to file it. The arrest was weeks ago, the husband was just released, and nothing is pending. I'm surprised Goh bothered writing it at all."

"Don't mention this to anyone, Lee. I'm just checking on Goh. I don't like him up here looking around."

"Sir, he did ask a few questions, simple things, like how Sergeant Jiawei was doing, whether she was coming back to work, apparently there are rumors she's retiring soon."

"Thanks, Lee, let me know if he comes back up here and who he talks to."

"Sure thing."

Sitting in front of his computer screen he opened Goh's personnel file. It was lengthy, over six hundred pages which wasn't unique for a twenty-year veteran.

It was boring and tedious, beginning with the man's application twenty-one years ago. Typical and average scores in the academy, a comment by one of his trainers that "Cadet Goh applies himself with just enough effort to pass academically," and another one, "Cadet Goh is not a team player and avoids social interactions with his fellow cadets."

Interesting. The man hadn't changed much in twenty years. Usually there was a bond between fellow officers, a camaraderie. Goh had chosen narcotics and went deep under cover. An assignment ensuring he would be working alone. Still, his evaluations had remained above average, and several commendations were sprinkled throughout his file. One noted bravery under fire, another lauded his ability to make huge seizures of cocaine and millions of dollars in cash. And then six months without a single notation in the file.

The next document referred to his transfer back to uniform patrol. No mention of a request to transfer, or disciplinary reasons for the obvious demotion in assignment.

Six months after his transfer, Goh was reprimanded for being involved in a domestic dispute with his wife while on duty. Kwan looked for the domestic report that should have been attached to the reprimand but found no reference to it. There were more reprimands: Goh had failed to honor court-ordered child support payments to his now ex-wife, a financial institute filed a complaint when the inspector wrote a series of bad checks, and there was another one for public intoxication.

Then Goh was transferred off the streets and into the fraud unit, and other than several routine satisfactory annual evaluations, his file ended.

Halim Hazlina had mentioned that someone must have owed Goh a favor, or maybe he has a godfather somewhere, someone with enough pull that Goh was protected.

Kwan started at the beginning of the personnel file, reviewing Goh's application. There was a list of personal references, people willing to vouch for the young man. There were six; three were his neighbors, who said they had known him all his life. "A good boy," they all said. Of course, who would ask someone they didn't get along with for a reference? However, one neighbor refused to talk to the investigators. That was odd. One of the references Goh listed was a relative, an uncle with a name that sounded familiar, Lee Tan. It was a common name, but Kwan had heard it somewhere and recently.

His desk phone rang and he closed the file.

"Kwan," he said.

"Superintendent, Sergeant Goh here. I remembered that name you mentioned, Tommy Fong. I think I handled a case involving him last year, a stolen credit card or something."

"Did you write a report?"

"No," Goh said. "I told him to contact his bank. I never heard back from him. I just wanted to let you know."

"Thank you, Sergeant."

He hung up the phone and leaned back in his chair. "Very convenient."

Goh was worried. Something or somebody had told him his name had come up with Fong's death, and he was desperately trying to cover his tracks. That supplement he wrote for Dian was bullshit, just an excuse to be snooping around for information.

Kwan went back to internal affairs.

"Hazlina, can you show me the GPS data for Sergeant Goh for the last two months?"

"Sure, let me get his ID number. You want me to send you a link? You can watch it, or I can send you a printout with his routes over a two-month period."

Each of the department's cars could be tracked by GPS, and their radios sent a signal out to the communications building, pinpointing their location. In an emergency, it allowed the dispatchers to send the closest officer to a call. It also allowed supervisors to ensure the departments' personnel were where they were supposed to be.

"Both if you can," Kwan said. "Something is up with this guy. I can feel it, but please keep it to yourself. We may have a leak, or Goh is the leak, I don't know."

Back in his office, he watched Goh's dot moving on a map as the man left the station at 8 a.m. two months ago.

CHAPTER 27

LEANN

"God, this is just as bad as New York City," LeAnn said as she fought traffic on her way back to the condo. But at least she'd never had to drive in New York, Uber and the subway were all she had ever needed. In front of her, several traffic lights were out and uniformed police officers were directing traffic. It took an hour for the typical fifteen-minute drive.

The condo was cool, dark, and best of all, quiet.

Stretched out on the bed, she took deep breaths, feeling her ribs rubbing each other, wincing as the now-dull ache in her chest reminded her how vulnerable she still was. The laptop chimed in the living room. It would hurt to sit up. It was less painful to roll onto her side and then stand, but lying where she was felt glorious. Then it chimed again.

"Dammit, what do you want!" Wait, it had to be Christopher's wife. She knows something!

It did hurt when she sat up, then she jumped up.

Sorry it took so long, but I found the site you wanted. These are serious people with serious skills when it comes to computers. No names here, please, but our friend made a stupid mistake and tried to interact with them. That's how they found him.

I'm still working on trying to ID the one you want, but there are at least six active people so far in this group. I have two IP addresses; one is here in the States, Maryland, I think. The other is in Singapore. The one in Maryland is the one with the serious encryption, government maybe. The one in Singapore is the weak link; I'm working on that one first, maybe it will help me get what you need. TTYL.

The next message was shorter.

I'm going to try something in the morning. If you don't hear from me, it didn't go well.

"What?"

Tell me what, she typed back and then deleted it. The woman would have said if she could, and less contact between them was probably best. LeAnn closed the laptop and went back to the bedroom. Christopher had made a mistake, his wife said. Hopefully, she'd find something with the link in Singapore because LeAnn had nothing.

"I killed my only lead, and the new girl is gone or dead. I failed her. Does that about sum it up, LeAnn?"

Another bowl of ramen noodles. They were beginning to lose their appeal. It was sleep she really needed. Five days now since Fong had slammed her into the wall, the pain had lessened some, now it was a dull nagging ache that never eased. Bastard! It would be at least two more weeks, maybe more, before she could hope to be whole again. She needed to be ready soon. Each night she crafted a different way to kill the Clean Man. Slowly was best, painfully was better. No garrote for him, that was too quick, although looking into the prick's bulging eyes as he died would be a pleasant memory. He had smashed Jie's finger for failing him once. Some type of blunt force seemed like a better plan. Maybe she'd crush his kneecaps.

Tonight, sleep was again elusive, too many ideas and too many plans. LeAnn was never any good at ignoring something undone, unfinished. Having no clue how she was going to find the Clean Man was the real problem; having to rely on some unknown woman half a world away was also a problem. "If I could just sleep, I can work this out, just one hour." Each time she nodded off, the destressing ache woke her again.

"Even if I find him, how will I kill him? He's twice my size. He's probably fought people all his life. The stun gun may do it, I should try it on someone first."

Staring at the ceiling, she went through one plan after another. She had the idea of calling Kwan, telling him everything she knew. But she was a wanted person. Interpol and the FBI would be looking for her and talking to Kwan would be a mistake. I can stay ahead of the local police, if I . . . Her thought trailed off as she remembered her brother saying those exact words.

Ramzi and Madinah had been inseparable; they were twins, after all. *Live together, kill together.* It made her laugh. They thought they were so smart. Both were dead now, but they had been dead to her for years. Once they started killing, they and her mother treated her like an outcast, too immature for their big plans, well, the authorities had finally caught them.

She was never going to make their mistakes. And working alone had always been her way. No one to depend on, no one to fuck up and ruin it all. "No, I'm not going to call Kwan." She told herself. "I'm going to kill the fucking Laoban, and let Kwan deal with the rest of them."

With the laptop she searched for a pain medication, but each one had an addiction warning. One of them caught her eye though, a fentanyl transdermal patch. No needles, no pills to swallow, just stick it on the skin like a Band-Aid and enjoy euphoria. Well, that's not exactly the way it read, but she liked the thought. Fentanyl would lead to a relapse, though, just as surely as heroin would.

Back in bed, she considered how she could use a patch like that in her plan. It was an easy way to drug someone, get a slight advantage on a bigger man, incapacitate him, and then kill them. It was almost like the stun gun. She finally slept, and in her first dream, she stood over him as he lay dying in a pool of his own blood.

CHAPTER 28

THE CLEAN MAN

James Soong stroked the unconscious girl's thigh, feeling the smoothness found only on the skin of the very young. This was the first time he had seen the fifteen-year-old Gemma in person.

"I don't understand the attraction," he said. "She is just a child. Where is the challenge in that, Sergeant? When I'm with a woman, I want her to be kicking and screaming at the end."

Goh looked like he was searching for a safe answer, but simply nodded.

"Yes, I suppose she will do well. Too young for my personal tastes, though. Her father is an important man, and a lot of heat will be raining down on us all, so we need to be meticulous. I am going to make a lot of money with this one, and you will too.

"Thank you, sir."

"Another four weeks, I think, I don't want to be premature again. That Moran bitch cost me dearly. Jie was worthless, of course, but I liked Khoo, and Tommy was a good man. He will be hard to replace. I may need you to step in and assume some of his responsibilities, and I will compensate you, of course."

"Anything you need, Laoban."

Soong nodded and then looked skyward as if thinking of something important. "One hundred thousand dollars," he said. "That was his final offer. That's a lot of money for one night of pleasure, and the senator will forget all about the mishap with Brianne during his last visit. He was excited when I told him the news. A young, beautiful girl, the daughter of a powerful politician, just like himself. He wanted to leave Washington right away, but I told him this process takes time, and I want it to be perfect.

"You should have seen his eyes when Brianne entered the room. His stoic facade melted away, like a child with a new toy. Lust is a powerful emotion, Sergeant Goh, and I knew how to play on the senator's needs. Brianne failed me in the end, she humiliated him, called him, 'an old fat man,' and she had to pay the ultimate price. Such a waste."

Behind Goh, the Ng cousins waited. Simon Ng, the older of the two, fidgeted while Kian leaned against the wall. Simon had worked in one capacity or another for Soong since he was twelve. His latest assignment had been transporting the older girls from one brothel to another, "the end game" as Soong called it, but this was his first assignment alone watching the girls. He had worked two shifts with Tommy Fong, and Tommy thought the boy was ready. This was a big step, and Soong didn't fully trust him yet, but the Moran bitch had forced his hand.

"Simon, we are going to leave you now, and your cousin will relieve you at 7 p.m., sharp. Isn't that right, Kian? Kian, are you listening to me?"

"Yes, sir," the twenty-year-old said.

Soong picked up a heavy claw hammer off his desk and slammed it into a file cabinet, crushing the top of it and both cousins jumped.

"Kian, it's yes, Laoban! Don't make me say it twice."

Soong's contorted face relaxed, and his cool demeanor returned as if he had already forgotten Kian. "Simon," he said. "I have given you written instructions. Be especially attentive, I would hate to be disappointed and find you like I found your predecessors. The girl is to be dosed with morphine every six hours. If she wakes, increase the propofol by one. That is the schedule for at least another week. You will sleep there tonight, and when Kian comes to relieve you, you will show him what he needs to know. Neither of you open the door for anyone else. Any questions?"

"No, Laoban," Simon said bowing so deeply, Soong thought he would collapse.

"Very well, Simon."

Goh and Soong walked out into the brilliant sunshine, leaving both cousins inside.

"You trust them?" Goh asked.

"No more than I trust you, Sergeant Goh," Soong said. "I'm joking, of course, but yes, I do. Simon's mother and most of his family work for me, and they are well aware of what happens when I'm disappointed. Kian is young and not very intelligent, as you can see. But he will follow instructions when he is properly motivated. He may lose a finger now and then, but just like Jie, he will follow orders."

Goh looked up and down the empty street nervously, while Soong smiled staring vacantly at the blue sky.

"What are you worried about, Sergeant?"

"I wonder how Ms. Moran knew where Fong lived," Goh said.

"One of the Sen brothers watching her thought he heard something in the alley one night. It could have been her, and to be safe, I shut that building down and brought Gemma here."

"That's why I'm worried," Goh said. "I feel exposed out here. The Moran girl seems unusually resourceful, and Kwan is no fool, I worry about him too."

"Yes indeed, just be careful. If I feel he is getting too close, I may have to see that something will distract him, something personal."

Goh looked at Soong, "I don't know if that's a good idea, it would enrage everyone in his unit, maybe even the entire department."

"Again," Soong said, "Don't worry yourself. Let me show you the rest of this building. I think it will work out quite well. The sewing shop was too small. This building is in a much nicer neighborhood, hidden in plain sight, if you will, on the outskirts of town, and away from prying eyes, I hope."

The two men walked to the far end of the building. At one time the building had been three separate warehouses, each with its own entry door, and the two outside units also had metal roll-up doors for unloading cargo. Above this door, "Used Restaurant and Kitchen Appliances" was painted in fading black Chinese characters.

"What do you think, Goh? I think it's the perfect ruse. Let me show you what's inside."

Soong opened the smaller door, and the stench coming from the darkened interior made Goh gag.

"You're smelling dead rats," Soong said. "I had Kian collect a few from the docks. Should someone actually want to buy a used oven, I think that smell will change their mind. But come inside, this will be brief. You see that new wall? Anyone who can deal with the smell will believe that wall connects to my office on the other side. Brilliant, isn't it? My girls will be safely hidden between the two of them. Come see for yourself."

Goh followed the man deeper into the warehouse where the lighting was dim, passing dozens of grease-encrusted broilers and fryers. The light fixture above them was hanging by its wiring, and the fluorescent bulb was missing. In the low light, the new wall looked similar to the others around it, but between the smell and the lighting, Goh wanted to leave.

"Can you feel her? Gemma is just a few feet from where we are standing. She could scream, but the other side of this wall is soundproofed. I should have thought of this months ago. But the best ideas are happenstance, are they not?"

"Yes, Laoban," Goh said, trying not to breathe.

"Four weeks, Sergeant, four weeks, and our little Gemma should be ready for some action, and her first and only client is very eager to meet her. Let's get out of here. The smell will have penetrated my suit by now, and I want to change."

"You said her only client?"

"It's a one-time agreement I have with the senator," Soong said.

Back in the sunlight, Soong motioned for Goh to pull the overhead door down and gave him a set of keys.

"Keep them, I may need you to use them one day. For now, the cousins will take care of the girl."

"Yes, Mr. Soong."

"I would prefer that you continue to address me as Laoban. Names mentioned too often can be troublesome."

"Yes, Laoban."

"I have the Sen brothers scouring the docks looking for some new product as we are speaking, so I expect to hear from them soon. Anything new around the station? Any pearls you have gleaned from my adversaries?"

"No, Laoban. They are still going through Fong's computer, but I've heard nothing new about the Moran girl."

"That bitch! I saw it in her eyes, you know. I knew she was special, and I mistook that as being in my favor. By now she knows I killed her friend in New York. I still want to know how she heard of the Blue Room. Jie and Khoo may have said something, but of course, that thread has been severed."

As the two men drove south in Soong's pearl white Mercedes AMG coupe, Soong could smell the stench of death on his suit. It wasn't that he was uncomfortable with the smell, but it reminded him too much of growing up in the slums of London, and that *was* uncomfortable.

"You are my only eyes and ears within your department, tell me if anyone asks you anything about the girls, and any gossip you may hear, no matter how trivial. Are we clear on that?

"Of course, Laoban."

"Fong is out of the picture now, so I'm going to need you to supply all the narcotics. Three months' worth. Figure four women, six weeks each. Here is a list, you should have no problem locating any of it."

Goh read the list and nodded.

"None of the cheap stuff?"

"Not yet, we will switch them to black tar once they are broken in, and I have plenty of that. I want pharmacy-grade drugs until then, no more accidental overdoses. I lost two girls to cheap heroin and it set me back weeks. Tonight, I will begin opening bids for a girl we don't yet have, hopefully the Sen brothers will be productive, and I will have a photo of her."

Soong pulled into the Sheraton Towers lot and parked next to Goh's unmarked car. Somewhere in the lot, one of Soong's men would be ready to pick up surveillance on Goh as soon as he drove away.

Soong had learned years ago to know everything about the men working for him, especially his contacts in law enforcement. Goh had worked for him for two years now, doing minor favors, but now Goh would be his introduction man, the face his clients would see when they arrived. With the loss of Fong and the two other men, he needed to trust Goh with some of Fong's responsibilities, but there was also something untrustworthy about him; he lacked loyalty, and that was troubling.

CHAPTER 29

LEANN

The chime on her laptop meant a new email from Christopher's wife. Another faceless, nameless person. It was driving her crazy, and she had forced herself to start calling the woman simply, *The Wife.*

The email directed her to an encrypted link, and then to another. The woman was being overly cautious, it seemed, but her husband had been killed, and she knew more about the internet than LeAnn ever wanted to know.

Sorry again that it's been a while, but I have a real job. I have to make a living. Anyway, I've jacked one of the user's computers; he's an ex-politician in Singapore named Chan Heng Casmir. He seems to be a lowlife and bit player compared to the others that use that chat room. His fire wall sucks; it's like from the '90s, but that's fortunate for us. I've attached several of his emails for you to read. Most of them were encrypted, but the good news is the encryption program was on his hard drive. Bad news is they're all in Mandarin, so I used a translator program to convert them to English, but I'm not sure how accurate it is.

The chat room uses a better encryption program, an expensive one to text each other. It took a while, but I found and bought the program to crack it online. Still, they use a lot of code words, like "product," I think that is obviously a girl. "Juice" is probably a narcotic because addiction is also mentioned.

So, here's what I've learned so far—in the last six months, it appears that eighteen different people have communicated in this chatroom. I have

IP addresses on some, but all of them appear to be asking and answering questions from one person, like the boss or the room's moderator. And you will see all of the communications to and from Casmir.

In my opinion, this scumbag politician and the boss are doing each other a favor, some type of revenge thing for the guy, and the boss is going to help him get this revenge. Read the back and forth and you will see what I mean. There is also a police officer mentioned, an informant maybe; the boss gets pissed when the politician brings him up and the guy apologizes.

From what you told me, I was able to put a lot of it together. There's an address mentioned several times that must be important. I looked it up. It's a house on Toh Avenue, out near the airport, and it's registered to a catering service that does business with a few of the airlines.

Still no luck on the IP in Maryland, that's the one that scares me.

You asked me for anything I could find on Kwan Kim Lai. He is a superintendent, some type of supervisor I assume, he's squeaky-clean, married, no children and lives within his means. I listed his home address and cell phone number. That's all I can find on him.

No sign yet that these people know I'm snooping, but be careful. If they are on to me, they may be able to track you down too. Keep switching phones, TTYL.

Reading through the ex-politician's files was difficult until she put them in chronological order. Six months ago, he asked for a favor relating to an upcoming election and how he would be grateful if something unfortunate were to happen to their mutual problem.

"Maybe Gemma is the answer," was the reply.

The politician answered, "That would be unfortunate," with a smiley-face emoji.

What is a Gemma?

Apparently, Christopher's wife had downloaded everything from the politician: billing statements, credit applications, and love letters to several different women from as far away as Ethiopia.

Chan Heng Casmir was divorced, apparently in debt, and had

been defeated in an election ten years ago. He had continued to run and had been defeated in each election since. His successor had moved on to bigger things and was now the Deputy Speaker of the Parliament. Casmir, it seemed, was a bitter man. Maybe Gemma was a code name for an execution.

LeAnn searched the rest of the files and couldn't find anything relating to any of the abductions or to the Clean Man.

She went through all the information on Kwan, and she had to admit, he did look squeaky-clean, but was he the informer? As a supervisor, he would be the ideal man on the inside for someone like the Clean Man.

She looked at an aerial view of the house mentioned in the Blue Room, did a GPS route, and saw it was thirty-five minutes away. She grabbed her keys, backpack, and binoculars and was driving past the house just after noon.

A six-foot-high cinderblock wall restricted her view, and all that she could see from the street was the roofline. The winding road back to the highway was elevated enough so that the house's gated driveway was visible, but finding a place to park and not be obvious to passing cars was going to be difficult. A small hill provided some cover, and she parked the Honda facing one side of the house, which was almost a quarter of a mile away. Using the binoculars, it was clear the driveway was empty, and the house looked unoccupied.

Two hours later, a mid-sized cream-colored sedan pulled up to the wrought iron gate, and the driver's window opened. From her view, she couldn't see what he was doing, but the gate slid to the right on a track, the car pulled inside, and the gate closed behind it.

The driver stepped out of the car. He was an average-looking, middle-aged Asian man. She focused and then refocused the binoculars, trying to zoom in on the driver, but she was just too far away to see anything unique about him. He could be thirty— or fifty.

The man disappeared from her view, either he went inside or was behind the house.

The car was also nondescript, a four-door with no distinguishing marks, except there was a white decal about three inches square on the back window.

"Dammit!"

She needed to be closer, and using the Nikon, she searched for a better vantage point, something with some cover and closer, but this house seemed to be in the middle of open ground. If the house had a couple of good cameras, any car coming or leaving could easily be seen and for all she knew, she was being watched right now.

As she thought about being watched, the man returned and the car backed out and through the gate.

The car turned toward her and began winding its way up the hill. The driver was middle-aged, maybe forty, with jet-black hair and wearing dark sunglasses—and he was staring right at her. He crept closer, maneuvering through the sharp left and right turns. She eased down in her seat, put the binoculars on the floor, and started her engine. She heard the other car now, its engine straining against the steep incline, tires squealing with each sharp turn. He was going to pass right next to her. The stun gun was in her backpack on the floorboard, she grabbed it and waited, listening to the car as it came up the hill. There was no other road, and if the car stopped in front of her, she would be blocked in.

Her head was below the windshield; she couldn't see anything. All she could do was listen to the car straining. It was loud now, probably right next to her, its engine idling, then it revved up and moved past her, the sound steadily fading. She inched up and peeked through the review mirror in time for it to make a final turn and disappear.

She took a deep breath, too deep and her ribs screamed in response. Putting the car in gear, she drove back down the hill, past the house, and kept going. Something told her she had been made. Had he gotten her license plate? Was he coming back even now?

She drove straight to the airport and returned the car.

CHAPTER 30

DREW MENDOZA

Nine thousand miles away, Drew Mendoza, wearing latex gloves, sifted through one of New York's Department of Sanitation's garbage cans. She needed a specific cup, and she lifted one out and examined it in detail—a Starbucks Grande, still with a bit of coffee in the bottom and light pink lipstick smeared on the rim—perfect. She bagged the cup and walked across the street to Astor's Internet Espresso Bar and sat behind a Dell desktop computer.

It was time to take a fresh look at the IP address in Maryland. This was her first time at Astor's, and like her husband, she made it a point to never use the same café twice when hacking into sensitive sites.

Today was going to be a poke–and–prod mission. She wanted to set off a few alarms and see what happened. If this was somebody connected with the government, she probably had twenty minutes before the big black SUVs would show up.

"Here goes," she whispered, setting the timer on her phone.

Knowing she wasn't going to get past the fire wall, but wanting to try anyway, she began a simple login crack program and watched the numbers and letters scroll on the monitor. She kept her face looking forward, certain that somewhere at least one camera was pointing at the row of cubicles, and with luck, she would look like half the teenagers in New York City in her oversized gray sweatshirt, matching yoga pants, New York Mets baseball cap, and Ray-Bans. Underneath, she was wearing something quite different.

As her timer reached the fifteen-minute mark, she picked up her backpack, placed the empty cup next to the monitor, and went to the restroom. In the stall, she stuffed the sweatshirt and pants into her backpack, put her blonde wig on and checked herself in the mirror. It looked right, good enough really, and she walked out through the front door.

Across the street, she ordered black coffee and sat under a green-and-white umbrella and waited. Twenty-one minutes now and not a Suburban in sight. Maybe she was being paranoid, but she wasn't going to take a bullet for anyone.

At the twenty-four-minute mark, a gray–and–black step-van with Priest and Sons Plumbing painted in block letters pulled up and parked right in front of her, blocking the view of the café.

"Of all the fricking places you needed to park," she said to herself and moved two tables over.

No one got out of the van until an identical one parked three spots down. Two men got out of the second one and walked inside the café, and neither of them looked like plumbers. Both were in their early thirties, had military-style black boots, and looked like the beefcake firemen she had seen on a coworker's calendar.

Then the doors of the van in front of her opened and a man and woman stepped out. The woman, also in her early thirties, adjusted an earpiece, and Drew could hear a radio broadcast coming from inside the van. It was a woman's voice, and she watched the woman's lips mimicking the same words.

"God dammit," she whispered. They were right in front of her.

These two joined the others inside the café, and Drew watched them through the window. They were standing next to the desktop computer where she had just been sitting.

Ten minutes later the four of them walked out, and one of them was carrying the computer, another held a clear plastic bag with the cup inside.

"Good luck with that," she said.

That was all she needed to see.

Two blocks north she stopped at her favorite café, opened her laptop, and sent another message. *A really big fish took the bait, watch your ass.*

CHAPTER 31

LEANN

Four more days passed before her ribs felt like they were healing. They still moved when she took a deep breath and when she sat up in bed, but today, it was bearable.

Her new rental was a gun-metal gray Volkswagen Passat. The underground parking lot was full, and like the Honda, the VW blended in with the other cars. LeAnn pressed the lock button on the key fob; the VW's amber lights flashed, and she walked over to it.

It would be dark in an hour, and she had found the ideal place to watch the house on Toh Avenue. It was a busy liquor store high on a hill and closer to the house. In the dark, she would be invisible to anyone on the road.

Christopher's wife had sent a message that something was going to happen tonight at the house near the airport, "something big" she had said. Hopefully whatever it was would include the Clean Man. She had not heard anything about him in weeks, and she felt like she was tracking a ghost, an infuriating dilemma for her.

Set up on the hill, she watched the last of the day's rush hour traffic. Thousands of red taillights moved along the interstate, but little traffic was on the smaller residential street winding down toward the walled-in house.

The lights from the liquor store lit up most of the parking lot, but the outer edges were dark, and her VW was in the last spot, backed in, giving her the best view through the windshield. Customers came and went, young men mostly, and she watched them through the rearview mirror.

Two hours now and nothing was happening in the house below her, it looked deserted. Then the landscape lighting switched on, and the empty driveway and security gate were visible, even without the binoculars.

Bright lights lit up the inside of her car, and she jerked upright as a dark-colored limousine parked behind her. Through the mirror, she watched a middle-aged man open the driver's door and get out. He looked American and was dressed in a black suit and shiny shoes. Even in the suit she could tell he was muscular, and he walked like an athlete. There was something arrogant about him, and she watched him walk all the way to the store's front door.

Through the limo's tinted windows, she made out the silhouette of a man in the back seat and possibly someone else next to him, the tint was too dark to be sure.

Five minutes later, the driver returned carrying a brown paper bag. The limo backed out of the parking lot, its light illuminating the inside of her VW as it turned, and then drove down the winding road, headed to the freeway.

The parking lot behind her was empty now, and she sat up straight, watching the limo as it neared the house. Brake lights flashed. Grabbing the Nikon, LeAnn saw the automatic gate opening.

"It's happening, and the bastards were right behind me."

The landscape lighting gave her a perfect view of the driver when he opened the door, a heavyset man, wearing a black suit. A similar man got out of the front passenger door. Both men scanned the front yard, then the neighboring houses, and finally did a 360-degree sweep of the area. A third man got out of the back seat and stood by the open door. This man wore a white, long-sleeve shirt, and LeAnn saw he was wearing a shoulder holster. While the first two walked around the back of the house, this third man stood next to the back door, as if guarding someone or something inside. The first two returned, opened the front door using a keypad on the lock and went inside.

This was a professional security team; they looked like military and reminded her of the men escorting the president. "This is the guy," she whispered. The one Christopher's wife feared. Someone with the government.

The two men came out of the house. The rear door of the limousine opened, and a fourth man stepped out. This was not another member of the security team; this man was old, in his sixties, maybe even seventy. His hair looked silver or gray in the light, his shoulders drooped, and she noticed he was using his hand on the car for balance, like a drunk leaving a bar.

Finally, a woman or girl got out and stood behind them all. She was wearing a black skintight dress, an FMD, they called it in college. She also was having difficulty walking, and one of the men held her by the arm and walked her to the front door. The old man and the girl went inside, and all three men went back to the limo. A light flared as one of the men lit a cigarette.

"You sick bastards," she whispered.

This is where the Clean Man made his money. This is where they brought Brianne and probably all the other girls too. Had she not killed Jie and Khoo, there was a good chance someone would have taken her there as well.

Four hours later, the old man came back to the limousine and spoke to the driver, who nodded and opened the rear door. The four of them drove away, heading to the expressway entrance, and disappeared in traffic.

What had happened to the girl? Was someone going to pick her up later, maybe a cleaning crew preparing the house and her for another customer. Maybe the Clean Man himself.

***

Thirty minutes later, she started the car and began backing out of her spot. She could pick that front door lock, even if it was one of the new keypad versions, and she could free this girl.

As she backed out, a gray sedan pulled up to the house's gate. LeAnn stopped where she was and watched. The gate opened and the car backed into the driveway. A single man got out and went inside.

LeAnn made a U-turn and parked again at the liquor store. She was thankful she had waited those last few minutes; this was the same gray car that had driven past the warehouse weeks ago. She knew that was no coincidence. It had been one of the Clean Man's men surveilling his business, and now that car was here, how many more of them were there?

She had expected two or three women to come in to freshen the place, change the sheets, and restock the minibar like a hotel crew after the morning checkout. Something felt different, or maybe he was just picking up the girl. She hoped so, she could follow him, and he would finally lead her back to the Clean Man. She would kill him, and maybe this man too, or all of them.

"I will kill you all," she said.

It was taking too long. This man wouldn't be there to change the sheets. If anything, he was there to bring the girl back, to force her if necessary. That would take five minutes, and it had been half an hour. "What's happening in there, God dammit!"

Soaked in her own sweat, all her alarm bells were ringing. Something had gone wrong inside that house. Maybe this new guy was raping her now? She didn't think so, it didn't feel right. Do I stay up here and wait, or do I call the police? Christopher's wife had given her Kwan's cell phone number, and she thought of calling him, waking him up and telling him to come get the girl, but that could take an hour, the police could be here quicker. But she would lose any hope of finding the Clean Man, and that was who she wanted.

In the end, she got out of the car and paced through the parking lot, keeping the house in view. Pacing helped, just moving was better than sitting in the cramped Volkswagen. Down below, the car's lights flashed twice, and the trunk opened. The man had opened it with a remote, and then he came out of the front door carrying a body bag.

She knew what it was. A black, six-foot-long, bag with straps, like an oversized duffle bag. He wasn't using the straps though, the body inside the bag was slumped over his shoulders.

"Oh no—no—no!"

Like a sack of garbage, the man dumped the bag in the trunk, looked left towards her, then right, and slammed the trunk closed.

Call Kwan, LeAnn, that's his job!

She had her phone in her hand and pressed the first two numbers . . . then squeezed her eyes shut and the Clean Man's image laughed at her and she was blinded with rage.

She threw the phone at the tree and then tried to smash it with her shoe, but the rubber soles just ground it into the gravel.

"Shit!"

The car was leaving. Pulling out of the driveway, it turned toward the expressway entrance and began accelerating.

Throwing the phone in the VW, she raced after the car's taillights. Following a car at night wasn't as easy as in daylight. At night, from a safe distance, all you could see were the red taillights, and they looked a lot like every other car's lights. But the driver in the car you were following had the same problem.

The VW strained as she tore out of the lot and headed down the road, the sedan disappeared around a curve. She was not a good driver, and she still wasn't comfortable driving on this side of the road. With the gas pedal to the floor, the tires protested, squealing and skidding toward the edge of the road. In one place where the hillside was steepest, she felt the car leaning to the point she was afraid it would roll over.

Idiot tourist dies in single car accident! She could see the morning headlines now.

Two more turns and the taillights reappeared. She took her foot off the accelerator and coasted as the two cars approached the entrance ramp to the Tampines Expressway.

The gray sedan was a four door Hyundai Elantra. LeAnn let three cars get between them and then relaxed, flexing her fingers, cramped from gripping the steering wheel. Traffic was smooth at this hour. No one was racing home, rush hour was long over, and she and the Hyundai cruised comfortably at 80 kmh.

She felt calm now and clear headed, seeing him toss the body bag in the trunk had triggered a rage so deep, she was blinded by it, and now her useless phone, its glass screen shattered, lay on the floorboard in front of the passenger seat.

The Hyundai's turn signal flashed, and her GPS showed the Seletar West Link was the next exit. As he turned, she lost two cars between them so she slowed even more, doubling the distance between them. To her left, the GPS showed the large green expanse of a golf course and to the right, the Seletar airport.

He's going to dump her body somewhere off this exit. It was near midnight. The closed golf course was pitch black and surrounded by tall trees and hedges, it would offer him privacy, but the body would be found at first light. The airport was a small commuter field, yet she saw the blinking lights of a big jet taxiing near the fence. Would he put her on a private plane? Could have that much power? Of course, he could. He could easily fly her out to sea and dump her in the ocean, and she would never be found.

The thought of a girl falling, tumbling over and over, distracted her, and she missed seeing him turn. A break in a row of hedges revealed a small paved path, wide enough for a golf cart or an ATV, it was the only place he could have turned, and his taillights were at the far end of it.

She switched off her headlights and made the same turn, following him down the path, small shrubs and larger limbs scraping the side of the VW.

The cart path ended suddenly in a large parking lot with the two-story clubhouse on one side and the Seletar Reservoir on the other. The gray sedan was parked near a dumpster hidden behind a row of golf carts, it's lights were off and the doors closed. She coasted to a stop fearing he would see her brake lights, then turned her engine off and waited.

Then the Hyundai's trunk opened and the driver stepped out. He stood still next to the car's open door and looked out into the dark parking area, then turned slowly and looked back at the reservoir. For two agonizing minutes, he stared in her direction, then bent over the trunk and lifted the bag out effortlessly.

How much did the girl weigh, one hundred pounds?

Through the binoculars, she rotated the focus ring, trying to get that perfectly crisp image of the man. He was dressed in dark slacks and a white shirt open at the collar—and wearing a badge and gun clipped to his belt.

Someone new was added to her list.

CHAPTER 32

KWAN

Morning light streamed through the sheer curtains in Kwan's master bedroom. Coffee was brewing in the kitchen, and somewhere in the house, his wife was singing. It was a glorious sound. Sitting up, he stretched, then made his way to the bathroom, humming along with Mei Lien's voice.

After splashing hot water on his face, he was brushing his teeth when he heard Mei Lien scream from the kitchen. He grabbed his gun from the nightstand and raced through the hallway, finding her standing near the front door. With an ashen face, she handed him a stack of papers and pointed to the open French doors in the living room.

In English, and in the same cursive handwriting he had last seen in a box with Hui Jie's bloody shirt, was a note addressed to him.

For a police officer, you are an idiot for not having an alarm system and better locks on your door. I used a pocketknife to open it. It's not just you, Kwan, it's Mei Lien and your unborn baby's life you need to think about. These men are killers.

You will find another body in a dumpster at the west end of the Seletar Country Club near a bridge. I watched as one of your fellow officers dumped her body there. He was driving a gray Hyundai sedan. Either you take care of him, or I will kill him in seven days. It's up to you, Kwan, all I want is the man he works for.

Also, I think these emails will help you figure things out.

—L

The Moran girl had been in his house while they both slept. She knew his wife's name and that she was pregnant. Who is this woman?!

His entire team was still at home, probably enjoying a bit of breakfast, so he called the station and had officers sent to the golf course, then called Chin and filled him in. "I'll be on my way in a few minutes, Chin."

The coffee was tasteless. He sat at the kitchen table with Mei Lien, but neither of them wanted to eat. The stack of cryptic emails trembled in his hands.

"I must go, Mei Lien. I have to go right now. Call an alarm company. See who your brother uses and I want a system installed today. Then call your parents and make arrangements to stay with them for a few days."

Tears coursed down Mei Lien's cheeks, and suddenly she looked so young, and so vulnerable. He held her until she stopped shaking, feeling their baby daughter stirring against his abdomen. He pictured Leila Moran walking through their house, probably standing at the foot of his bed as they slept. The image chilled him. And the woman knew things she shouldn't have known, and that angered him just as much. Rage, primal rage—blossomed in Kwan's chest. He wanted to break something—to smash something—anything. But that would terrify his wife, and she needed to see him in control.

"Kim, I'm so afraid."

"I know, honey. I'm going to have a car posted outside right away. I don't think this person means to harm us, but I will find her. You need to believe me."

Kwan arrived and found Haron Chin and several officers in uniform standing ten meters away from a green dumpster at the far end of the parking lot. A crowd of spectators had already begun to gather behind yellow crime scene tape stretched out between several of the patrol cars.

"Is she in there, Chin?"

"Someone's in there. I don't know who; someone small. There

is a black body bag on top of what looks like yesterday's garbage. No one has disturbed it since the first officer arrived.

Kwan walked toward it, his eyes focused on the ground, looking for anything other than asphalt. A cigarette butt, tire tracks, a scrap of paper, anything that might be evidence. But saw nothing but dead leaves and white sand.

The dumpster's lid was closed but still smelled like rotting garbage. He used his pen to lift one edge of the plastic lid. A black, heavy-duty plastic bag sat on top of several smaller ones. The shape of a face, legs, and even individual toes were visible through the thick plastic. Kwan, a Christian since birth, whispered, "Jesus, help us," dropped the lid and waited next to the rest of them.

"The crime scene technicians are on the way, ETA ten minutes," Haron said.

Kwan walked back to his car wanting privacy and called the deputy commissioner, his immediate supervisor, on his cell phone.

"I don't know if it's her yet, Commissioner. I'm waiting for the techs to get here before I look any further. You may want to notify the Speaker of Parliament that we have another body, and, sir, one of our own may be involved."

"What?" the commissioner asked.

"I'll fill you in when you get here."

He ended the call and tried to think of how he would tell the deputy commissioner that one of his abducted women, was a killer, that she had been inside his house, and that one of his fellow police officers might be involved as well.

Will he question my competence? Because I'm beginning to.

***

Thirty minutes later, with crime scene cameras capturing her every move, Claire Heng Chee the chief medical examiner unzipped the bag, revealing Gemma Balakrishnan's bruised and bloody body. She was nude, and the injuries, and probably the cause of death, were centered around her throat.

"She was probably strangled with a half inch braided rope. You can see the ligature marks on the soft tissues around her trachea," she said pointing to the serpentine pattern of bruising. You can also see the petechiae in the whites of her eyes."

"Can you tell the time of death yet?" Kwan asked.

"I'd say a rough guess is between 9 p.m. and midnight."

Commissioner Teo Leng arrived, along with his deputy, and slowly the crowd of officers thinned out, none of them wanting to be around the bearer of bad news.

"Commissioner Teo," Kwan said, "I'm afraid it's her. It is Gemma."

"Tell me everything you know," Teo said. "The Speaker is on his way here now and let us hope he doesn't bring the girl's father."

***

By midafternoon, Kwan was in the internal affairs office with Halim Hazlina and the two of them were about to watch a recording of the last twenty-four hours of the GPS tracker on Goh's assigned car.

"Before we start, do you know how she got these emails? Because that's the first question the prosecutor will ask," she said. "You need to tell me, Kim, and how in the world did she end up in your house?"

"Hazlina, I have never met or even seen this woman, and I have no idea how she got my address or these emails. She's like . . . some kind of movie character . . . and a ghost."

"So, this tiny, abducted woman killed two of her captors, then tracked down a third grown man and strangled him, right in front of one of our senior sergeants?"

"Yes, Hazlina, that's about it."

"Well, I'm glad I'm not in your shoes, Kim. These emails trouble me. They link Chan Heng Casmir directly to Gemma's death. I'm grateful for the information, but they will never fly in court. We need our own link if we're ever going to prosecute him."

"Do you think I don't know it? Dammit, this girl was in my house!"

"Relax, Kim, these are the questions the DA is going to ask. Imagine yourself on the witness stand trying to explain this movie character victim of yours to a jury. I'm struggling to believe it myself. Casmir is a has-been politician, but he's still well-known and a pain in the ass in Parliament and here at the department. He's going to raise hell when he finds out we have copies of his personal emails. I mean, they are damning, of course. He refers to Gemma directly, who then winds up strangled, but a good attorney can have these emails sealed, and the entire case against him would be thrown out. And worse—he can blame it all on Goh and the department."

"It's a nightmare. If I could just catch this Moran woman, if I could just speak to her for ten minutes!" Kwan collapsed in the chair and closed his eyes. "I'm sorry. I'm just worn out. You should have seen my wife's face this morning."

"Okay, let's get back to Goh."

"Do you think Goh would be stupid enough to use his own car?" Kwan asked.

Hazlina laughed. "You'd be surprised, Kim. Most of the men like Goh think they're invincible. They think they're so much smarter than the rest of us."

The two of them watched the icon of Goh's car leave the station at 5 p.m. when his shift ended and drive west toward the Woodlands train yards.

"I've watched him take this same route every day. He will turn left up here and drive slowly down Woodlands Road, and then turn back east and head home. That road is far out of his way, so what's he doing? He never stops or even slows down."

"I have no idea," Hazlina said.

Goh's car remained stationary at his house, until 11 p.m. when the dot began to move again. "He's going east along the Tampines

Expressway toward the Changi International Airport," Kwan said. "Where the hell is he going? The golf course is in the other direction."

"He's turning," she said. "Isn't that a residential area?"

"It is. He's stopping, can we zoom in right there?" Kwan said.

"It's Toh Avenue. It looks like he's parked in front of that house. The lot is huge, it must sit on an entire acre."

"I've been in that neighborhood, Hazlina. Most of the homes are on an acre or more."

The dot remained stationary until 11:40 and then began to move, following the same course but in reverse and headed toward the golf course.

"He's passing the airport, now he's turning off the road. Where is he going? There's no street there," Hazlina said.

"Can you switch to a satellite view?"

The image changed and the golf course was clearly visible. Goh's car was on a cart path heading toward the clubhouse.

"It's going to stop there," Kwan said, pointing to the southwest corner of the clubhouse. "That's the dumpster right there. We have him, Hazlina."

Kwan imagined the man backing up, lifting young Gemma out of his trunk and dropping her inside. The thought turned his stomach.

"I want him in handcuffs before dark," he said staring at Goh's dot on the map. The program showed Goh arriving at the station on time this morning, and then leaving immediately and was now driving southeast on the West Coast Highway.

"Do we have enough for an arrest, Kim? You know more about this case than I do. But I know you have an anonymous witness with some serious moral issues who can put him at the scene of that house and at the dumpster. This recording may not be enough for an arrest warrant, but I'm sure it's enough to bring him in for questioning."

"You may be right, Hazlina. We should talk to the DA, but right now we have enough for a search warrant. We need to work fast. It's been almost eighteen hours since she was killed and the way he left the station this morning, he probably knows we'll be coming for him. We can let the prosecutors argue if he killed her, or if he just disposed of the body. Hazlina, I'm hoping Goh will talk once he sees what we have."

"Good point, let's get the DA on the phone and discuss our next steps. I can't wait to hear you explain your mystery woman," she said with a laugh.

***

At midnight, Kwan, his entire team, and the department's Special Tactics and Rescue unit began assembling at the station with a search warrant for Sergeant Goh's home and car. A second team was standing by for a simultaneous search of the house on Toh Avenue where the girl was probably killed. Fearing a leak within the department's ranks, only the STAR's team leader knew where the targets were.

"We will knock and announce," the team's leader told the six men and three women dressed in full raid gear. "Our target tonight is Senior Sergeant Goh Gan Kim. Most of you will recognize him. Give him a few seconds to respond and then we force the door. He is a suspect in a homicide, and we can assume he is armed. Remember, this is a search warrant, not an arrest, but he doesn't know that. Expect him to resist, and if he does, use whatever force is necessary to subdue him. You have your assignments: Lee, you're on point with the heavy vest; Tam, you breach the door, a recon shows it swings inward; three followers next and the rest of you on perimeter. Questions?"

***

Kwan watched the entry team rap on Goh's door. Seconds later, one officer swung a weighted ram and hit the deadbolt square on the face. The door swung open, and Kwan heard the unmistakable sound of a Heckler & Koch MP5 submachine gun.

There were two quick, three-round bursts and then the radio call: "Subject down, all clear."

A cold sweat soaked Kwan's shirt. Who was down? Was it Goh? Dammit, he wanted to question the man! Goh was his path to ending this nightmare, and now if he was dead, anything he knew had died with him.

The sharp smell of cordite from the six rounds fired permeated the air as Kwan stood on the threshold of Goh's front door. Everyone was assembled in the front yard, awaiting the CSI personnel. Not only was this an officer-involved shooting, but the dead man was a member of the department.

Goh had been sitting in a chair facing the front door, wearing a bulletproof vest and armed with his service pistol, a CZ-75 9mm semi-auto. At his feet was a bottle of Jack Daniels, an American-made whiskey.

Goh had been warned, knew they were coming, and was ready to fight it out. Was it suicide by cop, or was he supposed to die tonight? Maybe somebody wanted him silenced, to take one for the team. Somehow Kwan couldn't see Goh as a loyal sacrificial pawn. More likely he would rather die than go to prison.

The techs arrived next and began processing the scene. Like peeling an onion, layer by layer, they worked their way into the room, photographing everything, measuring the distances of shell casings to the body, blood patterns, and close-ups of the gun in Goh's lap. Every angle of the shooting would be scrutinized. Kwan had seen it all too many times before.

Hours later they brought Goh out. Two officers had each fired one three-round burst, hitting Goh four times in the upper chest, once through his neck, and once in the forehead. His vest had stopped four of the 9mm jacketed hollow points, but the other two found their mark. Two fatal hits in two seconds.

Kwan looked down at the body in disgust. If the man had ever been a valiant member of the force, any good he had done would never be remembered. He had broken his oath and tainted his badge.

The shooting of anyone by the STAR team meant there would be headlines in the paper tomorrow. The fact that a member of the department was killed would send the internet into a frenzy, and every politician in the city would be giving statements by dawn.

"So much for our interview," Hazlina said, standing behind him. "He's taking all his secrets to the grave."

"Yes," Kwan said, "but at least we still have Casmir."

"Did I tell you that I think it was Casmir who saved Goh years ago? Goh was his nephew and should have been fired but somehow kept his job. Casmir doesn't have that kind of power anymore, but you shouldn't underestimate him."

Kwan imagined another STAR team entry, and standing over Casmir's dead body, or an armed standoff. "I want him alive, let's call him, see if he'll come in and give a statement."

"Good luck with that. He has a grudge with half the department, me included," Hazlina said.

"With you, what started that?"

"When I first transferred to IA, he came in complaining that someone in the department had towed his car illegally. When I showed him a picture of his car blocking the reserved parking area at the courthouse, he stormed out. Three days later I got a notice that he was suing the department, the commissioner, and me for harassment. The suit was thrown out at its first reading, but ever since then he's let me know he hasn't forgotten me."

"I was new here when he was first elected. I don't remember any of this," Kwan said.

"He blames all of us for his loss during the last election because the union backed someone else. He thinks we stabbed him in the back, but he was always snooping around in departmental affairs. He even pushed for a Community Advisory Board to oversee the department, and he wanted to be its commissioner. I think that was the last straw."

"I've got questions for him, and I know he has the answers," Kwan said.

His phone chirped in his pocket. It was his assistant, Haron

Chin at the Toh Avenue house. Kwan had forgotten all about the team searching it.

"Chin, what have you got?"

"No suspects at the house, but we have quite a bit of evidence. We have some trace blood in one bedroom. The bedroom itself looks like something out of a pornography studio. And here's the good stuff, there are hidden cameras everywhere. There's a recording studio in a room upstairs. All of the recording devices had their hard drives removed recently, but get this—they were all backed up on a cloud storage app and we have access to it. We have it all. As sharp as they have been, Kim, this time they made a huge mistake. We have Goh on video picking up the Balakrishnan girl's body, then cleaning up the scene and it was Goh that removed the hard drives. I heard about the shooting. It's a shame we couldn't bring the bastard in."

"Yes, it is. Who else do you have, do you recognize anyone else?"

"No, sir. Several unidentified men are on video, but we should talk in person. There are dozens of encrypted files dating back to last year, hopefully the techs can open them."

"Ok, Chin, I'll be back at the station soon."

***

At 8 a.m., Kwan sat in Tanya Chua's office downtown. "This email is dated five weeks ago, Superintendent Kwan. I'm not going to give you a warrant based on an old email that you probably don't have the right to be reading. Bring Leila Moran into my office and we can discuss it. I don't like Casmir any more than you do, but I do know he isn't stupid. Without the Moran girl, he will have us all standing in front of the Chief Justice begging for our jobs."

Chua was the senior prosecutor and had been assigned to the missing tourist cases. She was strict but an excellent trial attorney. Kwan knew she was right.

"My advice," Chua said, "is to call him and see if he will come in for an interview. Maybe you'll get lucky and he'll confess. I doubt it but see where it leads. Oh—and after what happened with Goh—I wouldn't go to his home alone, Kim."

***

By noon, the sun was somewhere behind a bank of angry-looking clouds. Kwan was dialing Casmir's number when the first raindrops began hitting the windshield, then the wind began rocking the car as he listened to Casmir's recorded message. Even now the man sounded bitter.

"Chan Heng Casmir, this is Superintendent Kwan Kim Lai. I need to speak to you on urgent matters, please call me as soon as possible." He left the department's Special Investigation's number and ended the call.

***

Sitting at his desk, he let his eyes close for a minute and jerked himself awake as his head hit the wall behind him. Fifteen minutes had passed in what seemed like seconds. He needed to sleep.

"Chin," he yelled through his open door.

"Yes, Sir?"

"Chin, I'm falling asleep at my desk. I'm going home to catch a few hours' sleep. Tell me who's doing what."

"I have Koh and Teo at the autopsy, Chua Phung Kim is in forensics looking at Goh's home computer, and Rohan is cross-checking everything in the Tommy Fong case with what we know of Goh and Casmir. Two technicians are going over the data from the Toh house crime scene. I'm working on the after-action report that will take me the rest of the day and probably tonight."

"I'm sorry, Chin, I hate to leave you with such a mess."

"I'll be fine and tell Mei Lien I said hello."

"Will do, thank you. Call me if something big comes up."

***

Four hours later, something big did come up and Chin was on the phone.

"We have Casmir on tape," he said.

"What?" Kwan said rubbing his eyes. "With Goh?" Kwan felt like he could sleep another twenty-four hours.

"No, Kim, he's on video with what looks like a fifteen-year-old girl. We also have the Gemma Balakrishnan death. It's pretty gruesome and hard to watch."

"Who did it, Chin? Tell me it wasn't Goh."

"No, not Goh, some unknown guy. We have probably thirty different video files so far with multiple victims and subjects. We're trying to identify them now."

"I'll be right in. Oh, I left a message for Casmir to call, has he?"

"Casmir? No sir, not a word," Chin said.

***

Tanya Chua, the senior prosecutor, Kwan, and Chin watched Casmir on video with a barely adolescent girl. Both were nude and Casmir was clearly having sex with the girl, a girl Kwan thought might be one of his earliest victims.

"Chin, does she look familiar?" Kwan said.

"Yes, I thought so too," Chin said. "Here are the three victims we think look like the one with Casmir."

"Yes, I think it's one of these two sisters," Kwan said. "Both were taken from the Expo MRT station. They were seen getting off the train but never made it to their hotel."

"As hard as this is to watch, the next one is worse," Chin said. "This is Gemma Balakrishnan and an unknown white male. He looks like he's in his sixties or seventies, Caucasian, but nothing else to help identify him. After almost an hour of some strange foreplay, she resists and he beats her pretty bad."

Kwan and Tanya had a hard time watching Gemma after seeing her lifeless body mixed in with garbage just hours ago. Kwan watched the man slap her several times in the face and then punch her in the abdomen. None of the blows would have been fatal. Painful probably, but they weren't the killing blows.

The old man dressed himself, as Gemma crawled to the far side of the room. He was yelling at her, and Gemma sat with her knees up, rocking back and forth. There was no audio, but Kwan knew she was sobbing.

As the old man walked out of the room, someone threw a black dress on the bed. It was quick, but Kwan saw a man's right hand.

"You see that, Chin? Back that up and slow it down."

In slow motion, they watched a man's right hand clutching the black dress. There were three gold rings, one on each of the fingers except the thumb and pinky.

"That might be the man in charge. If those stones are diamonds, those rings could be worth a year's pay," Kwan said.

"Maybe two years' on a prosecutor's salary," Tanya said.

"Are you ready to see this?" Chin asked.

"Do it."

Chin moused over to the next file, and Kwan saw Gemma in a different room. She was kneeling, with her back to the camera and wearing the black dress. The old man walked into the frame, nodded to someone behind him, and wrapped a red-and-white braided rope around her neck. Gemma panicked and tried to stand and pull away from him, but the man pulled her back with the rope. She was clearly panicking. Her fingers were clawing at the rope as she kicked at the man behind her. For a second Kwan thought the old man was going to lose control of her, then Gemma's legs gave out and she collapsed.

Now another man came into view, facing away from the camera. From what Kwan could see of his face, he appeared to be an Asian, and much younger and in better physical shape than the older man. This was the man with the rings, huge rings on each of his fingers. He put his fingers on Gemma's throat and shook his head, then lifted her off the floor with the rope. Gemma hung like that, dangling like a rag doll, until the man let go of one end.

"She's dead!" Kwan whispered.

"Look at his other hand, the left one," Tanya said. "Those rings are very unique."

"Chin, see if you can get both men's faces enhanced, run them through facial recognition, and see what they can do with those rings, maybe we can ID both of them. Tanya, I think we have enough now to get a warrant for Casmir. He knows who that guy is. Let's bring him in."

CHAPTER 33

LEANN

LeAnn watched the white-suited crime scene technicians from the hilltop above Toh Avenue. One after another, the techs loaded evidence bags and computer towers into their van. What she wouldn't give to see what was on those computers.

It was late in the afternoon now and her stomach growled. She had been parked at the liquor store since seven watching the procession of marked police cars, vans, and television news trucks coming and going. This was a big deal to someone, but it did nothing to ease her anger. There was a chance that the Clean Man would be picked up by the police, or he would flee the country and getting to him would be impossible.

The FBI had captured her brother, and she'd been able to kill him anyway. She would find a way, she always did. Ramzi had been careless and made mistakes, and here she was sitting several hundred yards away from a dozen police officers, spying on them through binoculars in broad daylight.

Am I still focused, or am I making mistakes now too?

She put the binoculars down and drove out of the lot and away from the house. There was nothing more she could learn here. She was no closer to finding the laoban. LeAnn laughed, remembering how Jie had said that word, like the man was a messiah or something. "He's just a man, Jie."

The girl she had hoped to save was probably the same one the cop had dropped into the dumpster, like Brianne, she had served her purpose and had to be disposed of. Like garbage! That cop was dead now. She had watched them bring his body out of the house on the news. He would not be sitting in a prison, eating for free, watching TV, and sleeping comfortably. Kwan had saved her the trouble of killing him.

She drove through the light afternoon traffic, trying to come up with a new plan. She'd been close twice now, and both times the Clean Man, one step ahead of her, had vanished. He had probably already relocated, drugging new girls in another shithole warehouse.

So where is he? Where would I be? I would need to replace the house, someplace nice, but secluded. I would want my perverted clients to feel safe and secure as they enjoyed their night of ecstasy with a child. He would also need another rundown warehouse, and there were plenty of those. Real estate!

***

At the condo she logged on to her laptop and left The Wife an update.

The cop is dead, another girl is dead, that house on Toh Avenue was the guy's love shack, the police are all over it. I have to find another way to get to the boss. Can you check the catering company listed as owning the house on Toh? See what else they own.

She waited for thirty seconds, staring at the screen, watching the curser blink, thinking the woman would magically answer her.

She tried calling Kwan, but it went to his voice mail, so she called the police station.

In her best Mandarin, she said, "I want to speak to Superintendent Kwan Kim. This is Leila Moran, he is expecting my call."

There was some background noise and then silence as the employee muted the call. Seconds later a man speaking English came on the line.

"This is Senior Sergeant Razak, will you hold while I try and find Superintendent Kwan? He is on the road at the moment."

"Just tell him I called. Call him on the radio if you have to and tell him I will call him in thirty minutes and he better answer."

She hung up the phone, took it apart, got into her car and drove down the street to the park. Sitting in the shade of a Rain Tree, she waited until the thirty minutes had passed and put her phone back together.

She was dialing Kwan's number when the phone rang.

"Is this Kwan?"

"Yes, it is. Is your real name Leila Moran?"

"For now it is, Kwan. Good work on killing the detective, he deserved worse."

"What's worse than death?" he said.

She thought about it and answered, "Suffering."

"Ms. Moran," Kwan said. "Don't ever go near my home again and stay away from my wife. You may think you were trying to help me, but that crosses the line. I want you to be clear on that."

"I hear you. You speak English very well, Kwan."

"I would say that I want to speak face-to-face, but let's be honest, I'd have to arrest you. Whatever suffering you're experiencing, you can't kill everyone who has done you wrong."

"Can't I?"

She waited for him to answer: ten seconds, then twenty.

"Are you tracking my signal, Kwan?"

"Yes, I am, Leila."

"Well, at least you're honest."

She ended the call and disassembled the phone, throwing the pieces in different trash cans as she walked back to her Volkswagen.

CHAPTER 34

KWAN

Kwan stared at the phone, wanting to call her back. He would wait her out instead, she would call again soon.

He sat in the passenger seat of Haron Chin's unmarked car as his assistant raced to the south side of town to track down Casmir. "I have to find this Moran girl, Chin. She is so frustrating—a loose cannon and a killer that could ruin our investigation. Sixteen girls still missing," he said, "and how many more of them are going to die?"

Chin stopped three houses from Casmir's home, waiting for the marked patrol cars to arrive. The house was a single-family, wood-framed home built after the end of World War II in one of the better sections on this side of Singapore.

Casmir was an unemployed or retired businessman, depending on who you asked. He had been a powerful and popular man in his community at one time and easily won an election when he ran for an open seat in Parliament. But controversy had dogged him for years. Rumors of corruption and influence peddling finally caught up to him and the voters turned on him. Now he blamed the People's Action Party, the Prime Minister, and the media for his defeat.

Kwan watched the two white-and-blue Fast Response cars park in the swale in front of Casmir's house. "Let's go," he said, and both men approached the front door.

"Do you smell that, Chin?"

Kwan turned his face into the wind, "It's gone now."

"No, what was it?"

"Maybe nothing, I just hope we're not too late,"

"Ugh, I smell it now," Chin said.

Kwan pointed to the flies buzzing around the windows. "I'm afraid we are too late."

With a gloved hand, Kwan twisted the doorknob, and the door opened easily, swinging inward. The full force of human decomposition hit them simultaneously, and one of the two patrol officers gagged.

"I knew it," Kwan said.

Hanging from a roof truss, Casmir's body had already begun to decompose. The skin around his bare feet looked black and mottled, and his neck was too long for his body as his own weight had stretched the vertebrae a few extra inches. The only sound in the house was the buzzing of flies.

Both men looked at Casmir and then at the red and white braided rope.

"Recognize that rope, Chin. I'm sure it will match the ligature marks on Gemma's throat."

"I'm thinking two days, maybe three. I'll bet this happened right after she died," Haran said.

"At least two, definitely before Goh died. Maybe he was involved in this too."

"You thinking it's not suicide?" Haron asked. "The knot looks legit. Maybe guilt got the better of him. He tied the rope across the beam, stood on that trash can, and then kicked the can away. Pretty standard suicide."

Kwan walked toward a dining table where a single sheet of paper lay face up.

原諒我

Kwan read it aloud. "'Forgive me,' it says. Why would he use a printer instead of handwriting? Every suicide note I've ever seen was handwritten. This is too cold, and yet he's asking for forgiveness. This, and the matching rope? I'm not buying a suicide, Chin."

"I agree, and from what I've heard about Casmir, he's not one to apologize for anything."

"Chin, let's wait outside and let forensics do their thing before we look any further."

"Wait, look at this fingernail," Haron said. "It's broken and the break looks fresh and there's something under this nail that looks like flesh."

"Damn if it doesn't, "Kwan said. "Casmir put up a fight, but there's no sign of a struggle here. The house is clean, too clean, like the housekeeper just left. Let's assume this is a homicide till we know different. Remind me to check with the medical examiner and see if Goh has any similar scratch marks."

"You don't think the Moran girl did this?" Haron said.

"I thought of that too, but it doesn't feel like her style. She would want us to know she did it, she would want me to know what Casmir was. This looks too clean, too neat, and probably painless. Every one of her victims so far was brutally killed. That's her message to us, and maybe to the rest of this gang too. Heaven help them."

"I like her," Haron said.

"I'm trying not to, Chin. But I want to see these bastards in court and behind bars, not in the morgue."

"Me too, but I still like her."

"I need some fresh air," Kwan said, as Chin's phone chirped.

The air outside seemed sweeter than he could ever remember. Casmir had been dead for two days, maybe even three. It had been hot, and the heat would have sped up the decomposition, but it was still close to the time Gemma had probably died. Goh could have killed him, maybe somebody thought he would be a liability, or Casmir was simply consumed by guilt. But then there was the skin under the broken nail. Too many possibilities, too many unknowns, Kwan thought.

"Okay, thank you," Chin said and ended his call. "I have more bad news, patrol is reporting there is another abduction victim— two, actually. Two fifteen-year-old girls went shopping yesterday and haven't been heard from since. Their mothers thought the girls were at a sleepover and are just now reporting it."

"Tell them we'll be on our way once we're done here and send anyone who's free to interview the mothers. Have them start checking surveillance footage where they were last seen." Kwan sighed and shook his head. "Chin, this doesn't make any sense. Things must seem like they're falling apart for these guys, and yet they're still picking up new girls. It's insane."

Chin's phone rang again, and this time he had good news.

"One subject in the videos from the Toh house has been identified. Chua is going to text me the name and last known address."

"Excellent! No bullshit with warrants this time. Let's go get him as soon as the technicians get here."

***

The man was forty-two-year-old Yusof Menon, an assistant principal at a Malaysian primary school in Clementi, northeast of downtown Singapore. They found him in his office, feet up on his desk and reading a newspaper.

"Mr. Menon, I'm Superintendent Kwan and this is my assistant Haron Chin. We need a moment of your time."

"What is the meaning of this? Do you have an appointment? This is my free time, and I don't like being disturbed."

"I understand, but I need you to come with us. You can walk out of this office with us, or I can handcuff you and drag you out in front of your coworkers. What will it be?"

"I have no intentions of going anywhere with you, sir. I have important work here, and I am an important man. You can make an appointment with my clerk outside."

"Show him, Chin," Kwan said.

Chin found the file on his phone and showed Menon a three-second clip of himself nude at the Toh house. Menon's face paled, and it seemed he might faint and fall out of his chair.

"I, I . . ." was all the man could say, and Kwan lifted him out of his chair and pulled him toward the door.

"Handcuffs or no handcuffs, Mr. Menon."

"I can walk. I do want to call my lawyer, though."

"Chin, I want to seize the computer in his office, start a warrant for his house as well. Mr. Menon, we will discuss your call to a lawyer once we get to the station."

***

Menon sat quietly in the back seat for the forty-minute ride to the station, gazing out the window with a blank look on his face. The man's life as he knew it was over. A school administrator, a pedophile, raping a child no older than one of his students.

"Are you married, Mr. Menon?" Kwan said.

"Yes, I am. I don't want my wife to know about this."

"That will depend on how thoroughly you cooperate, and what you can tell us."

By the time they reached the elevators, Menon had lost all his swagger and looked like a beaten man. Shoulders slumped, he kept his eyes on the ground and refused to make eye contact with the inspectors and civilians they passed in the hallway.

Kwan sat him alone in the interview room and watched him through the mirrored glass for fifteen minutes. Thirty minutes was enough time to break most men, but not this one. Menon stood and paced back and forth within the small room, adjusting his tie, checking his reflection. The man was ready now.

Chin set a laptop in front of Menon and started the full video. Kwan watched the man's eyes focus on the screen for the first minute as he undressed, then Michelle Chong, a fourteen-year-old girl abducted eight months ago, sat next to him. Menon looked away.

"Let's talk about this, shall we? Or do you want your attorney to come in? We can call him, but of course, he will want to watch the video first. I'm not going to promise you he won't see it eventually; in fact, he probably will, but a lot depends on your cooperation. Do you understand?"

"Yes."

"I'm going to tape this interview, Mr. Menon. Now tell me, how is it that you came to meet this girl?"

Kwan wanted Menon to think they knew everything, when in fact all they knew was the girl's name, her age, and when she went missing.

"I met her through a dating app. I paid a man to have sex with her. He told me she was twenty-one."

"Look at her," Kwan said slamming his palm on the table. "She has braces on her teeth, does she look twenty-one to you? Do you think a jury will think so? Now stop with the bullshit."

Menon was in complete distress now, his eyes red and watering, his lip quivering. One more push, Kwan thought. "This could be on the evening news, and something like this could go worldwide. CNN has been asking questions about these girls, Yusof, which makes me worry about how well you'll survive the night in a cell."

"I . . . I . . .," Menon stopped trying to speak, looked at the floor and started wringing his hands, then looked up at Kwan and said, "A friend told me about a website with lots of beautiful girls I should look at, and I did. Then I got a message from someone asking if I wanted to see more, and if I wanted to meet any of the girls."

"Who was this friend?"

"I don't know his name."

"How can you call him a friend and not know his name?"

"We don't use our real names."

"Tell me about this website because something is smelling like bullshit again, Mr. Menon. Maybe your wife can help us figure it out."

Menon jerked up out of his seat like he had been hit by lightning.

"No, no! It was a site I found by accident once, just a bunch of guys looking at pictures of young girls. We trade pictures and talk about things."

"You were on a child pornography site, is that right?" Chin asked.

Menon didn't answer for a minute. His lip was still quivering and sweat began staining the collar of his shirt.

"Was it child pornography?" Kwan repeated. Kwan could feel his anger rising as he thought of Mei Lien sitting at home, eight months pregnant with their baby girl.

"Yes," Menon whispered.

"I couldn't hear you, what was that?" Chin said.

Menon turned and looked at Chin, then back at Kwan.

"Yes," Menon shouted, "Yes, it was child pornography!"

"Now we're getting somewhere, Yusof," Kwan said using the man's first name. He was ready to tell them everything. "I have inspectors picking up your home computer. If your wife is at home, she is probably not having a good day, if you know what I mean."

"She moved out months ago."

"Is that when this started, Mr. Menon, searching the internet for underage girls?" Chin asked.

"No, it was before that, she knew. She saw one of the pictures."

"Let's change the subject," Kwan said. "How did you come across this girl?"

"I got a private message one night asking if I wanted one of the girls I was looking at. At first I said no, but a few minutes later, I got another message. It was a video file from one of the girls, a private one. She knew my name, not my real name, but the name I was using. She was very . . . suggestive, and I agreed to meet with her."

"And you did? Was that when you went to the house on Toh Avenue?" Kwan asked.

"No, I never knew where the house was. I had to meet with a guy first. We met at the Tampines Mall. He asked me a lot of questions, and I thought he was a cop so I didn't want to answer at first. But then he said, if he was a cop, I would already be under arrest. Then he gave me a list of instructions. The fee would be $500 Singapore dollars for one night. I was to send a Visa gift card to an address and then they would be in touch with me once it was received."

"What did this man look like?"

"He never got out of his car, so I couldn't see his body. His face looked thin and he had an odd nose. He was about forty. Malaysian, I think, but spoke in Mandarin. He had a small scar on the left side of his face, on his temple."

Kwan opened a file and pulled out a stack of pictures, ten 3x5 color photos, including Goh's departmental ID, Tommy Fong's driver's license, and photos of Jie and Khoo lying in the morgue.

"Do you see the man you met in these pictures

Menon pointed at Fong's picture. "That's him. I recognize his nose."

"And what happened next?" Kwan asked.

"Four or five nights later, I got another private message telling me everything had been approved, and did I want the same girl I had seen, or would I like to look at others. I said, sure, let me see the rest. They showed me photos of six girls, and I chose the one you saw me with, Lei Lei."

"She told you her name was Lei Lei?"

"No, I never spoke to her. It was all text messaging."

"So, go on, Mr. Menon, tell us what happened next."

"On a Friday night, I think it was five months ago, I met the same man at the mall. Lei Lei was in the car with him, she smiled and said hello to me, very beautiful. The man said I had to ride with them to a house twenty minutes away. He put a cloth sack over my head, saying the house where we were going needed to remain a secret. I was scared to death, but I was . . . you know, excited too.

"So, we end up at a house near the airport. I heard planes taking off and could see them once they took the sack off, and then we went inside. He gave me a number to call when I was ready to leave."

"And?" Kwan asked.

"You know, what's on the tape. That's it."

"Tell me about Lei Lei."

"She was quiet, and a little clumsy. I think she was high on something because when she spoke, she slurred her words. She didn't want to talk much."

"And is this when you asked her how old she was?"

Menon looked at the desk and then at the ceiling. "No, I never asked."

"Okay, Mr. Menon, we saw what happens on the tape. Tell us what happens next."

"I was a little disappointed. She seemed willing at first, but then, I could tell she didn't want to be with me, her eyes told me that. So I called the number, and the same man picked me up and left the girl there. He put the sack back on my head and drove me to the mall."

"Do you admit having sex with Lei Lei?"

"Yes, you know I did. It's right there on the video, but just one time."

"Just one time. Is that because you are a man of honor?" Kwan said.

Menon didn't answer. He put his forehead on the table, moaning something Kwan couldn't understand.

"So, is that the end of the story?" Kwan said.

Menon didn't move, then exhaled and sat up staring at the wall behind Kwan.

"No, I saw another girl two weeks later."

Kwan handed Menon a dozen photographs taken off the videos and asked him to look through them. "Which one?"

"I don't see her here."

"Any name?"

"No, I didn't ask this time. I didn't want to know."

"And then the guy took you back to the mall. Anything else, did you see any other girls?"

"No, I stopped going on the website. I got a few more private messages from different girls, but I never opened them. You will probably see them on my computer."

"So that's it, you had sex with just these two girls and paid $500 each time with gift cards."

"No, the second time I had to pay twice that, $1,000."

"That's an expensive night for an assistant principal at a primary school, Mr. Menon, an expensive night for anyone," Kwan said.

"That's not all of it, sir."

"Oh God, now what?" Chin said.

"Two months ago, the man in that picture, the one that picked me up at the mall, came to see me at the school, just walked right in like you did. He sat down and showed me the same video you have. I guess they have a hidden camera. I remember looking for one, but I didn't see anything. Anyway, he said that he was sorry that I was no longer interested in doing business with him, but he would need $1,000 a month to ensure that the video remained private."

"So, you've been paying him $1,000 a month ever since?"

"Yes."

"Do you remember the address you sent these cards to?"

"I do. I keep meticulous records, Director Kwan, but the address isn't always the same."

Kwan could see a little of the man's bravado returning once the topic of underage girls was behind him.

"I need those addresses," Kwan said.

Menon looked through his wallet and handed a piece of paper to Kwan. "This last one is where I'm supposed to send the next payment."

Kwan looked at the addresses and saw one of them was the warehouse by the docks, where Jie and Khoo had been killed.

"Mr. Menon, do you recognize any of these other men?"

Menon looked through the ten photos, then pushed Goh's picture toward Kwan. "This one looks familiar. I'm pretty sure I've seen him, but I'm not sure where."

"Okay, Mr. Menon, if there's anything you want to add or say, now is a good time."

"No, I think I've said enough."

"Chin, get one of the guys to do a drive-by at this last address. Just a look and let me know what it is."

Kwan handed Menon a legal pad and a pen. "Mr. Menon, we have our conversation with you recorded, but I want you to write it all down, and anything else you might remember while my assistant and I discuss your case with the state's prosecutor."

As the door closed, Kwan said, "We're getting close now, Chin. Can you feel it?"

CHAPTER 35

LeAnn

The end of June brought the heat, the humidity, and the bugs to the city of Singapore. LeAnn sat on a bench in Labrador Park enjoying the sun on her face and watching ships of all sizes pass in front of her. Big cruise ships that looked like floating hotels, oil tankers and freighters with hundreds of brightly colored containers on their decks, all heading out to sea.

Today was her birthday, the 30th of June, not that she celebrated being a year older, she seldom celebrated anything. The closest she ever felt like celebrating was when something troubling her, some pressing issue that consumed her every thought, passed. That was the essence of her obsessive-compulsive disorder. A task not finished, a loose thread on her shirt, even something as simple as reading a book: once she read the first page, she had to read the entire thing, no matter how badly it was written, she suffered through it until she reached the last page.

In adolescence, the obsessions turned dark. She killed a man in Manila when he whistled at her. Just a vagrant on a park bench, not unlike the one she was sitting on right now. She could have ignored him, and she did try, but that simple whistle had blinded her with a rage that never waned.

The man haunted her in her dreams; she couldn't eat and couldn't sleep. Seven days later she stabbed him as he slept on that same bench. And then she was free. The relief was intoxicating.

She told Ramzi the story that night, and he laughed so hard she wanted to kill him too. She looked at her hands now in the sunlight, remembering that vagrant's blood under her nails, feeling the filth and germs seeping into her skin. She wanted to wash them right now, but there were no bathrooms anywhere. The only water was the brackish bay water right in front of her.

Using a new burner phone, she called Kwan, wanting him to answer, but something in the back of her mind hoped he didn't.

"Kwan," he said.

Just a single word, she had hoped for something more professional, or maybe more intimate.

"What was her name?" she asked.

"Is this Leila Moran?"

"You know it is. I need to know her name, Kwan!"

"Gemma Balakrishnan."

"Gemma," she whispered, and saying her name was painful. Was this the girl she'd seen through the window?

"Tell me, Kwan, did she have black polish on her toes?"

"Yes, she did. How do you know that?"

"I saw her. I could have saved her," she said, feeling hot tears run down her cheek. "I could have saved her, Kwan," she repeated.

Bawling like a child, she dropped the phone in the dirt at her feet. She had gone after Tommy Fong and left Gemma to die. The tears burned her eyes, her chest heaved as she sobbed, causing her ribs to cry out in pain. The image of that young girl lying strapped down was going to haunt her for years, maybe for the rest of her life.

Kwan was still talking; his voice was garbled, but she could tell he was shouting at her. She picked the phone up and brushed the dirt off the screen. She couldn't answer him yet, she couldn't think.

Grief. She had no time to grieve for a girl she didn't know. She pictured the Clean Man's face right in front of her, peering down at her, those big teeth, his hand on her thigh, and she let her hatred take control.

"Stop yelling at me, Kwan!"

"Tell me what you know, dammit," he screamed. "There are sixteen more girls out there, and each one of them is important to me."

She listened to the background noise on his phone, the sound of a horn honking, a distant siren, he was driving. She waited, wondering if he was trying to trace her phone again. He would probably need access to cell tower information, which he couldn't get behind the wheel.

"You killed three of the people who would have helped me recover those girls, Ms. Moran."

"Kwan," she whispered, "call me LeAnn. Have you made any progress, any arrests?"

Kwan was silent. The background noise had changed; the rustling sound of wind told her he had stopped somewhere.

"Okay, LeAnn, yes, I have made one arrest. But the people I really need to talk to keep dying. The police officer you identified is dead, and now a politician is dead too, suicide, maybe, but I don't think so. It wasn't you, was it?"

"No, the last man on my list is the boss, the Clean Man."

"The Clean Man?"

"That's what I call him. He's the boss. Jie and Khoo called him the Laoban. Do you know what that means, Kwan?"

"Yes, I do, everyone answers to him. It's an old expression for a shopkeeper, but used as you did, it means he is the only boss. Why do you want him? Are you going after him like you did Fong?"

"Fong, that bastard! I called Fong the Driver until I knew his real name. But it's the Clean Man I want now. I have to find him——before you do, of course."

"Why, LeAnn?"

"He touched me, Kwan—they all did. Jie and Khoo raped me. Can you imagine that?"

"No, I can't."

"That's a good answer, any other answer and I would have ended this call."

"LeAnn, is there anything you can tell me, anything else that can help me find these girls?"

"They may be dead already. You saw what they did to Brianne. I think once they've served his purpose, he gets rid of them. I heard him say something like that when I was there."

"If you saw Brianne," Kwan said, "then you know why I want to find the other girls. Help me, LeAnn."

"Brianne was a beautiful girl, Kwan, and I watched them turn her into a heroin addict. Then that day, the day I got away, I saw her in the back of the van. They got me addicted too, and I know I could have easily been the dead one, so don't think I'm naive or that you can talk me out of killing that bastard."

"You can't just murder people," Kwan said.

"You don't know anything about me, Kwan. You want my help? Let me tell you, I saw Gemma alive at that warehouse. The one with the sewing machine painted above the door. It was late, maybe midnight, and there was a young guy watching her. He was in his early twenties, real thin with long, straight black hair. That's all I could see. The next night there was a different guy; they look similar, like they might be related. One of them drives an old motor scooter. I don't know how the other one gets there. There was another guy too; he was older, short, and stocky. He picked up a girl from that place, she was young, and I think it may have been Gemma, and he drove a van just like Fong's, only older.

"That's how I found Fong. I followed him to that warehouse and then followed him home. I was going to try and get Gemma out of there that night, but I wanted Fong. I wanted him so bad that I left Gemma there. Fong broke my ribs, and I couldn't go back and get her. I think the Clean Man took her away right after that. I watched you at the warehouse, Kwan. I wanted to see you bring her out alive, and now she's dead."

Kwan was silent, she could hear him breathing heavily.

"I'm sorry," she said.

"You could have called the station."

"I know, but I didn't trust you or anyone else. That's why I came to your house. I needed to see how you live. That helps me decide sometimes—whether I should kill somebody or trust them. It's a fine line for me. I don't expect you to understand that. It was watching you sleeping next to your wife—that's what I needed to see, and I knew you were okay."

"Don't ever do that again, my wife still can't sleep."

"I told you I won't," she said, pausing. "Today is my birthday, by the way."

"Happy birthday," he said. "We should meet, you and I."

"You're a good man, Kwan, and from what I hear, a good cop––you would have to arrest me. I have to go now. I have work to do," she said, ending the call.

She took the phone apart, assembled another one, and dialed her sister's number, listening to the strange pops and clicks of an international call.

"Happy birthday," Araya said.

"Thank you, I needed to hear a familiar voice."

"What's wrong? Are you okay? Are you hurt?"

"No, I'm okay. I'm not doing heroin if that's what you meant, and I've gained most of my weight back.

"That's great, I haven't stopped worrying about you. How are you feeling? It's been a month now, any more withdrawal symptoms?"

"I'm okay, really. There's just been some complications with, you know, taking care of things."

"I'm afraid to ask. What about that guy in the van?"

"He is no longer an issue. Araya, they killed another girl. I saw her, and I could have helped her, but I went after the driver instead, and now she's dead. I feel responsible. I know it was my fault."

"LeAnn, please get out of there. Come stay with me right now. You don't need to do any of this."

"I wish I could, Araya, but I have one more loose end to tie up first. I have to finish this for that girl's sake, if not for mine."

"You need justice, LeAnn. Go to the police, let them put that man in prison. I want my little sister here with me, safe and sound."

"It's too late for that now. I would be the one in prison. I'll call you again when I'm heading home."

LeAnn ended the call. Another cruise ship was in the channel, close enough that people on deck were waving to those on shore, so close the acrid smell of its exhaust drifted towards her in the breeze.

The open sea stretched out to the horizon where a storm was building, and lightning flashed. She waited, hoping to hear the thunder, but it was too far away. Tonight, maybe it would rain. The sound of a storm, rain on a metal roof always soothed her. At the moment though, she felt drained. It was Gemma. She had never experienced grief, like an emptiness in her gut, a void she would never fill. She was grieving for a girl she never met.

***

A new email was waiting for her when she got back to the condo.

I have a few new leads. I saw some bits and pieces of new conversations in the Blue Room. There was something about Gemma. I'm guessing she is one of the girls. The boss mentioned finding a replacement for the dead cop. He also sent an email to a new player (no name yet) saying that he is worried about a politician and wants "that mess cleaned up."

The big guy in Maryland, the government guy, has some serious protection. I baited him with an attempt on his server and a half dozen agent-looking people showed up outside the café I was using. That guy has vanished from the site though, nothing from him since then.

I have a new address for you—he asked that new player to take care of the pickups at this address: 230C Pandan Loop. I don't know what is being picked up or who the person doing the pickup is yet. Working on that—ciao.

"Gemma is dead," LeAnn replied. "Yes, the cop and the politician are dead too. I'll check that address. Did you look to see what other real estate the catering company owns? TTYL."

***

Pandan Loop sounded familiar, and as her VW exited the Ayer Rajah Expressway, the hair on the back of her neck rose and bile churned in her stomach. She was heading toward her nightmare, now passing the little café where she had sat on a bench watching the police arrive so long ago.

An unmarked police car was parked at the end of the street, the man and woman sitting inside stared at her. She waved at them, hoping it looked casual. The woman waved back and looked away. She kept driving; 230C was three doors down from 230A, where she had killed Jie and Khoo. She turned another corner and parked two streets away.

The Wife was right about something happening here. The good news was she had another breadcrumb on the Clean Man's trail, the bad news was she had no clue what it was, and worse, the police were here first.

From behind her, the drone of a small engine grew louder. It sounded like a lawnmower or a chainsaw. In her side mirror, a red motor scooter was driving toward her, its engine belching smoke and sputtering. The rider wore a faded red helmet, and his long black hair was whipping around behind it.

Two weeks ago, that scooter was parked at the sewing machine warehouse, and the rider with the red helmet was inside with Gemma. It turned the corner on Pandan Loop, and she lost sight of it.

Any second now, the scooter would pass the police car. If he saw it first, he would keep going and exit on the far side of Pandan Loop. If he didn't see it and stopped in front of 230C, they would grab him and she would learn nothing.

Starting the VW, she made a U-turn and raced to the other end of Pandan Loop, hoping to see the scooter come out without a police car behind it. She parked in a crowded lot in the middle of a dozen cars and waited.

With her window down, she heard the engine first, its rhythm slow and steady. Then it passed her. She waited and watched to see if the police car was following it, then accelerated until it was in front of her.

The scooter was too slow to follow, twice she had to pull off the road and let the bike get far enough ahead of her that the driver wouldn't see her in his mirror. The third time, she lost sight of it. The scooter was gone.

Turning the car off, she stood outside and listened. The rattling sound was on the next block over, still moving slowly but steadily away from her. She hit the gas and made two quick turns just as the red bike turned into a garage. With her Nikon binoculars, she recognized the man as one of the two watching Gemma. He walked up a single flight of stairs, opened a door on the second level and went inside.

The lower half of the building must have been an automotive repair shop at one time. Car parts were scattered everywhere, and an old, rusted tow truck was propped up on blocks. The second level looked like an apartment; a satellite dish hung upside down next to a window, and a makeshift clothesline was strung across the columns on the porch. Three pairs of men's boxer shorts hung limp across the sagging wire.

She was in as good a spot as any and waited for nightfall. As dusk came and went, a single streetlight came to life, illuminating the bluish flicker of a television screen behind his closed curtains. She waited for two more hours.

The street was dark now. The single streetlight would flare up every two or three minutes and then wink out, making a buzzing noise that sounded like a hive of angry hornets. She waited and with its last flash, grabbed her backpack and sprinted thirty yards, then crept up the concrete stairs. In the darkness, she listened to the sound of the television and looked for any movement behind the curtains. In another minute, the light would flare again, and she decided to wait for it.

Right on time, the light flared, casting a sickly yellow aura on everything within fifty yards, then winked out. In those few seconds, she spotted the long-haired man on a couch, his eyes closed and mouth open, and two empty beer bottles sat on the table in front of him.

She turned the doorknob, slowly, feeling the bolt retracting silently and then releasing. The door swung open, and she stepped inside, listening to him snore.

It was a single room efficiency with a small bathroom just big enough for a toilet and a shower. There was no sign anyone else lived here: no girlfriend, no parents, and no friends.

She set her backpack on the floor and held the stun gun to his neck and waited for him to wake up. She had tried the gun at her apartment a few times. It made a healthy snapping sound, and a blue arc pulsed across the electrodes, but she wasn't about to try it on herself. Tonight, though, she would know how well it worked.

With Jie's knife in one hand, and the stun gun in the other, she said, "Wakey, wakey!"

His eyes opened—and she pressed the trigger. His scream was ear-piercing, a high-pitched keening, more like a small child than a grown man. She kept the pressure on the trigger. Every muscle in his body spasmed, and his forearm jerked, knocking one of the empty bottles off the table, the glass shattering on the floor. With the trigger still depressed, she counted to five, then released it.

His rigid body went limp, like a rag doll. His eyes were still open, staring vacantly at the wall behind her, but he was paralyzed. She tie-wrapped his hands and feet and bound them together with a two-foot section of rope and pushed him off the couch. Hog-tied, he hit the floor with an "oomph" as the last of the air in his lungs escaped.

With the stun gun pressed to his chest, she waited.

His eyes began to move first, then his breathing deepened. His eyes focused on the rug and the broken glass next to his face, then he turned and saw her standing over him.

"Who the fuck—"

She pulled the trigger again and counted to five.

The scream was shorter this time, but his recovery took longer. He was disoriented at first, then remembered her, hatred seething in his eyes.

"Shall I do it one more time?"

"No, no . . . what do you want?"

The anger was gone, but she could tell he wasn't ready, but she asked anyway.

"Who do you work for? What is his name?"

"You're crazy fucking . . .!"

She pressed the gun next to his right nipple and pulled the trigger. This time the gun left a burn mark on his skin.

"Did that hurt? I'm so sorry."

As he came around the third time, she held his boxer shorts up to his face. "You know what comes next, right?"

He looked down and saw the stun gun pressed to his scrotum; the pressure alone was painful. "No, no, don't do it."

"I need you to answer my question. Who is the Laoban and what is his name?"

"You're crazy . . ."

She stuffed his shorts in his mouth as a gag and then hit the trigger. The stun gun was losing power; the snapping sound was less intense, and the spasming wasn't as severe as it had been.

He was already alert and trying to talk. She put the stun gun in her backpack and took out a pair of pruning shears. "I'm going to cut off one of your fingers if you don't answer me. Nod if you're ready to talk."

His face went from bright red to crimson, and the tendons in his neck bulged as he tried to scream.

"I'll take that as a no."

It wasn't as easy as she had expected—it took both hands, but the bone snapped clean, spraying a fine mist of blood onto her face.

Jesus, she hadn't planned on blood. Blood on her skin was

something she had grown accustomed to, but she loathed the sensation.

Despite the dirty boxers stuck in his mouth, he was still able to make a lot of noise, his face was pale now, ashen, and as she watched, he lost consciousness.

Dirty dishes were piled in the sink—all of them. His cabinets were empty, as were most of the drawers. Two small roaches scurried for cover as she turned the faucet on. At least he had a bar of soap. She washed her face and hands with hot water, then looked for a clean towel. "I'm not going to use anything I find in here," she said, wiping her hands on her jeans. On a table near the front door, she found a stack of mail, all addressed to Gerard Sen.

Gerard was still unconscious, and from the kitchen she could hear him breathing. She took two bottles of Tiger beer from the almost-empty refrigerator, opened one, and took a long pull. "Not a bad beer, Gerard."

The couch looked clean enough to sit on; it was old and the fabric was worn, but it was comfortable. With her black Skechers resting on his back, she switched the channels on his TV until she found a local news program. Gerard moaned.

"Wake up, Gerard, we need to talk."

A deep groan vibrating through her shoes told her Gerard was starting to feel the pain. The groaning grew louder still, and his eyes opened. LeAnn put more pressure on his back as he tried to sit up. Then he saw the blood and began to wail, and she let him sit up.

"It hurts, doesn't it?"

His eyes darted back and forth, from her and the bloody shears, to his severed finger next to the empty beer bottle. His face had begun to color but paled again as he stared at the finger.

The man wailed, and it was surprisingly loud despite the underwear still in his mouth. She turned the television up to match the volume.

"You see this?" she said, pointing to his finger. "Yes, I'm sure it hurt, but I want you to think of poor Gemma. You remember

Gemma, don't you? I saw you through the window that night. You bound her like an animal, how much pain was she in? Do you know, do you even care?"

Gerard was silent now. Tears continued to run down his face, but he was staring at her.

"You're not going to get any sympathy from me, and I want to be honest with you—I want you to suffer the way she did. But I'm not going to kill you tonight, Gerard. You've suffered enough. I'm going to make your Laoban suffer though, and you are going to help me find him."

Picking up the shears, she wiped the blood off the blades using his thigh, then rested them on his groin.

"I want your boss to suffer, do you understand? I know my Mandarin sucks but nod yes if you do."

Another tear ran down his cheek as he nodded. He tried to say something, and LeAnn pulled the gag out of his mouth.

"If you scream, I'm going to cut your dick off, Gerard. Your name is Gerard Sen, correct?"

He nodded again.

"You can speak if you want."

"Yes . . . my name is Gerard. He will kill us all, don't you see. He will know you were here. We are already dead."

"Hush, Gerard. I'm going to ask you a couple of important questions now. He may kill us both tomorrow, but how you answer me will determine if I remove your dick tonight. Are we clear?"

"Yes. You're the Canadian woman. I speak some English."

"Great, tell me the Laoban's name."

"We never hear his name. No one is allowed to know, but one time I did overhear him on his phone, and he said his name is Soong."

"I want to find him, tell me how."

"He will kill me, and my brother too."

"He will be dead, Gerard."

"You don't know him. He will kill you and then come after me and my whole family, that is what he does."

"Why did you drive past that warehouse today? What were you going to do there, are there girls inside again?"

"No girls, just mail. I was going to get the mail from inside, but the police were watching."

"What mail? Why is the mail important?"

"It's his money. People send him Visa cards, American Express too, hundreds of them sometimes."

"Where is he right now Gerard? Don't bullshit me, you understand bullshit?"

"Yes, I understand. I don't know where he sleeps, or where he lives, but one of his offices is in Seletar, on Battersea Road. I haven't seen it, but my brother helps him there."

"Helping him with what?"

"My brother watches the girls too and does what the Laoban asks of him."

"Your brother, was he watching Gemma too?"

"Yes, he is learning."

"Gerard, you called me a bitch, and you said I was fucking crazy," she said, watching him shake his head no. "It's okay. I am a bit of a bitch, and a few of my recent friends called me a psycho. Even so, I'm going to let you live tonight, but a man I know wants to speak to you too. He's nicer than I am, and he won't remove any of your fingers, but if you don't talk to him, I will come back and remove both your hands. Do you believe me?"

He nodded.

"And Gerard, if you've lied to me, I will come for you and your family too."

She left him bleeding and hog-tied and called Kwan using his phone.

***

It was a good feeling, like progress had been made, maybe another step closer to finding the Clean Man.

In her condo, she stepped into the hot shower, wishing she

could lie in a tub full of hot water. So hot that the water would burn her skin because the pain would sterilize the filth she knew was on her flesh just from being inside Gerard's apartment, breathing his air, and having touched him.

CHAPTER 36

KWAN

As his eyes closed, he had a brief dream about soaring over acres of banana fields, the scent of fresh earth greeting his nostrils as workers armed with machetes harvested the crop below. As he drifted on the currents, his cell phone rang and, in the dream, he had no pockets. He panicked as the sail collapsed; he was free falling . . . and he woke up drenched in sweat.

"Yes," he said, answering the phone.

"Kwan, I have someone that you will want to speak with."

"Is he breathing?"

"Right now he is, but he won't be able to come to the door, if you know what I mean."

Now he heard nothing but footsteps receding and then someone whimpering.

"Mei Lien, I have to go," he said as his wife rolled over toward him.

"What is it? Who was that?"

"It was her, the girl, and I have to go."

"Please don't go alone," she said.

***

The small V6 struggled up the incline as he pressed the accelerator to the floor and then he was on the freeway. Trying to wipe two hours' worth of sleep from his eyes, he called dispatch on the cell phone and asked for two marked patrol cars to look for a mechanic's shop near the school, and to have Chin meet him there.

The shop wasn't hard to find. Flashing red-and-blue emergency lights lit up the entire block and more were still arriving. As he walked through the cluttered parking lot, paramedics arrived, adding to the crowd at the bottom of the staircase.

"Superintendent Kwan," one of the uniformed sergeants said. "We found Gerard Sen tied up upstairs. Sir, he says a woman severed his finger. We found it inside an empty beer bottle. He's in shock and barely able to speak. We brought him downstairs and the apartment has been secured."

Kwan saw the man sitting with his head between his legs as the paramedics rolled a gurney over to him.

Gerard Sen looked to be in his early twenties, skinny with long, oily black hair. Even in the poor lighting, his skin looked ashen, and the flashing lights of the police cars reflected off the sheen of his sweat. Gerard wasn't going to be able to talk to anyone for a while it seemed, and Kwan went up the steps and peered inside.

Resting in a bottle of Tiger beer was a finger, probably the end of Sen's pinky finger, submerged in an inch of red liquid. Kwan imagined the sensation of cutting someone's finger off, or having his own cut off. What he would do to be able to sit down and probe this LeAnn woman's brain. What horrors were locked up inside her?

Once Chin arrived, he let his assistant take over the scene and went home. As he parked, he hoped that he could return to his pleasant dream but knew that was not going to happen.

It was just after midnight as he walked in, and Mei Lien was at the kitchen table sipping hot tea.

"I was worried, and the baby was kicking, so I stayed up. Kim, will this woman come back, are we safe here?"

"Yes, I've talked to her on the phone several times now. She is a deranged woman, but I think she wants the same thing I do—

justice for these girls. It's just that we have a different idea of what that justice will be. Plus, we have an alarm now, so we are safe."

***

Kwan slept for another six hours and woke as the morning sun crept through his bedroom curtains. He felt rejuvenated and fresh for the first time in weeks, maybe even months. He showered and dressed and met Chin at the hospital.

Two uniformed officers sat outside the door to room 216 where Chin was waiting for Kwan. "Morning, Chin, our friend say anything last night?"

"He says he's a dead man, and he wants us to put his family in protection if we want him to talk."

"Interesting, let's see if he will reconsider."

Gerard Sen was sleeping. His color was healthier this morning, but his hair still looked like he used machine oil as a conditioner. His right hand was completely wrapped in gauze, and where the pinky finger should have been, a reddish-brown stain was seeping around the tape.

Kwan reached over and squeezed Sen's right hand, and like magic, Sen was wide-awake. Kwan suspected he had been sedated with plenty of pain killers, but he could see the grimace on the man's face.

"Good morning, Gerard, I understand you're making demands before you answer any of my questions. I spoke with LeAnn, the woman you met last night, the one who took your finger off. I can imagine that hurt, but she assured me you would be willing to talk."

"Yes, I want my mother and my brother moved somewhere safe first."

"Safe from what, from whom?" Kwan asked.

"You know who."

"I think I know enough about the Laoban already, so I'm going to release you from custody. I'm sure the Laoban has some of his own questions for you as well, and I'm sure you will want to talk to him."

"Wait, wait . . . I am a dead man if you leave. I'll bet he has people right here in this hospital that will do it."

"Who is the Laoban, Gerard?"

"I told the Canadian woman—I don't know his name, it might be Soong, but to speak his name is forbidden."

"So, you really have nothing to tell us, nothing we need to know. Why should we protect you, Gerard?"

"He killed the politician, Casmir. Casmir wanted money after helping him with a woman. There was a big argument about Gemma; Gemma is the girl I was watching. There was a lot of money, and Casmir wanted a bigger share."

"Why did the Laoban kill her? If she was worth a lot of money, he could have ransomed her."

Sen looked confused. "The Laoban didn't kill her, the American killed her."

"Are you sure, what American?"

"They called him, the Senator; he's a big shot that has been here many times."

Kwan couldn't believe what he was hearing. He remembered the old man in the video with Gemma, the man with the rope, and then the second man with the rings.

"Does the Laoban wear rings, big ones on each hand?"

"Yes."

"Chin, show him the pictures."

"Gerard, show me which man is the senator. Point him out and tell me he is the one that killed Gemma."

Gerard leafed through a dozen pictures, stopped at Goh's, and pushed them back at Kwan. "First, I was not there when it happened, but I know none of these are the man they call the senator."

"I see you know Senior Sergeant Goh though, what do you know about him?" Kwan asked.

"I don't know that name."

"This man," Chin said, pointing to Goh's picture.

"I've seen him in the car with the Laoban. But I don't know who he was."

"Chin, see how soon they can transfer him to the prison ward. I don't want to tie up two officers all day, and I don't want to hear that someone has killed our friend in his sleep. The Moran girl may still want another pound of flesh from him. I'm going back to the office. I need to look at something."

CHAPTER 37

LEANN

A message waited on her computer. *Progress report, call me.*

"I need to know your name," LeAnn said. "I have a condition where I need to know names, and I don't know what to call you."

"Drew."

"Is it night there, Drew?" she said.

"Not yet, listen," Drew said. "The Blue Room is like a ghost town; some of the small players check in, but no one is there to answer them. Some serious shit must be going on. Did you have anything to do with it? Tell me yes!"

"Maybe, I found another lowlife creep. One of his new guys, he was the one I saw watching Gemma."

"Is he dead yet?"

"No, Kwan has him now. I thought it would hurt the boss more if I kept him alive. That address you gave me was next to the warehouse that I woke up in, where I was held. Anyway, they are using it as a drop box. I think the Clean Man is running an extortion ring. Setting up important people and then blackmailing them.

"Something else though, the guy told me that an old man killed Gemma, he was an American and they called him a senator. Gemma was a politician's daughter; I think this was a snuff killing from the beginning, and I'll bet there's a video of it somewhere. I'm going to ask Kwan. I doubt he'll tell me, but I want to hear him say no."

"The Senator, holy shit!" Drew screamed. "This has to be the guy from Maryland. That's the only way this all makes sense."

"I thought so too. If he is, I want to take care of it before he disappears. Governments have a way of protecting their own. If I can find the Clean Man, maybe I can find out who he is. We can ruin the man."

"LeAnn, he killed Christopher. I don't want to just ruin him."

"Me either."

"I'll poke around for anything that looks like video files, but listen, I have two more addresses for you. I did a search on the house by the airport, that catering service is called In-Flight. It's a small-time catering service owned by a guy named James Soong. I—"

"Soong!" LeAnn cut her off. "That's the name the creep mentioned—it's got to be him."

"Well, I can't find much on him, believe me I tried, but In-Flight has a total of five other properties in Singapore and two more in Kuala Lumpur. Three of those you already know about; the other two are small warehouses. I did a satellite view, and they look similar to the one on Pandan Loop."

"Okay, send me the addresses and I'll do a drive-by first thing tomorrow."

"Kill the bastard, LeAnn."

***

She slept in, and the sun was directly over the city bathing it in summer heat. Traffic crawled along the side streets and the Volkswagen's air conditioner fought a valiant battle with the outside air.

The warehouse on Battersea Road did look like those on Pandan Loop, a long row of two or three small businesses under a single roof. There was a logo above the one farthest from the road, a profile drawing of a smiling man wearing a chef's hat above two crossed spatulas. Underneath that were several Chinese symbols, and she had no idea what they said.

There was no one around, no cars, no workers, and the road she was parked on was deserted. She drove into the lot of a business next door and parked the Volkswagen in the shade of an old tree and watched.

With her binoculars, she scanned the building looking for anything that might help her make a decision—get out and take a closer look—knock on a few doors—or simply sit and wait.

A closed dumpster sat between the two large roll-up doors; two smaller but empty garbage cans sat next to it. The two windows in front of her had newspaper plastered to the inside, so getting out to look through them would be a waste of time.

She drove out and headed across town to check the other addresses. It was an old gasoline station with the service pumps removed. Trash blew across the driveway and stuck to a chain-link fence that had been cut and repaired several times.

She parked next to the front door and looked inside. If any business had been done inside the office, it had been years ago. Everything of value had been removed, and only junk too big to carry away was left behind. She turned to leave, stopped, and walked back. Pressing her hands against the glass, she peered closely at the old metal-and-wood desk. It was a twin of the one Jie and Khoo had used every day.

"Shit," she said, closing her eyes. Fighting nausea, she tightened her stomach muscles and held her breath until it passed.

Sweat trickled down her back and the sensation of being filthy hung on her shoulders like a heavy robe. She could see Khoo sitting at that desk.

"You're a dead man Khoo, leave me alone."

***

For the second time that day, she showered in hot water until it began to cool. Even then, with her skin still red, she scrubbed her arms and legs with a coarse brush for the third and fourth time.

Lying naked on the cool tile floor had a calming effect, centering all her emotions, no clothes, no outside sensory distractions, just a cool dry surface allowing her to begin planning her next steps: What she was going to wear, what equipment she wanted to bring, and the route she was going to travel. She practiced every scenario she could imagine, down to the last-minute details.

Dressing in her black utility pants and black sleeveless T-shirt, she watched the clock and did the math in her head. She wanted to arrive as the last of the daylight lingered, giving her a daylight view before the night took it away.

At 6:45, she got into her car, and at 7:15 she turned right as she passed the Changi General Hospital and drove north on Battersea Road, parking her car under the same shade tree with the chef and his spatulas facing her.

Traffic on the road behind her was light. It was after hours, and most of the blue-collar businesses had already shut down for the day, but she made it a point to check each car as it went past her. One of them, a gray Subaru, slowed, and it looked like an unmarked police car, but the car kept moving and was out of her view before she could see the driver.

Just as dusk began to beat out the last of the sun's light, the Subaru returned and drove into the lot. Slowly, the car drove completely around the building, out of her view for a minute, and she was afraid it had stopped in the back. "What the hell is it doing back there?" she said aloud.

She was about to get out of her car and check when the car came around the corner, its headlights now casting twin beams of light in the darkness between this warehouse and the next.

At the closer side of the building, far from the grinning chef, the Subaru parked next to the front door and the driver got out. Even with the Nikon, she could only see a silhouette of the man, the light was too dim.

He put his ear to the closed glass door as if he was listening inside and then tried the doorknob. The door opened, and the silhouetted man was bathed in dim red light. He went inside, and the door closed. The front of the building was now in complete darkness.

CHAPTER 38

THE CLEAN MAN

James Soong swung his American-made Signature Series Louisville Slugger and slammed it into the drywall behind his desk, blasting a cloud of white dust into the air. It was one of his prized possessions, not that it was worth more than any other bat but for the fear it instilled in his employees. Just holding the bat while they were in the room excited him.

He had made it a point that whenever one of them needed to learn from a mistake, others were around to witness the lesson. Six of them were lined up against the wall when Brianne had to pay, and he noted each of their reactions. Those who quivered or showed weakness were moved far from his main source of income and placed in charge of the older whores that had lost their youth. Youth was where the real money was.

But now, things were falling apart.

"That fucking bitch!" he screamed as the bat cracked against the wall again, releasing another cloud of dust.

His best men were dying like flies, and Gerard was probably answering questions right now. The man didn't know much, but he probably knew enough, if he talked. Gerard had been one of the six who watched Brianne take the bat, and his knees had almost buckled as her blood flew across the room.

"Dammit!" he said, swinging the bat again, crushing a portrait of Charles "Lucky" Luciano, and sending shards of glass across the room. He had always admired the American mafia, studying men like Luciano, and he thought of the dead mobster as a role model.

The bat crushed another section of drywall, and this time a framed picture of Marlene Dietrich fell to the floor, adding more glass shards.

He was in a blind rage now, part of him knew it and fed off the destruction; the other part of him watched silently, afraid to step forward and take control.

Gemma had been his last moneymaker, one hundred thousand US dollars, paid in advance, for a single night of sex for an American senator that liked it rough, and at the last minute, another twenty-five thousand for the man's ultimate thrill—poor Gemma. But that last twenty-five thousand was probably gone, confiscated by the police just yesterday, along with how much more? The police had found the mailbox on Pandan Loop, and he had lost at least another one hundred thousand dollars.

"That bitch," he said, swinging the bat again, crushing his HP printer.

Fong and then Goh were both dead and they were irreplaceable. They had arranged and handled all the introductions, all the blackmailing and everything requiring a face-to-face contact. Who would take their place now? Simon Sen or his brother? The NG cousins? They were just out of puberty, all four of them were twits, simpletons that needed written instructions on how to change an IV.

Soong swung the bat again. His desk lamp flew across the room, shattering, and a small piece of the broken bulb ricocheted and struck him in the forehead. The wound stung, and he wiped a bead of blood on his pant leg.

Three new girls and four idiots to watch them. He looked at his watch, it was 7 p.m. and both the NG cousins were scheduled to arrive at midnight.

"Christ, Jie was a better man than any of them."

The bat flew on its own this time, slamming into the mahogany desktop, his father's desk, a beautiful thing that once belonged to the prime minister of Malaysia.

"Yes, Papa, your precious desk is ruined now."

His father had begun amassing his wealth in Kuala Lumpur, running everything from prostitution to gambling. In Soong's eyes, his father had been a small-time mobster, unable to see the big picture. And that picture included blackmail.

Introduce a wealthy old man to his darkest desires, a night of erotic sex, and then make him pay for it for the rest of his life, string him along and making twenty times what he paid for the whore in the first place.

For ten years, his perfected operation ran like a fine machine, making him a rich man, first in Kuala Lumpur, then Hong Kong and now Singapore. Then the Canadian woman, the witch, fell into his hands.

"Ten years," he screamed, slamming the bat into the desk again. This time the bat split, sending the heavy barrel flying. It punctured the drywall and hung there, like an obscene reminder of his failures.

"Oh, Leila," he screamed, "how you must pay!"

A drop of blood dripped from his forehead, down his nose, and landed on the desk. He stared blankly at the drop as the drywall dust absorbed it, then touched the cut on his forehead, and stared at the red smear on his fingertip.

"Yes, you must pay for all of this, Leila."

Who was she? There were plenty of Leila Morans, but none of them were his Leila. He had dismissed this one as an average acquisition, dull and lifeless. True, there was something in her eyes he couldn't read, something he mistook for mischief. But he had seen the photos of what she had done to Jie and Khoo.

"No, I don't think it was mischief in those eyes, little one."

He looked at the shattered bat in his hand, a foot-long piece of the handle, as if seeing it for the first time.

"I'll need a new one," he said to himself and set it gently on the desk. "And yes, yes, I must reorganize. I just need to start over, tonight, right now."

Sitting at the desk littered with white powder, wood splinters, and glass, he began writing in his journal, oblivious to all the debris in the room.

CHAPTER 39

KWAN

Somewhere, at least two more girls were being held captive, Australians this time, probably strapped down, drugged, or maybe even dying. Goh was dead. An unfortunate event, mostly because dead men can't talk, but Goh was known for being obsessive, and maybe he had left a clue.

The blue icon moved across the map on Kwan's computer. It was Goh's icon, and Kwan was watching video of Goh driving home on June twenty-fifth, and just like the day before, he drove randomly around the northeast side of the city, but both days he turned on Battersea Road. Gerard Sen mentioned a warehouse on that road, but the inspectors couldn't find anything.

Kwan restarted the program at June first. Every day, Goh ate at the Asian Café, one block east of the station at noon sharp, not ten till or ten after. At the end of his shift, he left the station at five in the afternoon and drove onto Timah Road, then the pattern became random. During the first week of June, Goh drove past the warehouse on Pandan Loop each day, until Jie and Khoo were killed. That day he drove straight home. The next week it was Yishun Avenue where Gemma had been held, and the week before Goh died, it was Battersea Road.

It was after seven and Mei Lien was having dinner with her mother and father downtown. No doubt Mei Lien was getting an earful of parenting advice from her mother.

At seven thirty, Kwan locked his office and headed downstairs, intent on driving straight home, but as he neared the Tampines, he turned right onto the entrance ramp, following Goh's last GPS route.

Let's see where you were headed, Goh.

Driving west on the expressway, he exited and drove north until he found Battersea Road, a commercial area near the Seletar airport. He slowed to a leisurely 25 kph and surveyed both sides of the road. There wasn't much to see on the left, trees mostly, but on the right were several fenced-in warehouses.

He slowed even further, rating them on how they compared to the others—the one he was looking for would need to appear vacant and unused, one with no visible security. Security would mean there was something inside that needed protecting, a fact Chin had noticed.

On his right were six large warehouses surrounded by eight-foot chain-link fences topped with razor wire. Kwan noted several panel vans backed up to the delivery doors, unloading cargo, and he ruled them all out.

Next, he came to a vacant field nearing the end of Battersea Road where two small strip warehouses stood alone. Both buildings looked like they had been shuttered for months, maybe even years, and were similar to the warehouse on Pandan Loop.

He drove on until he reached the dead end and made a U-turn, then headed back south, passing the first vacant building, and pulled into the parking area of the second. Through the front door, a dim red light flickered inside the office. He continued driving toward the rear and stopped by a dumpster.

The light was failing, and he switched on his headlights, then looked up and down the back of the building. He wanted an excuse to get out of the car, but nothing looked unusual, no alarm bells were going off in his head. Finally, he got out and opened the heavy plastic lid to the green dumpster and peered inside. It seemed empty, but it was too dark now to be sure. With his flashlight, he saw it was completely empty, not even a scrap of paper had been left behind. His inspectors had been right, there was nothing on Battersea Road.

But something on this street had drawn Goh here. He was surveilling something, but what? The thought gnawed on his consciousness. His instincts were telling him there was something here.

Back in his car he drove around to the front and stopped at the door. The dim light he had seen was from a fire exit sign on the far wall. A vinyl roller shade blocked most of his view, but the room was a mess; large holes had been punched into the walls, dozens of them, as if someone was searching behind the drywall.

Kwan reached for the door handle and instinctively pulled, and the door opened silently. Now the bells were ringing in his head. With his radio in one hand, and his flashlight in the other, he stepped inside. His gut told him to back out and radio the dispatcher, to at least tell them where he was. But he was focused on the chaos and destruction in the beam of his flashlight. He took two more steps inside and stood next to a desk. The office had been thoroughly vandalized, and recently. Dust motes floated through the bright beam of the flashlight.

Shards of glass crackled under his shoes, an old black-and-white portrait of a man hung sideways on the wall, its frame bent and the glass shattered, and the desk, which looked expensive, had been beaten and splintered.

On the far wall, something odd jutted out from the drywall. Kwan knew what it was, and walked over to get closer, his shoes still crunching on shards of glass.

It was the broken end of a baseball bat, and with his flashlight, he read the logo, Louisville Slugger. The part jutting out from the wall ended just behind the logo in jagged splinters.

Something was really wrong—the countless motes floating in his beam of light meant this damage was recent— instantly he realized he should have called it in. As he brought the radio up to his lips, steps behind him crunched the glass and something slammed into his side. His radio flew across the room, landing behind the desk. He looked at his side, where the other end of the broken bat stuck from his rib cage.

A man laughed. Kwan tried to turn around but was impaled by the splintered wood and the hand holding it. The man smiled, yanked the handle from Kwan's ribs and speared the bloody, splintered handle into his thigh.

Kwan fell backward, and from the floor, he drew his gun and fired two rounds blindly, then tried to aim at the man's silhouette and fired again. His flashlight rolled across the floor, the beam pointing uselessly at an empty wall. His attacker was bathed in dim red light, there was blood on his face, and the image reminded Kwan of a circus clown.

The man moved and Kwan fired at him two more times.

Kwan couldn't move and wondered if he was paralyzed. He knew he was in shock and was on the verge of blacking out. As his attacker crept closer, lips curling away from his giant, blinding-white teeth, cold blackness swallowed Kwan.

CHAPTER 40

LEANN

LeAnn stood in the open doorway watching the Clean Man looming over Kwan. The bastard was wearing his white suit again, but this time it wasn't so pristine. Blood dripping from his cheek and ear had stained the jacket's lapel, and more blood soaked the area around his right knee. In the red light, the blood was black.

"Well, if it isn't the Clean Man!"

The man turned and looked at her and his face went slack.

"Surprise, surprise," she said, stepping across the threshold.

Soong's mouth hung open and his skin looked gray in the red light. He was either surprised or in a lot of pain or maybe both. In her hand was Jie's pocketknife, the three-inch rusty blade extended.

"Ah, my little Canadian," he said. "Are you going to kill me with that? Are you going to try and gut me like a fish? Ha!"

Soong was holding the broken and bloody handle of a baseball bat. Behind him, the other end dangled from the wall.

"I'm not sure yet how you will die, Soong. Maybe I will gut you." She rolled the knife around in her hand like a toy. "You know, I killed Jie and Khoo with a screwdriver. And Fong—do you want to know how I killed him?"

Kwan was on the floor. Blood pooled near his thigh, and his shirt was soaked in blood too. As she spoke, she walked deeper into the room, trying to draw the Clean Man away from Kwan and the desk, out into the open and vulnerable. But so far, he remained where he was, the fear still in his eyes.

"He was a much bigger man than you, Soong. I put a wire around his throat and rode him like a horse. It was a wild ride, but in the end, he died like a pig on the floor of his own home."

The blank look on Soong's face began to fade and a smile formed on his lips. Still, an unmistakable bit of fear lingered in his eyes. "Go ahead, ask me," she said, but Soong remained silent, his mouth trying to keep the smile fixed while his hand shook.

"Remember what you said that day? I do. You said soon I would want to please you. Well, here I am, Soong. That *is* your name, James Soong, from a little shithole outside of London?"

Soong's lips pulled back into a grimace, his huge teeth glowing in the red light.

"I'm sorry, you little twit, but I think this day will be your last."

Soong moved away from Kwan, and LeAnn saw the spark of an idea in his eyes; he was planning his attack, thinking, judging distances, all while looking at her knife. She could read all his emotions—doubt, anger, arrogance. It was as if he were having an ongoing battle with himself. He was out of control now, his rage rampant, the need to punish himself was in charge—the destructive child, or the "death drive," as her psychiatrist called it. She moved one step closer.

Her move startled him and he froze. He had been probing her for a sign of weakness, something he could use against her. Soong was accustomed to being feared, it was part of his nature, and this small woman-child should be cowering in fear. He stepped back and away from her, wincing.

His leg wound was serious. LeAnn spotted a tiny black hole in his pants, just above his right knee, and more blood was there now than when she first walked in. A bullet wound—she thought she'd heard gunfire. The longer she could drag this out, the weaker he would become.

"I see the doubt on your face, Soong. Right now, you're wondering how this inept girl could kill your best men, aren't you? Yes, that's it isn't it, I can read you like a book. I think it's going to be you who dies today, Mister Clean Man. Oh, how many times I said that name each night as I fell asleep, the almighty Clean Man. But look at you, not so clean now, are you?"

Soong looked down at his white suit, now covered in his own blood.

"Just a flesh wound, my dear. Actually, I have never felt more alive, and it's me that holds all the cards, don't you see? You think you can overpower me? This policeman thought so too. Look at him now, he's taking his last few breaths of life, and soon you will join him."

"Your body says something different, Soong. You're holding a broken bat and gasping, and I'm breathing just fine," she said, taking another step forward.

"Ah, my bat! You know, this is the same one I used on Brianne, remember her? I'm sure you do. I crushed her skull with it. And maybe the bat is not what it used to be, but I think I shall cherish it after tonight, maybe frame it somehow and hang it on my wall."

"Your bat is broken, Soong, much like you, but in a different way. You're a narcissist and a coward. I knew it the first time I saw you leering at me in your fancy suit. I think it was the way you talked, playing with your accent as if everyone would be impressed. But deep down, you know you come from trash, don't you? I looked you up. It's amazing what you can find on the internet. Was your mama mean to you, Soong? Let's do this. Let's dance, you miserable twit," she said, using his own slur against him, and took two steps forward.

Soong almost tripped over Kwan as he backed up. He looked down at the officer, and she advanced again. Fifteen feet separated them. Three or four steps for him, at least half a dozen for her.

Soong began switching the bat between his hands, something she had seen Ramzi do when he was practicing with his knives, keeping his prey uncertain when and where the attack would come from.

He was ready, she saw it in his eyes, he was done talking. He was going to lunge and swing the splintered stump of the bat; it was his only logical move. But from which direction? She couldn't wait for him to decide. She needed to take him off guard. What would Shakespeare say if he were here, what tragic words would spill out across the page?

"The gloomy side of death," she said.

Soong hesitated.

"It's Shakespeare, you ignorant bastard." She said, racing forward, swinging the little knife backhanded from left to right.

Soong had just taken his first step and was startled by her move. He reared back as the knife sliced open his right cheek and cut through the cartilage of his nose. Blood sprayed out; some of it got in her eyes and blurred her vision. The hand holding the knife was slippery with his blood too. She had him off-balance, though, and spun around to cut him again when his bat handle caught her in the ribcage.

The blow knocked the wind out of her, and her healing ribs cracked once again. But this time, something deeper in her chest screamed with pain as Soong pulled the bloody stump of the bat from her side, the jagged two-inch-long splinters dripping with her blood.

Instinctively, she swung the knife again, still reeling from Soong's blow. The knife missed his throat and caught his chin, just scratching the surface. But it was enough to back him up, and he retreated again behind the desk.

He stood, silent, holding his cheek as fresh blood mingled with the old on the jacket. LeAnn leaned against the wall, trying to catch her breath; she was wheezing and some of the noise was coming from under her arm.

"It's just me and you now, my princess," Soong said. "It's you that's dying now. I foretold it, didn't I? But I still see that spark in your eye. I may have to pluck that eye from your pretty face just to snuff it out."

He waited a second, watching her. "What, no comment, no witty comeback?" he said. "Surely this was not what you expected." Then he wiped his cheek and examined the blood on his hand.

Her grip on the knife was slipping, if she didn't end this soon, she and Kwan would die.

If she could just draw the bastard over to her. Soong remained behind the desk. He was weaker now, breathing harder, shoulders slumped. He was losing blood too, but not fast enough. He was going to wait her out.

She knelt on one knee and leaned back against the wall. "Come kill me, you coward," she said. "If you're man enough."

"My little spitfire, you think you know me so well, but I don't think you have ever known the likes of me."

Soong stepped around the desk, and she saw his ego slip; she saw him as he was years ago: an angry man with big dreams and no future. His brow wrinkled and his thin lips quivered, he was coming for her . . . then stopped short. He laughed and his sickening grin returned.

He was at least four feet out of her range, and it would take an awfully lucky blow to hit him and do any damage. She had to bring him in closer.

LeAnn let the knife slip from her fingers, closed her eyes, and heard the "Dance of the Sugar Plum Fairy," picturing the ballerinas twirling across the stage.

Still on one knee with her back against the wall, she waited for Soong to move forward.

"I think you have had enough fun now, little one."

The crunch of broken glass told her he was right in front of her. He grabbed a handful of hair. The pain felt good, euphoric, compared to what she was feeling between her ribs. She let him do all the work, using every bit of strength he had to lift her off the ground, and as he did, she pulled the freshly charged stun gun out of her back pocket, pressed it into his throat, and hit the trigger.

The sounds were glorious. The snapping electric current and the gasping wet, noises from his open mouth were so . . . erotic.

Soong fell face first, his nose missing the edge of his Persian carpet and crunching against the black ceramic tile. LeAnn turned him over. Soong's eyes had rolled back and blood poured from his misshapen nose.

"You are no longer the Clean Man to me, or even a laoban. You are just another little man in a big, big world."

Her punctured lung gurgled with each breath, and she was breathing hard. Using Kwan's handcuffs and the rope from her backpack she hog-tied Soong into a fetal position, leaving him where he had fallen.

"Kwan, can you hear me?"

The man was barely breathing and his pulse weak. Soong's bat had done serious damage, wounding his abdomen and thigh. It was the thigh wound that was bleeding the most, and she took his belt off and used it as a tourniquet, wrenching it down as tight as possible.

"Just months ago, I would have left you right here, Mister Policeman, but I think you may be worth saving, for your child, at least."

Kwan moaned, and his eyes fluttered.

She looked back at Soong and saw he was staring at her. Taking a long length of leader wire from her backpack, she fastened a slipknot at one end and put it around his neck, then tied the other end to the rope binding his feet. Any pressure he put on the rope would choke him, maybe even kill him.

She had plans for Soong and dying alone wasn't one of them, but Kwan wasn't going to live without a good trauma surgeon.

"Kwan, wake up. I can't carry you. You have to stand up."

His eyes opened and tried to focus on her; he rolled over to his knees and struggled to sits upright.

"I'm going to bring your car up closer. Don't move, and don't touch him either."

Kwan looked over at the bound man and nodded.

LeAnn pulled the keys from his pocket and limped outside to the unmarked police car. Putting the car in reverse, she backed up as close to the front door as possible.

It took all the strength the two of them had, but she managed to get Kwan in the passenger seat, then she raced the two short blocks to the Changi General Hospital.

"Where is the goddammed emergency entrance!"

"Back . . . back there," Kwan said, pointing to the driveway behind them.

She hit the brakes hard, and Kwan cursed something in Mandarin.

"Sorry."

LeAnn parked right in front of the automatic doors, triggering the sensor, and a woman in green scrubs backed up, then ran outside toward them.

"Help me! This is my father. He's been stabbed."

Now several more employees raced out, and they got Kwan in a wheelchair and started pushing him inside.

"Wait! Stop her," Kwan said, pointing back at LeAnn.

LeAnn was already backing out of the parking lot, and no one was looking in her direction.

She had never driven a car as fast as she was driving right now, and with each turn, she struggled to control it, oversteering and running off the road right in front of the warehouse.

***

Soong was just as she had left him, his broken and bloody nose bent to the left and already swelling. He grinned when he saw her, those perfect white teeth now blood-stained looked ghastly.

"I got you good, didn't I?"

"You seem to be the one bound up like a hog," LeAnn said. A scream from a closed door behind Soong's desk startled her.

"Help us," someone screamed again.

LeAnn opened the door which led to another room, it too lit only by a red emergency fire exit. In the center of the room were four familiar cots. Three were occupied, and one girl stared at her, wide-eyed, whimpering as LeAnn walked over to her.

"It's going to be okay."

The girl must have been terrified at the sight of her, and LeAnn laughed, imagining how she must look covered in blood.

One at a time, she pulled the IV out of each girl's arm, using her thumb to stop the bleeding and the IV port's tape as a Band-Aid.

"Can you take these straps off?" the girl said in English.

"Not yet, but soon. Where are the drugs? Do you know where they keep them?"

"In the white cabinet."

Among a dozen bottles of liquid fentanyl, were two boxes of transdermal 11.0 mg fentanyl patches. Next to the cabinet, folded and on the floor, was a new wheelchair.

LeAnn turned to the girl. "If I unstrap you, will you help me? I can't lift anything."

"Yes, please."

"Help me get three of these on the guy out there. Don't panic or scream. He's tied up, but I want to get him in here and on an IV, can you do that?"

"Yes, he—"

"I know what he did."

Soong glared at them both. His nose was twice as big now, and he had to breathe through his mouth. At least he was quiet. She pulled his pants and boxer shorts down as far as the rope would allow and put three of the square patches on his thigh, then stood looking at the near naked man.

Soong's eyes widened and he hissed something she couldn't understand.

"How does that feel Soong, two young girls looking at your junk? Feeling a little embarrassed, are you?"

Soong closed his eyes.

"Three is a lot," the girl said, looking at the fentanyl patches

"Is it? I've wanted to try them, so he's going to show me how well they work. I don't want to kill him though, at least not yet. Once I get one of those IVs in him, I'll take them off."

Soong's eyes were half-open, and bloody mucus dripped from

his mouth. The girl did most of the lifting and by the time they got him in the chair, he was unconscious.

"I've never done this before, but how hard can it be, Mr. Soong?"

"I've done it," the girl said. "Well, not to a person. When my dog was sick, we had to use one to give him antibiotics."

"What is your name?"

"Colleen."

"Colleen, let's put Mr. Soong on your IV. You can do it if you want, but we need to get him on one of the cots."

"Why don't we just leave him on the floor?"

"I want to leave him like he left me, and you. He's got to be on the cot."

One girl moaned and opened her eyes. Colleen ran over to her and started undoing the straps.

"Wait," LeAnn said. "Leave her."

"She's my sister."

"Okay, just her. Maybe she can help us. I don't have a lot of time. I'm getting weak and I don't want to die in here."

With the sister's help, the three of them had Soong on the cot, strapped down and an IV in the back of his hand. LeAnn checked Soong's eyes. He was still unconscious and she pulled the patches off his leg, lifted her shirt and put one of them on her abdomen, trying not to think about what might be on the adhesive.

"I hope you live through this, Mr. Soong."

"Aren't you going to kill him?" Colleen asked.

"Do you want me too?"

Colleen's blank face stared at him for a minute and then she nodded.

"I want to, I've dreamed of it for weeks, but what I'm going to do will be better than killing him. I was in one of those cots a few months ago. Can, can you get the yellow shears from my backpack?"

In LeAnn's dreams, the Clean Man was awake and terrified, but now he would miss out on all the pain she had wanted to inflict on him. She wanted to see those perfect, oversized white teeth, to hear him screaming in his practiced English accent.

"You two may want to look away," she said to Colleen and her sister.

***

Sitting in her VW a block away, LeAnn looked through her binoculars and watched the first police car race into the parking lot where all three girls were huddled together wrapped in Soong's Persian rug. She should have left immediately, but she wanted to see them bring him out.

Twenty minutes later, two paramedics wheeled a gurney out through the door, it was Soong and he was screaming. She took a deep breath triggering a stabbing pain in her side, and felt the relief of something heavy leave her.

Warm blood drained down her side, the bleeding was worsening and the pain in her side had spread throughout her ribcage. A single fentanyl patch helped some but she was afraid two might be too many. She needed to drive and be alert enough to deal with the clinic near the condo. If she lived through the night, she would worry about relapsing tomorrow.

Staring out the windshield, she hoped to get another glimpse of Soong as she turned around on Battersea Road. He had stopped screaming and she wished she was closer . . . to hear him again, but he was quiet now. Maybe he died after all.

She drove fast, avoiding as many ruts and potholes as possible while thinking of Jie, Khoo, Fong, and now the Clean Man. She had warned them all, and they had laughed. She wanted to laugh now, but she could barely breathe.

Even though it was close to midnight, The Tanera Clinic was open. It was a dirty-looking building on the outside, white walls marked with years of smudge and grime. The inside was slightly better, but what were her options? The pain was excruciating now and blood was seeping into her shoes.

An older woman dressed in a white uniform sat behind a glass partition. She looked blankly at the blood oozing through LeAnn's black shirt and handed her a clipboard.

"Name and address, please. How will you be paying for your visit?" she asked in Mandarin.

"Cash."

"You need to pay now."

LeAnn felt her knees weaken, and she had trouble remembering the words she wanted to say in Mandarin. Tommy Fong's roll of cash was in her backpack. She leaned over to hand it to the woman and fell.

Everything went black, although she could still hear. The woman was calling for someone and she felt hands touching her. Some unknown person was touching her . . . and she welcomed the sensation.

"Please help me," she said.

***

When she opened her eyes, she was inside an ambulance; its siren wailing. The experience was dreamlike, and she wondered if she was on her way to prison or back to Soong's warehouse. She pulled on the straps holding her down but had no strength. Closing her eyes, she surrendered.

She was in the darkened halls of the New York University's auditorium, pushing a loading cart down the carpeted aisles toward the stage.

Both girls were bigger and heavier than she was, but with a bit of ingenuity, she got them propped up next to Olivia.

"There you are, my friends. You look so beautiful. I would brush your hair—I know you all want to look your best on your last day, but I forgot my brush."

CHAPTER 41

KWAN

Kwan woke in a darkened hospital room. Haron Chin was sleeping in the chair next to his bed, and two empty cups of coffee and a newspaper on a nightstand told him the man had spent the night.

Kwan was cold and trembling under a thin white sheet, and his left arm was taped to the handrail of his bed. The clear plastic line of an IV disappeared under a white gauze bandage on the back of his left hand, and it stung when he made a fist.

What the hell happened to me?

He remembered leaving the station and being on the Tampines Expressway, but why? His home and wife were in another direction. He closed his eyes and tried to swallow, but his throat was dry, it felt like he was trying to swallow sand.

He needed water and tried to open his eyes again, but they were so heavy. He struggled to keep them open and then gave up.

"Chin," he tried to say, but wasn't sure if he had. He closed his eyes and . . .

He was at the circus with his daughter. She was eighteen now and her long dark hair had been cut short. Kwan marveled as her brown eyes glittered in the spotlight. She was so smart. "LeAnn," he said to her in the dream. "Look out."

A clown had snuck up behind her. His makeup looked like blood, and his two front teeth were huge, like rabbit's teeth.

LeAnn's face faded, and the clown moved closer, then spoke.

"I'm not finished with you, Kwan."

Kwan closed his eyes, hoping it was all a dream. When he opened them, an ash-colored baseball bat handle was stuck in his side. He tried to pull on it, but it wouldn't budge, like a new appendage that he had to live with. I'm hallucinating. I must be. I'm in a hospital on painkillers.

Kwan opened his eyes, and Chin was still sleeping. The two coffee cups were gone though, replaced by flowers in a vase.

He looked down at his side. The bat was gone, and a white gauze bandage encircled his chest. He closed his eyes. It was just a dream.

***

"Wake up, Mr. Kim," a woman said. Someone was leaning over him, and the beeping of a monitor behind him stopped. His eyes refused to open, like they were glued shut. With his right hand, he rubbed his eyes until he could see her.

"I'll bet you're thirsty, try these ice chips. You're dehydrated and on an IV for fluids, but the ice is all I can give you now."

The woman was a nurse, and a pretty one. Another dream, he thought, and closed his eyes.

"Mr. Kim," the nurse said again.

He opened his eyes and for a moment, the walls in his room had big holes in them. White powder floated through a shaft of red light, and someone behind him laughed. The image faded, and the red light became the soft white light of a fluorescent fixture over his bed.

He opened his mouth as the woman pressed a Styrofoam cup to his lips. The ice was cold, but as the chips melted, they soothed the dryness in his throat.

"Thank you," he was able to say. "I'm having terrible nightmares."

"My name his Anamah Tan. I am your night nurse. Bad dreams could be from the medications. I will tell your doctor, maybe we can give you something else. Mr. Chin will be back shortly. He has been here since Tuesday night. He's a very nice man. And your wife and daughter were here a short while ago.

"My daughter," he croaked and tried to sit up, pulling on the IV at his wrist.

"Yes, Mr. Kim. She delivered a beautiful baby girl last night while you were in surgery."

"What happened to me, what surgery?"

"Your friend will help you with that. All I know is that you were dropped off here with a wound to your side and another to your thigh just below your groin. Your blood pressure was near zero, and you coded before they could get you into surgery. The ER staff said your daughter dropped you off and ran away, but that's not true, your friend will explain."

"Can I see my wife and my baby girl?"

"She was being discharged, but I did talk to her, and she said she would be back tonight. I think she left with her mother. How is your pain, Mr. Kim? Your wounds will be painful; you have several fractured ribs and a punctured lung. Your last dose of Dilaudid will be wearing off soon."

"I don't feel much pain, and I really want to remain alert—this fog I'm in is frustrating. I need to know what happened that night."

There was a knock at the door and Chin walked in.

"Well, the dead man is awake," he said.

"Your friend wants to know what happened to him, and I'm glad you can tell him. When you first feel the pain, press your call button. If you don't, the pain can become excruciating."

As the nurse left, Chin pulled the chair closer and asked, "So, Kim, what do you remember?"

"I left work, and I was headed home, but then I remember being on the freeway. I keep seeing myself in a room that had holes in the wall, someone behind me laughing, and a piece of wood in my side. I think I remember being in a car, but a lot of that is like a dream."

"The emergency room staff said you were dropped off by your daughter, driving your car. She raced away and then the phone call came in."

"What phone call? What was it?"

"It was made on your cell phone by Colleen Walker, one of the Australian victims. We traced your phone and found her. There were three of them in a hidden section of that warehouse."

"So three girls are safe? I don't remember any of that."

"Kim, are you ready for the best news?"

"Tell me, Chin. Tell me you have Leila, or LeAnn Moran."

"Better—you called him the Clean Man. We have him downstairs."

"The Clean Man," Kwan repeated. "The Laoban!"

"Yes, his name is James Soong. I can piece together what I think happened, but Colleen, the Australian, won't confirm anything."

"Tell me everything, Chin, don't make me pull it out of you. Damn, this is starting to hurt."

Kwan lifted the sheets and looked at all the bandages. His whole chest and left leg above the knee were covered in white gauze and surgical tape.

"The Moran girl went back after she dropped you off here and found the girls in a hidden room. It was just like the warehouse on Pandan Loop, but with four cots. She freed them and bound Soong to one of his own cots, then she left, and we haven't seen or heard from her since. The Australian said Moran was pretty beaten up too, bleeding profusely from her side."

"LeAnn did all this?"

"There's more, Kim. Soong was near death, strapped down with an IV in his arm, so sedated the paramedics couldn't find a pulse at first. Kim, she cut every one of his fingers off. I think Jiawei was right when she called her the devil. I never want to be on the wrong end of that girl."

"She told me that he'd touched her," Kwan said. "That's why she took his fingers. But I can't believe she let him live."

CHAPTER 42

THE CLEAN MAN

"I'll need a pen and paper, please," he said to one of the two men standing at the door.

What a mess. First it was the Canadian woman, and now I'm stuck in this damn hospital surrounded by idiots.

"Can I make a phone call? I can't seem to find my cell phone. Do you have it?"

The two men looked at each other without answering.

"I should have transferred everything to Myanmar weeks ago," he said aloud.

He watched a woman wearing a suit enter the room and speak to both men, then take a chair next to him.

"Mr. Soong," the woman said. "I'm Tanya Chua. I am the lead prosecutor on your case. I—"

"What can I do for you, Ms. Chua, is it a donation you want, employment maybe? I do have openings as I have lost several employees recently. It's the nature of my business, you see. Just leave one of your cards with my men there," he said, pointing to the two uniformed officers, "and I'm sure I can find something for you."

"Mr. Soong, do you know where you are and why you are here?"

"Not exactly, but I can tell you it's damned inconvenient."

Soong lifted both of his bandaged hands, bringing them close to his face and studied them, turning them over and looking at his palms.

"This is also inconvenient," he said, gesturing to his hands. "I will need a pen and some paper."

He watched as the woman opened her briefcase and took out a stack of 8x10 color photos.

"Do you recognize any of these girls?"

One after another he examined them, shaking his head after each one. Then he stopped, staring at the last one. It was a passport photo.

"This one!" he screamed. "This twit is the one responsible for everything!"

He began biting at the bandages on one hand, chewing and ripping the tape away until the stubs of his fingers were exposed.

"Look," he said. "She did this!" Soong slammed his palms into LeAnn's photo, over and over, until her picture was covered in blood and then shook his fists at Chua, speckling her suit with blood.

It took both officers to hold him as an orderly strapped him down and injected him with a sedative. Soong's eyes darted back and forth as he bit a chunk of his lip off and spat it out on the floor next to the prosecutor.

"She is a monster, I tell you. Don't let her touch me ever again!"

Slowly, the drug began working on him. His face went slack, and his screams began to slur, finally he closed his eyes.

"Holy Mother of Christ," Chua said. "I have never seen anything like that."

Tiny red drops of Soong's blood covered everything, including the walls behind him. Most of the bandaging had been ripped free from his hands, and each finger, including his thumbs, had been severed between his palm and the first knuckle.

"What did the girl do with his fingers?" Chua said to the officers. "I almost don't want to know."

"I heard that she put them in his suit pocket," one of them said.

"If I were a drinking woman, I would want to sit down and have a drink with this girl."

Soong looked peaceful enough as the nurses and their aides changed the sheets and mopped the floors and walls while a surgeon began sewing the skin around the reopened wounds.

In Soong's dream, his suit glistened in the sunlight as the girls, strapped down in their cots, paraded around him, circling him like wagons in the old westerns as he sat in one of Tottenham's filthy gutters sucking his thumb. Then one of the prostitutes took his lunch money.

Soong moaned as the doctor wrapped one hand and started on the other.

CHAPTER 43

KWAN

Kwan shuffled down the hallway toward the nurse's station, dragging his IV pole behind him. The elevator chimed and Chin stepped out as the doors opened.

"What is it, Chin? I'm afraid to ask."

"Good news, of course. First, Soong kept meticulous records, all handwritten—can you believe that? Using his records, we located another two victims. That's five now, and they are being reunited with their parents as we speak."

"How are they, are they okay?" Kwan had wondered if any of them would ever be recovered, and if so, what condition they would be in.

Chin's smile slipped. "Both were in Kuala Lumpur. Heroin addicts, I'm sad to say and working for small-time pimps. The authorities have made several arrests over there, and two of our senior sergeants left this morning to coordinate with them. Kim, I don't know if the girls will ever be the same, but they are alive and that's a start."

"That's great news," Kwan said. "But what about the American senator, the man that killed Gemma?"

"His name is Douglas Nelson. Parliament officials have notified the United States Embassy, and I don't know what's happening with it now. We gave them copies of everything we had, and now I guess it's a wait and see."

"I don't like the sound of that, Chin."

"I know. Politicians. You want to see Soong? He's still downstairs. Prison Services will be transferring him soon, probably to the Changi Prison Complex."

"I'll need a wheelchair; this is about as far as I can go on my own."

***

Kwan was disappointed. Except for the sutures in his face, the man looked like any other patient, too normal and too relaxed. He expected an evil psychopath, like the American Charles Manson, or the Nightstalker he had read about. James Soong looked like just another man.

"Has he talked?"

"Kim, I don't know what he was before, but this man is insane. He thinks he's in charge here: giving orders, asking nurses to take messages, and he talks to himself in the first person. Just this morning he ordered me to 'bring Mr. Soong's car around, he is ready to leave.'"

"I can't remember much of him that night. I have a lot of gaps that I can't fill. But I think he laughed at me, and I keep hearing that laugh in my dreams."

"Do you remember shooting him?"

"Not really. I wish I did. I dream about it, but in the dream, my gun jams each time I pull the trigger, or when it does fire, the bullet bounces off him or just falls out of the barrel."

"You hit him twice. You took a piece of his ear off and hit him in the thigh just above his knee. The girl did that to his face," Chin said, pointing at Soong behind the safety glass, "and the fingers of course."

"Yes, pretty gruesome."

Every few minutes, Soong would lift his hands up to his face and study them.

"I've seen enough, Chin, and I'm tired. Walk me back to my room."

***

As Chin left, Anamah Tan, his first nurse in ICU, walked in and closed the door. "How are you today, Mr. Kim?"

"Better than the last time you saw me. Are you working my floor tonight?"

'No, sir, I came to tell you that one of the patients on my floor asked to see you. She seems to be a very private woman and wanted me to ask you discreetly if you would see her."

"Who is she and why me?"

"She was brought to the hospital two days ago by ambulance and says her name is Leila Haddad. She has a lung injury and is being treated for septic shock. Maybe you know her?"

***

Anamah Tan pushed him down the hallway and into the elevator. On the third floor, she stopped at a private room, and Kwan saw a young woman sleeping in a room like his. Both her arms were taped to the railing of her bed with white surgical tape.

"Is she violent?" he said, seeing the restraints.

"No, but she thrashes out in her sleep and has pulled the IV out of her arm each time. She asked for the bindings."

Kwan rolled over to her bedside and studied her. With her eyes closed, it was hard to tell. He tried ignoring the short hair, and this woman's face was thinner, even gaunt.

"Did she say how she was injured?" Kwan asked.

"She said she fell in a park and didn't think her injuries were serious, then went to a clinic for treatment. That's all she can remember."

"I do think I know her. Do you mind if I wait here until she wakes?"

As the door shut, the woman opened her eyes.

CHAPTER 44

LeAnn

"Hello, Kwan."

He was an attractive man, with piercing, intelligent eyes. He rolled his chair over closer, almost touching her bedside.

"Aren't you afraid of me?"

"You're bound to the railings of your bed, should I be?"

"Maybe, I was diagnosed once a long time ago, as a sociopath."

"I don't feel afraid," Kwan said.

"What if this tape is loose, and I have a scalpel under these sheets?"

"You asked to see me. I don't think it was to cut my throat, LeAnn."

She pulled her right arm out from the tape and set the stainless-steel scalpel on her tray table. Her hand shook as she reached for her water, and it took all her strength just to hold the cup.

"Septic shock, they said. Another day and it might have been fatal."

"Where did you learn to speak Mandarin?"

"Right here. I've been here several times, although this is probably my last visit."

Kwan looked down at his lap. He was thinking something.

"What?"

"Thank you for saving my life. I don't remember much, but I think I remember you bringing me here."

"You're welcome, Kwan."

"I also remember finding the letter you left inside my house. I knew that if you wanted to kill me, it would have been then."

"I needed to see you face-to-face, it's a flaw I have, or maybe a compulsion."

"I want to know everything, LeAnn."

"First," she said taking a painful deep breath, "my legal name is Leilah Haddad, I have several other names, but I prefer LeAnn"

***

Kwan listened to her story, what happened to her family in Iraq, and the madness that followed.

"You see, Kwan, when I feel I've been wronged, no matter how slight, my only recourse is justice. Before Gemma, or maybe even when I saw Brianne, I'd never experienced remorse, or grief. I didn't understand the meaning of the words."

She could see the torment in his eyes, the conflict as he digested the magnitude of her crimes, and he glanced at the scalpel on the tray table a few times. "I'm confessing, Kwan. I have one more thing to do before I can sleep peacefully again. It's Gemma. Her death weighs on me. I promised her I would save her, not that she heard me say it, but I did say it to myself, which is the same thing, to me anyway. I'm a little OCD, remember? I can't let something like that go unfinished—the man has to pay."

Kwan looked at his hands, then felt the bandages around his chest. He was weighing his options.

LeAnn measured the distance to the door, then dismissed the beginnings of her plan to run. She was done running.

"How do you propose to make him pay? He is thousands of miles away, behind some fortress probably, protected by crooked politicians. I know what you will be up against. We have the same problems here."

"I'm very resourceful, but I'll need your help."

"I can't be involved in this. Like you, I would never be able to sleep. I've sworn an oath."

"So, did I, and Gemma is still dead."

"She is . . . what exactly do you need?"

Chapter 45

KWAN

Kwan wheeled himself out of LeAnn's room, into the elevator and down to the one section of the hospital controlled by Prison Services.

The two guards at Soong's door nodded, and Kwan waited outside, looking at the man through the Plexiglas window. Soong was awake now and motionless. He turned slightly, and locked eyes with Kwan. It was there now, the evil behind the brown eyes, the ruse of insanity was gone, replaced by something intelligent, something cunning, and everything that happened that horrible night came crashing back into his memory and some reflex caused him to reach for his side. He felt the bandages, and remembered the sound of the broken glass under his shoes.

"Sergeant," he said to the guard closest to him. "How many men do you have on this floor?"

"Ten, sir."

"Do you need more, is ten all that you need?"

"I think we're ok. I have two cars out in the parking lot and every entrance is secured."

"This man is up to something—I can feel it. He looks harmless, but don't discount the fact that he has people on the outside, maybe even inside this hospital. Be wary of anyone on this floor that you personally don't know."

***

It had been seven days since LeAnn dropped him at the emergency room, and he was ready to go home and spend time with his wife and new daughter. Doctors said they would release him first thing in the morning, which meant by noon if he was lucky, but tonight after seeing Soong, he wasn't going to spend another night there without his gun.

Chin answered on the first ring. "Chin," he said, "are you busy?"

"No, sir, what do you need?"

"I need my gun. I may be feeling paranoid, but the bastard is just a couple of floors below me, and I'm telling you it's giving me bad feelings. Maybe it's the drugs they're giving me, but I would feel a lot better if you could go by the house and get my other gun. Also, Mei Lien is making up a bag of clothes for you to bring, can you do that for me?"

***

When Chin walked in with Kwan's gun and bag, Kwan told him about visiting Soong earlier. "I'm telling you—he was a different man, Chin. He may not be as crazy as we think.

"Something else, remember what Gerard Sen told us? Soong has a network of people that will do anything for him. I don't think they would try something here inside the hospital, but maybe during the transfer to Changi, or during a court appearance. I will sleep better with my gun here."

"I'll do a walk through before I leave and see if I can pick up on anything. I'm going to put a uniformed officer at your door too if you don't mind, someone we know."

"Thanks, Chin, and can you tell my nurse I need her?"

When Chin left, Kwan put his head on the pillow, feeling the ache in his neck muscles. He felt like a fool. Soong had no fingers and was strapped down, and his room might look like a hospital room, but it was a prison cell—Soong wasn't going anywhere. Still, the gun felt good under the sheet.

He gave the bag of clothes to his night nurse and asked her to give them to the woman in room 307.

He closed his eyes and had a brief dream of being in the dimly lit warehouse, listening to the sound of broken glass and grit as he walked toward a battered desk.

Broken glass crunching under his feet startled him awake. He was burning up and a bead of sweat rolled down his forehead. Opening his eyes, the room was cool, sunlight streamed through the open blinds, and LeAnn Haddad was sitting in a wheelchair staring at him.

"Good morning, Kwan, how do I look?"

She was dressed in Mei Lien's old sweatpants and T-shirt. They were a little baggy on the girl's thin frame, but she looked better today than she did yesterday.

"Better. How did you get in, aren't there guards at my door?

"I told them we were related, they walked me in and sat with me while you were sleeping. They're still at the door, I must not look very threatening, but they look in now and then."

Kwan laughed. "I know better, but you do look good."

Thanks, I guess. They don't want to release me, but I can't stay here another night. I've got a week's worth of antibiotics, and I want to be far away from here by then."

"I saw him again last night," he said, "and he's in my nightmares now.

"I should have killed him, Kwan, but I thought leaving him crippled would satisfy me—and you too. I didn't want you to hate me."

"Hate is a powerful word. I don't hate you. I believe I understand who you are now. Soong is pure evil; I saw a little of that last night. I hope I'm never in the same room with him again. But you never know," he said, holding up his 9mm. "There will be an endless number of court appearances. Maybe killing him would have been a better choice."

"He's not that different from me, Kwan. There are people out there who hate me that much. Maybe I deserve it. Anyway, I'm glad we met, and that we both lived through the experience."

She said it so seriously, it caught him off guard, but he saw the slight grin, and for the first time saw a bit of warmth in her eyes.

"Will I see you again?"

"Maybe on the news, but you never know."

With that, the strangest woman he had ever met, rolled herself out of the room, and he thought of another dozen questions he should have asked.

CHAPTER 46

LEANN

LeAnn stood next to the seventy-four-year-old senator and his new wife. She was a pretty thing, sprawled nude across the satin sheets, snoring quietly. LeAnn looked around the room, admiring someone's taste in the decor. Probably not the senator's, she had read Douglas Ian Nelson's bio weeks ago, written by some aide most likely. He was a shallow man, three times divorced, each divorce coinciding with the women's thirty-fifth birthdays. This young woman of twenty-six was about to become wealthy, and there would be no divorce in her future.

The three fentanyl patches she had placed on the inside of the senator's elbow were working. Twenty minutes was all they needed. She had timed it on herself, twice, just to be sure. His breathing continued to slow until the snoring stopped.

The sweet scent of alcohol, wine probably, filled the gap between her face and his. She wanted to look him in the eye as he died, but waking him would complicate her chore. He was known to be a heavy drinker, and spidery veins branched from his nose to his cheeks. The alcohol would amplify the effects of the fentanyl, maybe even kill him, if she chose. However, she wasn't going to let him die a graceful death.

The stiff leader wire slid between the gap in the pillow and under his neck. He never moved, his breathing still steady, his ghostly white skin glistening in the moonlight coming through the windows. His pretty wife was still also, her single patch would keep her in a deep sleep for hours.

"Time to pay up," she said, pulling the wire tight.

She felt him twitch through the wire, once, twice, and then he was still. Just to be sure, she counted to sixty in her head and then relaxed, leaving the wire around his neck. She felt his carotid artery for a pulse . . . nothing.

He deserved more than this painless death, but he was a US senator, and by early morning the entire might of the FBI was going to be focused in this master bedroom. His reputation would be ruined, he would die disgraced, and that would have to be enough.

With her still-gloved hand, she pulled the patches off his arm and left the one on his wife's thigh. The wife moaned and a smile formed on her thin lips, maybe she was dreaming something pleasant. Tomorrow she was going to have one hell of a headache, but that would be the least of her troubles.

If her timing was right, the videos of the senator and the now-dead Gemma would be arriving at the FBI's Washington headquarters, the *New York Times*, the *San Francisco Chronicle*, and each of them would get her final quote:

"Cowards die many times before their deaths,
The valiant never taste of death but once." – William Shakespeare

ABOUT THE AUTHOR

Jeff Shaw was a police officer in South Florida for twenty-four years. Not long after retiring, he began writing a memoir on his career in law enforcement. The memoir is a collection of some of the most memorable cases he worked and how they affected him at the time, and how they still affect him today. That memoir, *Who I Am: The Man Behind the Badge* was published in 2020.

On March of 2022, he published his first crime novel, *Lieutenant Trufant*, the first in a series titled, *The Bloodline*.

LeAnn and the Clean Man is the second in that series.

When not writing, he spends his time reading, playing golf in the mountains of north Georgia, or just relaxing with his wife Susan.